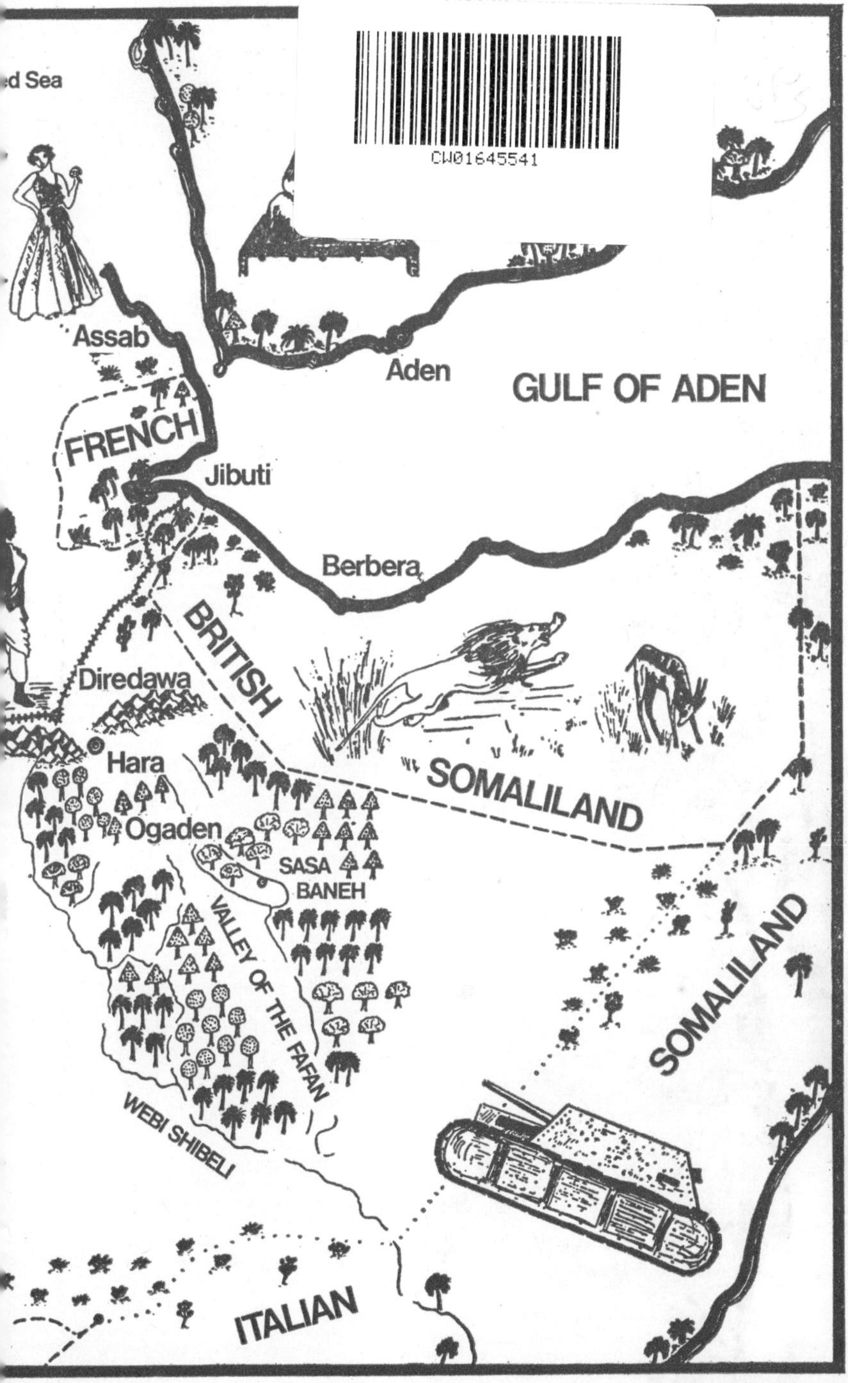

ed Sea
Assab
Aden
GULF OF ADEN
FRENCH
Jibuti
Berbera
BRITISH
Diredawa
Hara
SOMALILAND
Ogaden
SASA
BANEH
VALLEY OF THE FAFAN
SOMALILAND
WEBI SHIBELI
ITALIAN

THE SECRET WAR

Sir Anthony Lovelace had liked the handsome young American at their first meeting, but if he had known that Christopher Penn was one of the celebrated *Millers of God,* who condemned to death all those who profited from war and threat of war, he might have thought twice before associating with him.

He certainly would have done so could he have guessed that he would find himself pledged to assist in the 'elimination' of an Armenian gentleman named Paxito Zarrif, and that the keeping of his word would lead him on a chase through Europe and Africa to the heart of Abyssinia, and into a series of situations guaranteed to whiten the hair of any less intrepid man. As it was, only his love for Valerie, Christopher Penn's fiancée, carried him through, and in Addis Ababa his unspoken devotion reaped its reward.

The Secret War is told with all the verve and skill which millions of readers throughout the world have come to expect from Dennis Wheatley and which have so rightly earned him the title of 'the Prince of Thrillers Writers'.

THE LYMINGTON EDITION

BY DENNIS WHEATLEY

NOVELS

The Launching of Roger Brook
The Shadow of Tyburn Tree
The Rising Storm
The Man Who Killed the King
The Dark Secret of Josephine
The Rape of Venice
The Sultan's Daughter
The Wanton Princess
Evil in a Mask
The Ravishing of Lady Mary Ware
The Irish Witch*
Desperate Measures*

The Scarlet Impostor
Faked Passports
The Black Baroness
V for Vengeance
Come Into My Parlour
Traitors' Gate
They Used Dark Forces

The Prisoner in the Mask
The Second Seal
Vendetta in Spain
Three Inquisitive People
The Forbidden Territory
The Devil Rides Out
The Golden Spaniard
Strange Conflict
Codeword—Golden Fleece

Dangerous Inheritance
Gateway to Hell

The Quest of Julian Day
The Sword of Fate
Bill for the Use of a Body

Black August
Contraband
The Island Where Time Stands Still
The White Witch of the South Seas

To the Devil—a Daughter
The Satanist

The Eunuch of Stamboul
The Secret War
The Fabulous Valley
Sixty Days to Live
Such Power is Dangerous
Uncharted Seas
The Man Who Missed the War
The Haunting of Toby Jugg
Star of Ill-Omen
They Found Atlantis
The Ka of Gifford Hillary
Curtain of Fear
Mayhem in Greece
Unholy Crusade
The Strange Story of Linda Lee*

SHORT STORIES

Mediterranean Nights

Gunmen, Gallants and Ghosts

HISTORICAL

Old Rowley: A Private Life of Charles II (*Illustrated by Frank C. Papé*)
Red Eagle (*The Story of the Russian Revolution*)

AUTOBIOGRAPHICAL

Stranger than Fiction* (*War Papers for the Joint Planning Staff*)
Saturdays with Bricks*

SATANISM

The Devil and all his Works* (*Illustrated in colour*)

All these books, with the exception of those
marked*, are available in The Lymington Edition

DENNIS WHEATLEY

THE SECRET WAR

THE LYMINGTON EDITION

HUTCHINSON OF LONDON

Hutchinson & Co (Publishers) Ltd
3 Fitzroy Square, London W1

London Melbourne Sydney Auckland
Wellington Johannesburg and agencies
throughout the world

First published 1937
Reprinted eight times
The Lymington Edition 1963
Second impression 1966
Third impression 1976

Printed in Great Britain by litho by
The Anchor Press Ltd and bound by
Wm Brendon & Son Ltd
both of Tiptree, Essex

ISBN 0 09 041592 2

For

ANTHONY

CONTENTS

THE SECRET WAR

CHAPTER I

ANTHONY LOVELACE HEARS OF THE *Millers of God*

"WAR," declared Christopher Penn, "is the most terrible of all evils. Pestilence and Famine are natural ills which civilisation is gradually bringing under its control. Fire and Tempest, Earthquake and Flood—they at least are short-lived localised horrors which it's impossible to prevent. But War is man-made. It's a wilful, inexcusable act of barbarity. It entails the committal of mass-murder, mass-mutilation and every other crime in the calendar, by one set of normally peace-loving people against another. Nothing—nothing, I say, is too terrible a punishment for those who set it in motion."

The two other men at the table—fair, fat, red-faced Billy Van Der Meer, and grey-headed Hythe Cassel—were silent for a moment; they were a little taken aback by this unusual vehemence in the slim, frail-looking young man opposite them. His pale face was ascetically handsome, with features as clear cut as a cameo, and its natural pallor was in striking contrast to the jet-black hair above his high forehead.

Van Der Meer shrugged his broad shoulders. "Well, I don't see what you can do about it, Penn. There always has been war in the world and it looks as if there always will be."

"Nonsense!" expostulated Cassel. "Two hundred years ago people said the same about duelling, but public opinion condemned it, so duelling, or private war, was stamped out. Nowadays, public opinion has advanced to a stage where it condemns national war, so why shouldn't that be stamped out too? This Italian invasion of Abyssinia is sheer unprovoked aggression."

The war in North-East Africa had already been raging for six months. Ever since the Wal-Wal incident Mussolini had been massing men and material in Eritrea and Italian Somaliland. All through the previous summer he had parleyed with the bickering League, outmanœuvring the anxious diplomats at every turn. In the autumn he had withdrawn Italy's representatives from the Assembly and, contemptuous of world opinion, marched into Abyssinia without even a formal declaration of hostilities. He was "adjusting his frontiers" he said, and quite a lot of people were exceedingly worried as to where he would ultimately decide that the frontiers of Italy's African possessions should be. Some thought that the modern Cæsar would not be satisfied until the whole of North Africa was again a Roman province; others, experienced in hill fighting against hardy tribesmen in hideously difficult country, that he had burnt his fingers and would never reach Magdala, let alone Addis Ababa. Yet by the spring he had avenged Adowa, captured the sacred city of Aksum, and his legions were steadily advancing into the interior, building solid motor roads for their supporting artillery and supply columns behind them as they went. The problem still uppermost in the minds of most thinking people was, what would be the final issue of the campaign and would the dilatory League come to the assistance of the Abyssinian Emperor in some really practical manner.

Thin-faced, grey-haired Hythe Cassel; castigating the Italians for their attack upon a free people, as he sat with his friends, young Christopher Penn and red-faced Billy Van Der Meer, had voiced the opinion of many.

As he spoke, a newcomer entered the room in the Union Club where the three were talking: a tall, soldierly figure, brown-haired, his temples just touched with grey, brown-eyed, thin-nosed, with a small up-combed moustache making a dark line above his tight mouth and long chin. He was an Englishman and only an honorary member of the Club for the short period of his stay in New York. He did not know many of the men who were sitting or standing about the big room, but he was aware that they were not of the type who make spectacular money overnight and drop it again next morning. Most of them came from families who had governed the destinies of the United States for several generations, and approximated very closely to the landed gentry of Great Britain. Quiet, exclusive, travelled, very sure of themselves, they were of the class that makes its spirit felt, at any crisis, in the best interest of their nation.

Christopher Penn caught sight of the newcomer and beckoned. "Come and join us, Lovelace. We're talking Abyssinia and you know the country."

"Thanks." Sir Anthony Lovelace had met the young American, casually, on only two previous occasions, but Penn's strangely beautiful face had aroused his interest. He was introduced to the other two, and sat down, stretching out his long legs. "Don't know," he went on, "that I can tell you much about Abyssinia, though. I wasn't there for long. Only on a visit to see the Emperor's coronation in 1930."

"I was just saying," Cassel began, "that the League of Nations ought to enforce sanctions to their fullest possible extent, so as to put an end to this senseless slaughter."

"The League!" Van Der Meer's plump face held an expression of disgust. "What's the good of the League, anyhow? There are seven major powers—the United States, Great Britain, France, Germany, Russia, Italy and Japan. For all practical purposes in this dispute only three of them, Britain, France and Russia, are in the League. All talk of collective security is just hot-air so long as four of the seven big boys remain outside the ring."

"You're wrong!" Cassel was protesting hotly. "Even a weak League is better than no League at all. It's still the only international instrument for the maintenance of peace. Even with ourselves, Germany and Japan outside it, the League is strong enough to smash Mussolini and restore peace if it really wanted to."

"That'd mean revolution in Italy, though," Lovelace said slowly, "and there are a lot of people who would hate to see a Bolshevik state in the middle of the Mediterranean."

"Hi! Steward!" Cassel caught the attention of a passing waiter. "What will you drink, Sir Anthony?"

"A dry sherry, please." Lovelace hunched his lean figure in the chair and pulled out an ancient pipe.

Cassel gave the order. "I've nothing against Mussolini personally," he said, "and no one wants revolution anywhere, but such considerations should not be allowed to affect the high purpose of the League. The tragedy is that members of the League betray it whenever it suits their own ends best to do so. France wants to keep Mussolini in power, and so she's put every difficulty in the way of applying sanctions that she possibly could."

"Well, you can't say that of Britain, although it wouldn't suit us to have Italy go Red."

"On the contrary, Britain's playing her own hand every bit as much. She's only backing the League this time because she doesn't want Italy to have Abyssinia."

Lovelace began to fill his pipe with deliberation. "I don't think you have any real justification for saying that. We've all the territory we need without trying to grab this last chunk of Africa."

"Still, the fact remains that the League has world opinion solidly behind it, and if only Britain and France would act together, with real determination, they could stop this war, and make a new landmark in the history of humanity."

"You don't think it might be in the interest of—er—humanity if the Italians were allowed to occupy Abyssinia?" There was just the suggestion of a twinkle in Lovelace's brown eyes.

"What!" Cassel sat up with a jerk. "You can't be speaking seriously?"

"Not altogether, but the place is a bit of a mess. The Emperor is quite enlightened, I believe, and probably he does his best, but he's almost single-handed, and conditions there are—well—quite mediæval."

"They're building schools, you know, now, hospitals and modern prisons as well."

"Perhaps, but that's only since Italy threatened to take the country over and it became vital that Abyssinia should win the sympathy of civilised nations by showing that she meant to mend her manners. They only abolished slavery as the price of admission to the League, and nine-tenths of the population are still completely barbarous savages."

Van Der Meer grinned. "Is it true that if a chap wants to marry a girl there he has to show her proof that he's bumped off another fellow before she'll have him?"

"Yes, among certain of the tribes."

"Golly! Did you see anything of that sort when you were out there?"

"A number of old warriors I met had pretty gruesome necklaces, and in some parts it's still extremely risky to travel without a big escort. You see, there's practically no law outside the principal towns, and unless you pay your way with constant presents you stand a good chance of being murdered for your rifle or a couple of dozen rounds of ammunition."

"You're right, then. The place should be taken over by somebody."

"I disagree entirely," Cassel cut in. "Under the present Emperor conditions will improve very rapidly and, if once a white race were allowed to get a grip on the country, it'd be the end of the blacks. They'd be exploited in the interests of capitalism and become wage slaves in two generations. The only hope for the Abyssinians is to keep the white man out. It's their country and they have the right to do so."

Lovelace had filled his pipe and applied a match. Little imps of laughter were dancing in his eyes as he looked over the flame at the aggressive pacifist. "I'm afraid you're wrong there. The greater part of Abyssinia doesn't really belong to the Abyssinians. They only took it over with fire and sword themselves less than half a century ago. It's still peopled by completely alien races."

For a moment Cassel chewed morosely on the butt of his cigar. "It's easy to see you're a hundred per cent. pro-Italian," he burst out.

"No, I'm not, but, if I cared to, I could make a pretty good case for Italy." Lovelace's sherry arrived at that moment, and as he raised the glass he added: "Well, here's fun. Aren't you joining me?"

Cassel stood up and shook his grey head. "No. If you'll forgive me, I'm afraid I must be moving now. I fear we'd never agree, Sir Anthony, but all the same, it's a pleasure to have met you."

"Same here." Van Der Meer rose beside him. "I'm with Sir Anthony, though. Let Italy have the place, and anyhow, the League's a washout."

Christopher Penn had sat quite silent listening intently to the discussion. Now, as the other two moved off, he spoke for the first time since Lovelace had joined his table.

"What a tragedy it is that the League should have failed! Wilson intended it to embrace every nation on the globe, and now it has shrunk to little more than the old *Triple Entente*—Britain, France and Russia in alliance under another name. When Germany and Japan left it they put the clock back to 1914, and if they joined Italy the three would form a block every bit as strong as the old Triple Alliance—stronger, in fact, since Japan would prove a far more powerful ally than was the case with Austria-Hungary."

Lovelace nodded. "That's so. Half the people in Europe refuse to face the fact that the nations are divided into two great camps. In the event of a blow-up some of the smaller states would come in with us, of course, just as they did in the last Great War, but others would remain neutral, and others, again, would be forced to join the anti-League block, because of their geographical position. As things are, neither Britain nor France can possibly afford to back the League to the limit. If they did, either of them might get let in for a war on account of some trivial sideshow, which would give the nations outside the League an excuse to combine against them. Whatever happens, we mustn't risk another wholesale slaughter."

"You think Van Der Meer is right, then, and that as there always has been war in the world there always will be ?"

"God knows I hope not, but it looks like it."

For a moment Christopher Penn did not speak. He was staring across the room with a far-away look in his eyes. "There will be," he said softly, "as long as there are people like the man who is coming to speak to me now. I've been waiting for him."

Lovelace followed his glance with quick interest. "Who is he ?"

"Sergius Benyon. They say he's made another couple of million out of this war already."

Benyon was a big, jolly-faced fellow with little twinkling eyes. He paused at the table and nodded cheerfully. "They told me outside that you wanted a word with me, Penn."

"I do. Sit down a moment. This is Sir Anthony Lovelace."

"Glad to know you." Benyon drew up a chair. "Well, Penn, how's the lovely Valerie ? I see she broke another record with that plane of hers the other day."

"She's fine, thanks."

"That's good. Now what's the worry?"

"It's yours, not mine, I think." The grave dark eyes of the younger man's pale face held the other. "I suppose you're doing pretty well out of this Abyssinian trouble?"

"Sure thing! Long may the battle rage, my boy—not that I wish the poor devils any harm, of course, but we'll pay a dividend this year it'll be grand to handle. You'd better get your broker to nail you a wad of our shares before the mob get in. They'll go a lot higher yet."

"Thanks. You'd really like to see this war go on, then, and maybe spread to other countries?"

"Well, war certainly is a terrible thing, but it happens to suit my business. It's not our affair if they want to go cutting each others' throats on the other side. We're neutral and we'll keep neutral, so no harm's coming to us. Think what it means to our people! Employment for thousands of extra hands! Big bonuses for all the regular workers! Why, it's the best break my company's had in years. But—what are you driving at?"

"I was wondering if you really felt that way: so, well—so completely detached. Able to enjoy your profits without a thought that they're the product of human suffering."

A frown creased the big man's jolly face. "What the hell's bitten you, Penn?" he asked in a puzzled voice. "I'm just an ordinary business man, aren't I? Where d'you get these fool ideas, anyway?"

"From something that happened to-day." Penn spoke very quietly. "Have you ever heard of the *Millers of God*?"

"What!" Benyon clutched at the arms of his chair and half rose out of it. His face showed sudden intense anger and, Lovelace thought, just a trace of fear. He hunched himself forward and glared into Penn's pale face. "What the devil do *you* know of this bunch of thugs who call themselves the *Millers of God*?"

"Nothing, but it seems that you *have* heard of them before."

"By God I have! Rumours, that's all, but nasty rumours. One or two friends of mine have been—well, never mind." Benyon suddenly banged his fist upon the table. "Look here, Penn, you've *got* to tell me what you know of this devilish organisation."

"I know nothing," Christopher Penn repeated evenly.

"Then why the hell should you mention it after leaving word that you wanted to have a talk with me?"

"Because I was stopped by a stranger in the street to-day. He just said: 'You know Sergius Benyon. For his own sake give him this message: "The *Millers of God* are watching his activities. If, during the next month, the export figures of his companies exceed last year's for the same period by more than 10 per cent. it will be taken as proof that he is amassing riches by supplying material used for the furtherance of mass-murder. As an accessory to murder, before the fact, Sergius Benyon will then be formally condemned to death by the *Millers of God*."'"

"Hell!" Benyon slumped back in his chair. A faint perspiration had broken out on his forehead. He fumbled for a silk handkerchief and began to mop at his face, then he muttered: "So they threaten *me* with death now, do they? What else did he say, Penn, what else did he say?"

"That's all. Word for word as near as I can remember. And before I had a chance to open my mouth, he'd disappeared in the crowd."

"But I can't go and cancel all my contracts and—" Benyon suddenly seemed to recover his nerve. "I'm damned if I would if I could, either. I'm not going to be scared into ruining myself to please a bunch of half-baked pacifists. If it comes to a showdown I'll bet they haven't got the guts to try and do me in."

Lovelace's eyes were on Penn's face. It was grave and impassive as he answered. "The chap who sent you this message looked as though he meant it."

"Did he ? You could describe him, of course ?"

"Yes. The whole episode was so astounding that I should recognise him again anywhere."

"Good !" The big man jumped to his feet. "I'm going down to Police Headquarters right away. 'Fraid they'll want to bother you for your story later, but I'm not taking any chances, and the sooner these *Millers of God* people are chased out of town the better. It may be some bughouse religious organisation, still—you never know. I've heard some queer things lately. So long."

As Benyon swung easily away Lovelace raised his eyebrows. "This sounds like a secret society which is out to kill off war profiteers. Seems a bit drastic, doesn't it ? Although, of course, they're a rotten lot of blighters."

"They are," agreed Penn, "as a whole. Benyon's a decent enough fellow really, and I'd be sorry if anything happened to him. However, I've passed on this mysterious warning, so let's hope he'll take notice of it. You were saying just now, by the way, that you could make a case for Italy, if you wanted to. I'd be interested to hear it."

Lovelace looked up in surprise. He would have liked to speculate further on the possible activities of the *Millers of God*, but Penn was obviously determined to change the conversation. "All right," he said, "but you mustn't take this as my own view. I'm neutral. Most English people are at heart, I think. We hate to see the poor little Emperor done down because, believe it or not, we're a sentimental lot, and our sympathies usually go to the weaker party. On the other hand, we do know that the Emperor isn't strong enough to cope with the terrible abuses which still go on in his country. Of course, what it needs is a real good spring-cleaning.

On the other hand, we admire Mussolini for pulling Italy together after the war, and we've always had a genuine liking for the Italians."

While Penn listened attentively, the Englishman then outlined the amazing changes which had taken place in Italy since the Great War. He laid particular stress upon the fact that she had not sufficient arable land to support her population. "And, after all," he finished, "Mussolini is only proposing to do what Britain and France have done on innumerable occasions in the past. What's more, he gave many months' notice of his intention."

Penn nodded. "That's a very able argument, but, d'you realise you are admitting that Britain is as much to blame as anyone else for this wretched muddle? You say Mussolini gave many months' notice of his intention. If Britain had made it clear then that she meant to support the League, the presumption is that there wouldn't have been any war."

"Perhaps, but I'd rather you didn't father it entirely on us. Britain has voiced the feeling of the smaller nations, but she couldn't do that before she knew it. This is the League's business, and we had to wait for the League's decision."

"You mean you never fancied the idea of having the Italians in Abyssinia, because you feared they might prove awkward neighbours for you in Egypt. But you preferred to wait before making your protest until you could appear as the champion of the League."

Lovelace grinned. "You're a pretty shrewd young man, aren't you?"

"Not particularly. I've studied these questions rather carefully, that's all. Another thing: that argument about surplus population is a complete fallacy. Did you know that although the Germans had a very considerable colonial Empire before the war, there were actually a greater number of their nationals in Paris, the enemy capital, on the outbreak of hostilities, than in the whole of their overseas territory? It's been proved time and again that colonies are not essential to the expansion of a people. Look at the number of Italians and Germans we have here in the States!"

"There's a certain amount of truth in that."

"There is, and ingenious as your case for Italy appears on the surface, if I were Cassel, I should tell you it's just the sort of argument that Britain can be guaranteed to put up when she wishes to justify her own annexations. A delightful essay in hypocrisy!"

Lovelace laughed. "Oh, everyone accuses the British of being hypocrites. It isn't true, though. It's just that our statesmen are so slow in the uptake that quick-witted foreigners always suspect their noncommittal attitude to conceal some deep-laid plan. Generally, before our people have even had time to formulate a policy."

"Nonsense," smiled Penn; "they're the astutest bunch of diplomats in the world. Still, even granting that all you have said is honestly believed by the great majority of Italians, you don't believe it yourself, do you?"

"Not altogether." Lovelace was frank. "I was only arguing for fun just now. Actually, I'm sailing for Abyssinia on Saturday—as a non-combatant, of course—but I shall be helping Abyssinia as far as a neutral can."

"Really?" Penn looked up with quickened interest. "But it's a bit late in the day, isn't it?"

"Why? Of course, if the League can make some face-saving arrangement by which Mussolini comes off with flying colours a peace may be agreed to-morrow. Again, if the Italians start using poison gas the Abyssinian armies are so ill-organised that they might break up and the Emperor find himself compelled to throw his hand in. But that's unlikely. In six months the Italians have penetrated the country to the depth of about a hundred-and-fifty miles. They still have two-hundred-and-fifty to go before they reach Addis, and the rains are due in about a month. The probabilities are that the Italians will have to dig in then and wait till the next dry season before they can advance further. Even if they succeed in taking Addis Ababa they will not have conquered the country. The tribes will still put up a stiff resistance in the western mountains. I should have been out there months ago if I hadn't been held up by other, rather important, personal affairs."

"I see," Penn hesitated; "but what is it you are going to do out there?"

"I don't quite know yet," Lovelace said quietly. "I have a little money of my own. Not much, but enough to make me independent, so I've knocked about the world a good deal, and I've rather a gift for languages. I've been mixed up in the tail ends of half a dozen wars too, and know how to handle native labour, so there are plenty of jobs the relief organisations would be glad to give a fellow like myself."

"I see. You make a habit of being on the spot in any war that's going. But why? Is it because you like the excitement?"

"No." Lovelace fiddled with his pipe, and seemed a little shy as he gave his reason. "You'll probably think me a queer bird, but if you've never seen it you can have no idea of the incredible misery and suffering which afflicts the population behind a war zone. And since we can't stop the war, I feel it's up to those of us who can afford to chuck up the easy life to go and do the little that's possible to make things just a shade less terrible, particularly for the women and children."

"That's fine," said Penn softly. "You're really a war hater, just as much as I am, then. I'm afraid I've done you rather an injustice."

"Oh, that's all right. It just amuses me to pull the leg of theoretical pacifists like Cassel now and again, that's all."

Penn passed a hand over his jet-black hair. For a moment he was silent. "You know," he said at last, "there's lots of things I'd like to talk to you about. D'you happen to be fixed up for this evening?"

"No. I was going to a show but the man I was going with has gone sick."

"Well, I can't ask you to dine in New York because it's essential I should go out to my Long Island home to-night. But, if you don't mind the drive, we could dine there and the car could run you back, or I could put you up for the night, just as you prefer."

"Thanks. I'll come with pleasure."

As they stood up to leave, Lovelace glanced at the pale ascetic face of the young American again. "I wonder," he said suddenly, "if there is really anything except pacifist bluff behind this *Millers of God* business. D'you think the police will stand any chance of tracing the man who gave you that message?"

Christopher Penn's beautifully chiselled mouth curved into a faint smile. "Not the least," he said firmly. "I don't mind telling you now that whatever description I give will be completely mythical, and that the *Millers of God* are in deadly earnest. I am one of them myself, you see."

"I had an idea that might be the case," murmured Sir Anthony Lovelace.

CHAPTER II

MURDER?

AS Penn and Lovelace left the warmth and security of the Union Club, the outer world seemed doubly grim by contrast.

Manhattan Island was still in the grip of winter. Spring might be on the way, but the towering blocks of steel and concrete flung their pinnacles towards a grey and lowering sky. An icy wind bent the tree-tops in Central Park and howled down the man-made canyons, causing the down-town crowd to draw their wraps more closely round them as they hurried homewards from their offices.

During the forty-mile drive the two men hardly spoke. Penn, at the wheel of his long low car, was intent on the swift-moving traffic as it hurtled towards them, while Lovelace, naturally a rather silent man, was busy with his own thoughts.

The car swung right after passing through Baysbore and turned in through a pair of tall gates with a lodge on one side. The drive wound through ancient trees, and ended in a wide sweep before a long, low, rambling house. Lovelace saw just enough of its front, as the headlights swept the porch and balconies, to realise that it was old, creeper-covered and mellowed by time. Actually it was the original home of Christopher's branch of the Penn family, and except that its big stables were now garages and the house had all the additional comforts that modern science could supply, it was little altered from what it had been when Abraham Lincoln was a boy.

As a servant came out to take over the car, the deafening roar of an aeroplane engine sounded overhead.

"That chap's flying pretty low," remarked Lovelace.

"It's not a chap; it's Valerie, I expect. Her people are our nearest neighbours. Have been for generations. She's my fiancée, you know."

Lovelace looked at the young American with some surprise as they passed into the house. He could well understand any girl falling for such a handsome fellow. Women would be certain to find his black eyes beneath their curling lashes "romantic," and his unusual pallor "interesting." Yet he did not strike the Englishman as a woman's man at all. It was difficult to imagine him making love. He seemed such a spiritual type—almost as though he lived in a world apart.

"Hardly flying weather, particularly for a girl," Lovelace added after a moment.

"Oh, Valerie's all right." The reply was casual. "She can fly as well as most men, or better, and anyhow, she'll have landed and be safe at home by now. Come along in."

He led the way into a square, book-lined room and pushed a couple of arm-chairs up to an old-fashioned open hearth, upon which a bright fire was burning. "You'll excuse me for a moment while I give some orders, won't you? There are the drinks and cigarettes. Help yourself. I shan't be long."

"Thanks." Lovelace poured himself a drink and sat down, thrusting his feet forward to the blaze, but a moment later he drew them sharply up again and leaned forward to peer at a solitary photograph which occupied a prominent position on the mantelpiece.

It was that of a girl, and he judged her to be about twenty-five. The style of hairdressing showed that it was quite a recent portrait, but it was difficult to guess if her hair were golden or brown. The eyes were large, but rather pale in the photograph, which gave them an almost magnetic look and made Lovelace suspect that they were grey. They were set under dead-straight brows, giving the young face a look of tremendous personality and determination. It would have been almost forbidding had it not been for the mobile mouth and for an enormous, but somehow quite incongruous dimple under the curve of the left cheek.

Certain in his own mind that he knew the original of the portrait, he stood up to examine it more closely, but he searched his memory in vain for a clue. He was still gazing at it when his host returned.

"Sorry," Lovelace apologised. "You must think me an ill-mannered fellow staring at your friend."

"Oh, no. That's Valerie, the girl we were talking about just now."

"Yes, I think I guessed that; but the strange thing is I'm sure I've met her, and for the life of me I can't think where."

Penn laughed. "That's easily explained: she's Valerie Lorne, the flying ace, and she holds all sorts of records. You must have seen photographs of her in the Press a hundred times."

"Of course, how stupid of me!" Lovelace shrugged. Yet although he had never seen the famous air-woman in the flesh he was certain now that her hair was not fair, but chestnut, and that those compelling eyes were grey. He could not account for the queer impression that he had been face to face with her on some occasion.

Half an hour later the two men sat down to dinner. The mahogany was of an earlier period than the house, and the chairs were of the broad-seated comfortable variety: a memory of more spacious days when people liked ample elbow-room and men sat long over their wine. The Georgian silver was no purchase from an auction-room, but had come to the family straight from its maker in the hold of a sailing ship, when steam transport was still undreamt of.

An elderly butler and one footman waited on them; they served a meal that was good but unpretentious. Christopher Penn drank only water, but Lovelace found the Burgundy, which was served with the duck, excellent and *chambré* to a nicety. The port, too, was a pre-prohibition vintage, which had lain undisturbed, steadily approaching maturity, during the years that the Volstead Act had been in force. Yet there was not the least suggestion of glitter and display in the quiet room, and Lovelace felt that he might have been enjoying a pleasant dinner with one of his less well-off friends at home, rather than with a young man who controlled enormous vested interests and was several times a millionaire.

During the latter part of the meal the two discovered a mutual interest in fishing, and talked of flies, tackle, and of the red-letter days on which they had made their best catches.

The heat, the dust, the rains of Abyssinia all had faded from the Englishman's mind, and he was thinking of the brown trout which frequented a pool he knew on the Findhorn, when he realised with a little shock that, unobserved by him, the servants had left the room, and that his host was speaking.

"I want to talk to you seriously, Lovelace, about the real possibilities of stopping war."

"Yes; this society, the *Millers of God*, eh? I'd be most interested to hear more of that, if you care to tell me. It was taking a bit of a risk though, wasn't it? To admit you're a member, seeing that I'm, well—a comparative stranger."

Penn shook his dark head. "I don't think so. You see, I've rather a gift for sizing people up, and I felt I could trust you all along. When you said that about chucking the easy life to go out and make things just a shade less terrible for the innocent who suffer in every war, I was certain that, even if you didn't approve our methods, you wouldn't give me away in a thousand years."

"That's so, of course. Has your society been operating for long?"

"It started at Oxford just after the Great War. Quite a lot of men went up there to take their degrees who should have gone up years before. Many of them were broken and bitter. You know how it was, they'd been through it all and come out three parts wrecked in mind and body. There were others, too, who hadn't seen the fighting but spent the war years at their public schools. Half starved, poor devils, and deprived of all thc natural fun which goes with boyhood. They had listened on Sundays, week after week, to all those long lists read out in chapel; fathers, jolly uncles, chaps who had been in the eleven or fifteen a few terms before, cousins and friends; one by one posted as dead, casualties, or missing."

Lovelace sighed. "Yes, it was pretty grim."

"Well, some of 'em got together. They watched the Versailles Treaty in the making. Like a few of the more intelligent diplomats of the old school, who weren't allowed to have a say, they felt that it was an instrument of vengeance which must lead to further war—instead of a step towards a permanent peace. They had no faith in Governments, either Democratic or run by some big political Boss. They'd been let down too badly, and they saw that the best of Governments were only puppets pushed and tricked into acting on the will of ignorant multitudes. The people; who are swayed first one way and then another. A dozen of those embittered men met constantly. In private they surveyed the whole situation with the logical cynicism engendered by their wrecked lives and cheated youth. They came to the conclusion that there was only one way to stop future wars: to declare war themselves on the men who stir the multitudes to demand that their Government shall take action: *the men who sit behind it all and reap the benefits of war.*"

"But surely you're too young to've been at Oxford just after the war?" Lovelace cut in with a puzzled frown.

"Oh yes. I was only speaking of the origin of the society. There are branches of it in a dozen Universities now. It's become international, and I became a recruit, through my tutor, at Yale."

"I see, and what have the *Millers of God* done so far?"

"Well, the Mills of God grind slowly, you know, even if they grind exceeding small. Still, we've a certain amount to show. Each of us is prepared to use every penny we possess, if necessary, and all the influence we've got, to preserve peace. The Neutrality Bill has been put through in this country largely through our efforts. There's not a great deal in that. It's only an example which we hope other nations will follow. Then, much more important, there is the new law that all armament factories are to become the property of the State. That is a great step forward because it cuts the throat of the munition racket—at all events here."

"Yes, and there *is* a real hope that other countries may follow your lead there, even if their obligations prevent them going permanently neutral. There's nothing to stop them controlling armaments, except the armament people."

"Ah, there you have it. That brings me to the grimmer side of our organisation. If, after due investigation has been made, it's proved beyond doubt that a certain individual is actively working against the maintenance of peace, sentence is passed on him, and one of us undertakes the execution of that sentence."

"Have there—" Lovelace hesitated a second—"have there been many cases like that?"

"Quite a number. The first was Eberheim, the nickel man. He played a big part behind the scenes in inciting the Greeks to try and mop up all that was left of Turkey after the Armistice. One day he disappeared from his headquarters in Smyrna and he's never been heard of since. Then there was a fellow called Pirradow. He was in oil, and he died suddenly on the way out to make new contracts with the Bolivians during their scrap with Paraguay—after he'd been warned to stay at home." Christopher Penn fiddled nervously with the stem of his glass as he spoke. It held only water yet, judging from his flushed face, he might well have been drinking heavily of the potent wine. His dark eyes glittered like those of a fanatic as he went on. "Rechmanitz was another. One of his own hand grenades went off unexpectedly, just as he was getting in his car one day to go off and do a demonstration for the benefit of a Japanese buyer whose employers were anxious to blow the guts out of a few more poor devils in China. Verdino is supposed to have broken his neck in a fall. Dowling was found dead in his bath. Olagnoff was drowned at sea."

"I must confess," Lovelace interrupted, "that I've never heard of any of these people."

The younger man shrugged. "That's hardly surprising. The enemy work together you know. In a loose sort of way theirs is an organisation as well, and their power over the world Press is enormous. They suppress all but the barest mention of these 'accidents', as far as they can. They're getting a bit rattled now, though, and we're picking off the worst of them one by one."

Lovelace thoughtfully fingered his little moustache. "Then what it comes to is this. Your organisation is actually perpetrating a series of murders. It *is* murder. You can't get away from that."

"Well, what if it is?" Christopher Penn suddenly stood up. "That's the fault of our law which executes a poor devil who's too drunk to know what he's doing when he kills another in a brawl, and yet gives these arch-murderers, who deliberately ferment mass-slaughter, its protection. Call it murder if you like, but no executions according to the law of any state have ever been ordered for the protection of human life with more justice."

"My dear fellow, I agree with you in theory. It's the practical part which revolts me personally. That's against all reason, perhaps, but it's a fact, and as a decent man I believe at heart you must feel the same. I understand your using all your influence to support your organisation's political moves, and even issuing warnings or threats on their behalf, as you did a few hours ago to that man Benyon, but if they actually picked on you to hunt a man down and kill him, I don't believe your conscience would allow you to go through with it."

"It would. If I failed to carry out my pledge, and all the others failed too, new wars would break out that would take either us or our children. We've *got* to stop it somehow! Isolation's no good. The League's no good. Ours is the only way, and we must not falter." Penn's mouth tightened for a moment and then he suddenly cried: "I had my notification yesterday. It's horrible, isn't it? Horrible, but—I've got to commit murder!"

The door had opened. The girl of the photograph stood on its threshold. Her eyes were wide and staring. "You—commit murder?" she stammered. "Oh, Christopher, what *do* you mean?"

CHAPTER III

VALERIE LORNE TAKES A HAND

SIR ANTHONY LOVELACE stared at the girl. He had been right, her hair *was* chestnut, and her eyes *were* grey.

After her first exclamation she recovered almost instantly, and stepped firmly into the room. "What did you mean, Christopher, when you said you had *got* to commit a murder?"

"Darling, I'm sorry—sorry if I scared you; but you took us rather by surprise." He waved a hand towards his guest. "This is Sir Anthony Lovelace. Lovelace, my fiancée, Valerie Lorne."

As she acknowledged the introduction Lovelace thought her eyes showed a sudden flicker of interest, but she turned abruptly to her fiancé. "I let myself in and I quite thought you were alone."

"That's all right, sweet," said Christopher swiftly. "Until I heard your plane come over I didn't think you'd be back before to-morrow, but I meant to call you later. Let's go into the other room."

They followed her out across the hall to the book-lined sitting-room. Christopher shut the door behind him. "It's come," he said facing her. "Somehow I never thought they'd select me; but they have. It came yesterday morning."

"You mean—the thing you told me of when we became engaged?" She lit a cigarette and Lovelace gave her full marks for the hold she was keeping on herself.

Christopher nodded.

"Well," she appeared to consider for a moment.

"That's pretty hard on both of us: but, if you've got to, it will not be murder."

"Lovelace here seems to think it is."

"Please forget I said that." Lovelace was feeling the awkwardness of his position. "Look here, Penn, you'll naturally want to talk this thing over with Miss Lorne. Don't let's stand on ceremony. Ring for your car to be sent round and it can take me back to New York at once."

"Thanks, but I'd rather you didn't go yet. I've still got something I want to say to you."

The girl picked up a log and threw it on the fire. As she dusted her hands, she said thoughtfully: "It is obvious Christopher has told you about the *Millers of God.* Don't you think that the end really justifies the means in the work they're doing?"

"To a certain extent," Lovelace agreed uneasily, "but I find it hard to stomach the actual fact of killing some fellow who, however blood-guilty he may be in theory, considers himself a perfectly innocent business man going about his normal job."

Valerie Lorne spoke with sudden fervour. "I expected the infidels considered themselves innocent when they turned Our Lord's sepulchre into a Mohammedan mosque, yet thousands of Christians gave their lives to recapture the Holy Land. This, too, is a Crusade!"

"Perhaps, but surely that was different. It was a war like any other. There was no question of stealthy assassination. Still, this really isn't my business. Your fiancé seems determined to carry theory into practice and you, apparently, agree that he's right to do so."

"I've very little option," she said slowly. "I don't know how long you have known him, but Christopher Penn is Christopher Penn. He told me this might occur when we became engaged, although neither of us thought it likely then. Now it's happened I mustn't allow my personal feelings to interfere with—well—what he considers to be his duty."

Lovelace was several years older than either of the others. He sensed the young man's feeling that he had pledged himself to a horrid business and the girl's loyal acceptance of the fact; yet her abhorrence of it. He felt that he must make some effort to straighten out this tangle, so he said: "Is there some very unpleasant penalty to be faced if you decided to back out, Penn?"

"No, none. The society is very elastic and there's very little mystery about it. No passwords or secret signs, or that sort of bunkum. Most of us are even rather ashamed of the name under which it's run, but it had to be called something. There are no oaths of secrecy, so we can speak of it quite freely to anyone we like, although of course we never do, except to people we feel we can absolutely trust. Even if our judgment were at fault, and somebody broke a confidence one of us made to him, it couldn't do much damage. You see, we have no offices or fixed meeting places: nearly all our communications are carried by word of mouth and as most of us are wealthy people we travel frequently so there's no difficulty in passing on suggestions or decisions from one part of the world to another. There are no penalties for anyone who ceases to be an active member, either. If I refused to do this job it'd just be put up to someone else. But conviction and—well, honour if you like—are tighter bonds than any oath, and I could never respect myself again if I ratted on the others now."

"You see, Sir Anthony, that's Christopher." Valerie smiled for the first time, giving a queer little twist to her mouth. "Difficult chap for a girl to love, isn't he? The most pig-headed, quixotic fool between Panama and Alaska I should say—but I happen to like him. Anyhow, I'm afraid there's nothing to be done except for his friends to help him as far as they can."

Lovelace cast an eye on the decanter. "D'you mind if I mix myself a drink?" He wanted time to think up another argument.

"Please do. I'm so sorry I forgot to ask you. I so rarely drink anything myself, you see," Christopher said apologetically.

While he measured out the whisky with careful deliberation Lovelace's brain was working overtime. The boy was a fanatic and the girl was in love with him. Pretty hard on her but, by Jove, she was behaving magnificently. Where the devil had he met her? Somewhere in the past—but that didn't matter now. She had hypnotised herself into an active sympathy with this society of madmen; but were they mad or terribly, logically sane? Anyhow, she didn't want him to become a murderer for all her talk about Crusades. He wasn't liking the idea either now it had taken concrete form. Probably doubted his ability to carry the job through. Case of the spirit being willing but the flesh being weak. Perhaps he could be scared into chucking it. That seemed the only line to try. Tumbler in hand, Lovelace turned back towards his host.

"Ever seen an execution?"

"No. Why?"

"I have, several. Saw a Chinese coolie's head chopped off once. He took it pretty stolidly, but an Armenian spy in the pay of the Greeks who had to face a Turkish firing-party didn't take it half so well. Neither did a young Spaniard who was hanged during the South American trouble. I can hear his screaming now as they fixed the noose round his neck. To look at he was rather like you."

"Why are you telling me this?"

"Only because it may happen to you one cold grey morning. On an empty tummy perhaps, when dreams are unsatisfactory fare. The police must know something of your organisation by this time, and if they get you after you've done this job you'll see the inside of the death cell for certain."

Christopher shrugged a little contemptuously. "The police! Their job is to keep ordinary crime in check but they're up against an utterly different proposition in the *Millers of God*. No one of us ever commits a second crime. Each of us is a completely reputable person, who has other activities to cover his operations, and other equally unsuspected people to assist in his get-away. None of the deaths we are responsible for has any apparent motive, so there is never any case for the police to formulate against us. We're completely outside their natural orbit so we haven't a thing to fear from their attentions."

"I see. Well, would you care to give us some particulars as to how you propose to set about this er—killing?"

"With an ether pistol discharging a deadly gas from some special shells. It's silent, painless, and practically instantaneous. All our executions are carried out that way, although whenever possible we arrange things afterwards to look as though death had been caused by an accident. I received the pistol and shells yesterday with my instructions."

Lovelace's tanned face looked very grave. He was still seeking a way to divert the younger man from his terrible purpose as he inquired: "Where will you try and get Benyon—in his home?"

"Benyon!" Christopher exclaimed. "But it's not him. I should never be called on to execute a man I know—that would be too awful. It was only just because I did know him I was asked to give him his warning before I left the States."

"This—this job means your going abroad then?" said Valerie.

"Yes. To Paris first where I shall receive my final instructions from one of our people. After that I don't know. I was told to get my passport visaed for all countries bordering on the Mediterranean, or the Red Sea, and Abyssinia, though; so it looks as if they may be sending me to the seat of war."

"But, darling!" Valerie protested, "you would be

absolutely lost in a place like Abyssinia. You know how impractical you are and you don't speak a single foreign language except French."

He nodded gloomily. "I know, sweet. I've never been farther east than Rome, even as a tourist, and I'll be horribly handicapped if I have to go on to Asia Minor or Eritrea or Abyssinia itself. That's just what's worrying me at the moment."

A hint of amusement showed in Lovelace's brown eyes. "So that's it, eh? That's why you got me out here. When you heard that I was a pretty useful linguist, and had been in Abyssinia before, you hoped to rope me in as your assistant in the chase."

"Yes," Christopher confessed quite frankly, "that was my idea. When I heard you talking in the Club this evening it almost seemed as though God had sent you there specially to help me."

Lovelace shook his head. "Nothing doing I'm afraid. Because I hate war and all the senseless misery that it causes, it doesn't mean for one moment that I'm prepared to lend a hand in an assassination."

"I don't ask you to. I only want you as a friend who knows the ropes if I have to go to Africa. Please come with me. You're going out there anyway. It won't delay you much if we have to put in a day in Paris on the way. Forget what I'm going out there to do if you like. We'll never speak of it again, but I do wish you'd travel with me."

"I'm sorry." Lovelace shook his head again. "What you propose to do is murder: the killing of some unsuspecting man. I can't be a party to that."

Valerie Lorne had been silent for a time. Now she spoke again. "Won't you? I wish you would. Christopher will be like a child in those tropical countries. He needs a friend like you so badly. Even if you can't forget his mission you need take no part in it. Surely you won't refuse to let him travel with you to the Near East if he has to go there."

Somehow Lovelace found the girl's appeal harder to resist. In some queer way, which he could not explain to himself, he felt as though she had some sort of claim on him. Yet he still stubbornly shook his head.

"I can't. Perhaps that's because I'm not big enough to scrap all the rather foolish prejudices with which most of us have been brought up. If it were a question of giving my own life to stop another war—well, I'd try to screw my courage up to that because I've seen so much of war in its worst aspects. But to aid and abet a murder in cold blood; that's too much. I just can't do it."

Valerie sighed and turned to Christopher. "When must you sail, darling?"

"I've booked on the *Europa* which sails to-morrow night. It's urgent and they wanted me to leave as soon as possible. I pulled a few strings with the diplomatic people yesterday and they got my passport back for me with all the necessary visas this afternoon. I've made arrangements with my bank to have funds at my disposal in all the larger towns I may have to go to. I only hope the enemy organisation doesn't find out what I'm up to and try to prevent my leaving the country though . . ."

As the door opened they all started and looked towards it. The elderly butler stood there with his eyes on Christopher. "The telephone, sir," he said. "The person who called you refused to give his name."

"Excuse me, won't you." Christopher went into the next room.

The interruption had broken the tension. Lovelace walked over to Valerie who was leaning with one elbow on the corner of the mantelpiece. He was a good head taller than she was and stood looking down at her.

"We've met somewhere before, you know: where was it?" he asked abruptly.

"Don't you remember?" She turned her face up to his and a smile deepened the dimple in her cheek.

"No," he confessed. "I've been racking my brains for the last hour to place it; but I can't. Tell me."

Slowly she shook her head and her grey eyes grew dreamy. "Why should I? It may have been long ago. It may even have been in some previous existence. What's it matter where it was if you have forgotten?"

As she turned away Christopher rejoined them. His beautiful, ascetic face seemed colder and harder than ever, yet there was a faint nervous tremor in his long pointed fingers as he lit a cigarette.

"That call was anonymous," he said. "The man at the other end of the wire didn't mince matters. He just told me certain people know what I've been put up to do, and that if I stayed in the United States no harm would befall me, but that if I set foot outside the country I'd be dead within a week."

Valerie laid a hand on his shoulder. "You mean to go on, Christopher?"

"Certainly. This'll make things more difficult—that's all. I'll have to regard every person in the ship as an enemy who is out to get me."

"You won't," she said with swift determination. "I mean to fly you over the border into Canada before morning. You'll be on the water then before they even know you've sailed."

Christopher's face brightened. "Valerie, you're a girl in a million. If you'll do that it will give me a clear start and a safe passage over. Once I'm in Europe I'll go to earth, and they'll have the devil's own job to find me. Bless you, darling."

"How long will it take you to pack a bag?"

"I'll be ready in an hour. I've got a few papers to see to, that's all, and we can look up to-morrow's Canadian sailings in the news sheets. I'll order the car for you, Lovelace, to take you back to New York."

"Thanks," said Lovelace quietly. "I'd be glad if you would. But why are you in such a desperate hurry? Surely if you're over the Canadian border by dawn that will do? Plenty of time for me to collect my bags in New York and return here before you set out."

"Return here?" echoed Christopher.

"Yes. This is a very different business from what I thought it a few minutes ago. If the enemy are organised and have sent you an ultimatum your job's no longer assassination, but an act of war. I'm game to help you now, so I'm coming too."

CHAPTER IV

THE ROMANCE OF A QUEEN

IN the bitter cold of early dawn Valerie flew the two men up the coast of Maine, then across the Bay of Fundy to Halifax, Nova Scotia, where she landed them safely by half-past ten.

Their passports were all in order. Christopher's had been renewed only two days before, Lovelace had travelled so much in the last ten years that he made a practice of keeping his up to date for most countries he was likely to visit, and Valerie possessed a special *laissez-passer* granted to her by the State Department soon after she began breaking air records.

No question was raised when they landed and from the flying-field they went straight to a Travel Office. There they learned that the s.s. *Pomeranzen*, 10,500 tons, was due to sail for Rotterdam at eight o'clock that evening.

The Dutch vessel carried cargo as well as a hundred-and-twenty cabin-class passengers. She was a nine-day boat but there was plenty of accommodation vacant in her and they would have had to wait three days for the larger C.P.R. liner which was scheduled to dock in Europe half a day later.

Christopher's orders were urgent. He should have sailed in the *Europa* from New York that evening and landed at Cherbourg on April 5th. His change of plans meant that he would not reach Paris until the 11th, six days late, and he felt that he must not delay his arrival by even half a day more for the sake of travelling on the bigger ship. He said at once:

"All right. I'll take the two best cabins you've got on the the Dutchman, with bathrooms, of course, and a private drawing-room, if you can get me one."

Lovelace smiled to himself. He usually managed to travel in reasonable comfort, but he was not rich, and he felt that it would be fun to voyage *de luxe* for a change in the company of this young multi-millionaire.

Valerie cut in on his thoughts. "We'll need three staterooms, Christopher, and they must make arrangements to ship the plane as well."

Both men swung round on her at once. "We can't take you with us . . ." Christopher began.

"Why not?" she lifted her chin. "I'm due for a trip to Europe anyway; and in Paris I can get some frocks."

"We'd love to have you along, darling, but . . ."

"But nothing," she cut him short. The dimple in her cheek deepened as she smiled and squeezed his arm. "You want to get to Paris at the earliest possible moment, don't you? I'll fly you there from Rotterdam and save you the best part of a day in the train."

Christopher gave way without further argument and Lovelace was soon to find that he always did so when she took charge of a situation. She was far the more practical of the two and mothered her pale-faced, handsome fiancé as though he were some precious, wayward infant.

By the time they were two days out of Halifax Lovelace was thoroughly glad that she had elected to come with them. Without her it would have been a gloomy crossing, for Christopher was silent and moody. Each day he sat staring out across the grey waters of the North Atlantic with dark unseeing eyes, occupied, to the exclusion of all else, with the terrible secret war in which he had pledged himself to take human life.

Lovelace tried to put that out of his thoughts. To him no academic reasoning, however powerful, quite seemed to justify the sinister operations of the *Millers*. He had constantly to remind himself that Christopher's life was threatened too, and that they were engaged in a battle of wits, rather than the planning of a cold-blooded assassination.

Valerie seemed to accept the fact that her fiancé was pledged to his gruesome task and appeared to have no doubts as to its justice. She spoke of it little and it was a great relief to Lovelace that he was able to forget it while in her company. They talked happily enough of the thrills she had had in breaking air records, and of his experiences when travelling in foreign countries, or as a relief worker behind the lines in numerous wars.

He puzzled his wits in vain as to where he had met her before. Her dead-straight eyebrows below the white forehead and chestnut hair, the big, grey, almost magnetic eyes and the deep dimple below the left cheek were strangely familiar to him. For some reason that he could not fathom, she continued to make a mystery of it, insisting that their first meeting must have been in some former life, and refusing to aid his memory with any sort sort of clue.

It was not until late on the last afternoon of the voyage that, settling herself beside him in a steamer chair, she broached the subject of Abyssinia.

"You'll look pretty foolish," she said thoughtfully, "if the war is over by the time you get to Addis Ababa."

"Christopher may, but I shan't," he answered dryly. "Anyhow, I think it unlikely the war will be over for some time to come."

"Why? Look at the victories the Italians have gained recently. They captured those two big mountains, Amba—something, weeks ago."

"Amba Aradam and Amba Aladji you mean. Yes, that was at the end of February."

"Well, ever since the Italians have been smashing up Abyssinian armies right and left. Ras Kassa and Ras Immira have both been defeated and Marshal Badoglio is pressing on now into the interior."

Lovelace shook his head. "The Abyssinian armies are very different from ours. If a modern army sustains a serious defeat its organisation breaks down and the whole thing may go to pieces, but these people have no organisation worth talking about. The Rases' troops are just great hosts of fighting men in which every man's his own Army Service Corps. You can launch an attack which will send the whole lot running helter skelter one day but twenty-four hours later ninety-five per cent of them will pop up again ready for another scrap."

"Yes, I know that, but what's to stop the Italians just keeping them on the run? How can they put up any really serious resistance? Why! The British won a war against the Abyssinians with the old-fashioned sort of guns and rifles they used fifty years ago. The Italians have machine-guns and tanks and aeroplanes; things undreamed of then. With such a tremendous advantage in armaments I can't see why the Italians shouldn't march straight through to Addis Ababa now and mop the whole thing up."

"Can't you?" Lovelace laughed. "When we defeated the Abyssinians the whole situation was entirely different. The tribes were in revolt against the bad old Emperor Theodore and we only went in to give them a hand pushing him off the throne. The bulk of the population welcomed General Napier with open arms and, anyhow, he only got as far as Magdala. It's another thing altogether to have to fight your way through that devilish country with every hand against you."

"Is it? Even with tanks?"

"Lord, yes! Ask any of the fellows who've seen fighting on the North-West Frontier of India. It's much the same kind of terrain and the Abyssinian is own twin to the Pathan as far as bravery, cunning and cruelty go. Columns are ambushed and shot to pieces in every gully and you hardly ever see a tribesman. They fade away into the rocks and you can't imagine where they've got to until they start shooting you up again from a new niche at the next turn of the road. What's the good of tanks in that sort of warfare?"

"How about planes? The airman ought to be able to spot their hiding-places and bomb them out."

They try, of course, but it's mighty expensive on ammunition. No real targets to go for, you see, only handfuls of snipers scattered about the precipitous hillsides. They may kill a man here or there and scare his nearest pals for an hour or two; but planes can't really help much when the fighting is in such mountainous country. The Italians have only penetrated to a depth of about a hundred-and-fifty miles so far. They've still got two-fifty to go and nothing short of a miracle in courage and endurance could enable them to cover that in the month to run before the rains come."

"Will the rains make further progress quite impossible?"

"Utterly. You've no idea how it rains out there. Every gully becomes a mountain torrent and tiny rivers swell to hundreds of yards in width. It just comes down like a cloud-burst for days on end and it seems as if half the country's going to be washed away. If all the engineers of the finest armies in the world were concentrated there they couldn't transport their troops and stores through that welter of mud and foaming water."

Valerie sighed. "But supposing the League persuades the Emperor to agree to a peace with Italy after all. That would let Christopher out, wouldn't it?"

"Not necessarily. Abyssinia's only one act in the game as far as the *Millers* are concerned. Their campaign is world-wide. They may not be sending Christopher to Africa at all for all we know."

"As he was told to get his passport visaed for all countries bordering on the Mediterranean and the Red Sea it looks as if Abyssinia is almost certain to be his destination. What's it like there, Anthony? The people are Christians, aren't they?"

"Well, hardly. Most of the wilder tribes are still dyed-in-the-wool pagans. In the towns there are many Mohammedans, particularly in Harar, which is an old walled Arab city, but most of the ruling caste have been

Christians of a sort since the dark ages. Before that they followed the Jewish faith."

"Are they Jewish by race, then?"

"Oh, no, but they consider themselves the Chosen People because they've been in possession of the Ark of the Covenant for centuries. One of their kings pinched it when he was on a visit to Jerusalem. They'd adopted the Jewish faith before that owing to the lapse from virtue of the Queen of Sheba."

Valerie glanced at him suspiciously from under her level brows. "You're pulling my leg. She wasn't a real person, was she?"

"She was indeed," he protested, "and by all accounts a darned good-looking girl, into the bargain."

"Tell me about her."

"She was the Virgin Queen of Ethiopia in King Solomon's day. The country was already rich and powerful. Probably much more civilised than it is at the present time through the influence of Egypt and Babylonia. Anyhow, her merchants used to trade as far as India and the Sudan. She's said to have lived in great luxury and been very wise and beautiful, of course an Arab type—a sort of Egyptian Shahrazade. The report of Solomon's wisdom came to her so she determined to visit him.

"It must have been a tough journey for a woman; trekking on under the blazing sun week after week with very little water, almost trackless deserts to cross, and most of the route infested with bands of marauding Arabs. But she did it—and legend relates that, when she arrived in Jerusalem, her state chariot was drawn by sixteen zebras; although they're always said to be untamable." Lovelace picked up a book he had been reading before Valerie came on deck. "The whole story's here if you're interested."

"What is it?" Valerie asked, taking the book from him.

"Wallis Budge's translation of the Kebra Nagast

That's the Abyssinian Bible, or rather their own particular version of the Old Testament, mainly. I'll find you the bit about how the wily Solomon did the dirty on the lovely Queen, if you like." He lent over and turned the pages until he came to the passage. Then Valerie read:

And King Solomon sent a message unto the Queen, saying, "Now that thou hast come here why wilt thou go away without seeing the administration of the kingdom, and how the meal(s) for the chosen ones of the kingdom are eaten after the manner of the righteous, and how the people are driven away after the manner of sinners? From (the sight of) it thou wouldst acquire wisdom. Follow me now and seat thyself in my splendour in the tent, and I will complete thy instruction, and thou shalt learn the administration of my kingdom; for thou hast loved wisdom, and she shall dwell with thee until thine end and for ever." Now a prophecy maketh itself apparent in (this) speech.

And the Queen sent a second message, saying, "From being a fool, I have become wise by following thy wisdom, and from being a thing rejected by the God of Israel, I have become a chosen woman because of this faith which is in my heart; and henceforth I will worship no other god except Him. And as concerning that which thou sayest, that thou wishest to increase in me wisdom and honour, I will come according to thy desire." And Solomon rejoiced because of this (message), and he arrayed his chosen ones (in splendid apparel), and he added a double supply to his table, and he had all the arrangements concerning the management of his house carefully ordered, and the house of King Solomon was made ready (for guests) daily. And he made it ready with very great pomp, in joy, and in peace, in wisdom, and in tenderness, with all humility and lowliness; and then he ordered the royal table according to the law of the kingdom.

And the Queen came and passed into a place set apart in splendour and glory, and she sat down immediately behind him where she could see and learn and know everything. And she marvelled exceedingly at what she saw, and at what she heard, and she praised the God of Israel in her heart; and she was struck with wonder at the splendour of the royal palace which she saw. For she could see, though no one could see her, even as Solomon had arranged in wisdom for her. He had beautified the place where she was seated, and had spread over it purple hangings, and laid down carpets, and decorated it with *miskat* (moschus), and marbles and precious stones, and he burned aromatic powders, and sprinkled oil of myrrh and cassia round about, and scattered frankincense and costly incense in all directions. And when they brought her into this abode, the odour thereof was very pleasing to her, and even before she ate the dainty meats therein she was satisfied with the smell of them. And with wise intent Solomon sent to her meats which would make her thirsty, and drinks that were mingled with vinegar, and fish and dishes made with pepper. And this he did and he gave them to the Queen to eat. And the royal meal had come to an end three times and seven times, and the administrators, and the counsellors, and the young men and the servants had departed, and the King rose up and he went to the Queen, and he said unto her—now they were alone together—"Take thou thine ease here for love's sake until daybreak." And she said unto him, "Swear to me by thy God, the God of Israel, that thou wilt not take me by force. For if I, who according to the law of men am a maiden, be seduced, I should travel on my journey (back) in sorrow, and affliction and tribulation."

And Solomon answered and said unto her, "I swear unto thee that I will not take thee by force, but thou must swear unto me that thou wilt not take by force anything that is in my house." And the Queen laughed and said unto him, "Being a wise man why dost thou speak as a fool? Shall I steal anything, or shall I carry out of the house of the King that which the King hath not given to me? Do not imagine that I have come hither through love of riches. Moreover, my own kingdom is as wealthy as thine, and there is nothing which I wish for that I lack. Assuredly I have only come in quest of thy wisdom." And he said unto her, "If thou wouldst make me swear, swear thou to me, for a swearing is meet for both (of us), so that neither of us may be unjustly treated. And if thou wilt not make me swear I will not make thee swear." And she said unto him, "Swear to me that thou wilt not take me by force, and I on my part will swear not to take by force thy possessions"; and he swore to her and made her swear.

And the King went up on his bed on the one side (of the chamber), and the servants made ready for her a bed on the other side. And Solomon said unto a young manservant, "Wash out the bowl and set in it a vessel of water whilst the Queen is looking on, and shut the doors and go and sleep." And Solomon spake to the servant in another tongue which the Queen did not understand, and he did as the King commanded, and went and slept. And the King had not as yet fallen asleep, but he only pretended to be asleep, and he was watching the Queen intently. Now the house of Solomon the King was illumined as by day, for in his wisdom he had made shining pearls which were like unto the sun, and moon, and stars (and had set them) in the roof of his house.

And the Queen slept a little. And when she woke up her mouth was dry with thirst, for the food which Solomon had given her in his wisdom had made her thirsty, and she was very thirsty indeed, and her mouth was dry; and she moved her lips and sucked with her mouth and found no moisture. And she determined to drink the water which she had seen, and she looked at King Solomon and watched him carefully, and she thought that he was sleeping a sound sleep. But he was not asleep, and he was waiting until she should rise up to steal the water to (quench) her thirst. And she rose up and, making no sound with her feet, she went to the water in the bowl and lifted up the jar to drink the water. And Solomon seized her hand before she could drink the water, and said unto her, "Why hast thou broken the oath that thou hast sworn that thou wouldst not take by force anything that is in my house?" And she answered and said unto him in fear "Is the oath broken by my drinking water," And the King said unto her, "Is there anything that thou hast seen under the heavens that is better than water?" And the Queen said, "I have sinned against myself, and thou art free from (thy) oath. But let me drink water for my thirst." Then Solomon said unto her, "Am I perchance free from the oath which thou hast made me swear?" And the Queen said, "Be free from thy oath, only let me drink water." And he permitted her to drink water, and after she had drunk water he worked his will with her and they slept together.

"Well!" Valerie exclaimed, closing the book with a bang. "What a rotten trick to play. Jollying a girl into a promise like that and then saying she'd broken it just because she took a drink of water."

Lovelace grinned. "If that line hadn't come off he'd probably have thought up another and I'll bet there wasn't much forcing about it. The Arabs have a saying, 'The fate of every man is bound about his brow,' and she must have known what to expect when she consented to sleep in his tent. The Eastern peoples have always been fatalists, you know."

"What happened? I suppose she had a baby?"

"That's right. Menyelek, her only son, whom Solomon afterwards acknowledged as his heir. The boy became king of Ethiopia and the present Emperor's directly descended from him. Now you know why the ruling caste in Abyssinia always followed the Jewish faith from Sheba's day until they were converted to . . ." Lovelace suddenly broke off and pointed. "Look, the voyage is nearly over. There's Cape Gris Nez looming up on the horizon."

The weather was warmer now. Those nine April days at sea seemed to have put the wintry cold and sleet of Halifax among things long past. For the last twenty-four hours they had been steaming up the English Channel; all day the sunshine and light balmy air had held a foretaste of true summer.

The last rays of the westering sun caught the white cliffs of the French coast as Valerie stared out towards them. In a few hours now she knew that the ship would berth at Rotterdam.

On previous voyages she had always felt a little thrill of joy on catching her first glimpse of Europe. It meant that she would soon be seeing old friends again; a prospect of change, new scenes, and jolly parties. Now, in the fading light, with the dark shadows of night gathering about them as the ship headed up the Straits of Dover, her heart was heavy with foreboding.

CHAPTER V

THE INTRICATE WEB

THE Hotel de Bayonne et Biarritz is situated in a quiet side street behind the Gare St. Lazare. It is small, old-fashioned, and unpretentious.

Christopher Penn had always occupied a suite at the Crilleon on his previous visits to Paris but, in their peculiar circumstances, Sir Anthony Lovelace had considered it imperative that they should avoid all their usual haunts. He had selected this modest hotel as their headquarters. Valerie Lorne had flown them from Rotterdam that morning and was still with them. They had only arrived half an hour before and were still busy with a breakfast of hot coffee and crisp rolls.

All three of them were waiting now, while they ate their hurried breakfast, in the stuffy little private sitting-room of the hotel, with its old-fashioned gilt-framed mirrors and worn red plush furniture, for the man who was to give Christopher further instructions which might carry him to Italy, Malta, Egypt, Eritrea, or even, perhaps, Abyssinia.

"When this chap turns up how shall we know that he is one of us?" asked Lovelace suddenly.

"Naturally he will be," Christopher replied a little irritably. "I was given his name before I left the States and I wired him from Rotterdam soon after we landed last night, directly we'd settled where to go to earth when we reached Paris, in fact. I showed you his reply, which was waiting for us here when we arrived, saying he'd been expecting me for nearly a week and would call this morning."

"Yes, but as the *Millers of God* have no secret sign or password, what guarantee will you have that he's actually the man you believe him to be? We'll be in a fine mess if the enemy have intercepted your wire and send one of their own people to lead us into a trap."

Christopher shrugged. "That's most unlikely. Anyhow it's better we should have to take such an outside chance than that the society should have permanent centres and an organised membership. With only our leaders meeting to formulate decisions, which are passed on by word of mouth, it makes it far harder for the police, or anyone else, to fix anything on an individual member. When I've done my job I shall just fade out, as others have, and there won't be a single document or tie in existence to prove I did it."

At that moment the shabby waiter ushered in a short plumpish, smartly dressed man of about thirty, and waved him towards the little party at the table.

Christopher got up to meet the visitor who, as the door closed again, said quickly; "Mr. Penn—yes? I am Paul Barrotet. I had expected to find you alone for discussion of our business."

"My fiancée, Miss Valerie Lorne, and Sir Anthony Lovelace." Christopher introduced the others. "They both came over with me and know all about this thing."

"All?" The Frenchman asked sharply, raising a pair of bushy black eyebrows.

"Yes. I exercised my discretion, as members are entitled to when they need help. Won't you sit down."

Barrotet bowed to Valerie and then his black boot-button eyes rested for a second on the tall, brown-faced Englishman. He bowed again before pulling up a chair and said gravely, "One sees in Sir Anthony the type which has made the justice of his nation respected all over the world, and it is a war of justice which we wage. Only through the work of the *Millers of God* can there be any true hope of a permanent world peace."

"Miss Lorne has only come as far as Paris with us," said Lovelace slowly, "and I only volunteered to join

Penn because I know the countries to which you may be sending him, whereas he's never been east of Rome. He's told me quite a lot about the *Millers of God* in the last fortnight, and I understand that your aim is to stop future wars by killing off the war-makers. Any number of people must profit out of war though, and what I don't quite get is where certain of them reach the point when the *Millers* decide that they should be er . . . executed?"

The short, dark Frenchman leant back and spread out his hands. "It is simple—no? Is it agreeable to you that we should speak in French which is easier for me?"

A succession of nods greeting his suggestion, he went on quickly: "Many who contribute in a small way to the making of wars are unconscious agents, guilty of no more than lack of thought for the general good in the means they employ to earn their daily bread. With them we do not interfere. It is those few, wealthy, intelligent, unscrupulous, who deliberately aggravate national grievances in the hope that wars may result from which they will profit, upon whom we pass sentence."

"I give you an example, *hein*? Certain of our members keep constant watch upon the International Press. Day after day they find paragraphs in the Italian papers which say:

" 'Britain is secretly backing Abyssinia.'

" 'British rifles have been found in the hands of captured Abyssinians.'

" 'Britain has put an embargo on the sale of camels in her African territories; in consequence Italian soldiers are suffering the torture of thirst, because not enough camels can now be purchased to ensure regular water transport.'

" 'Britain is turning innocent Italian business men out of Malta and Egypt on false charges of espionage, so that British merchants can secure their trade.'

"And so on, and so on. Meanwhile, in the British papers it appears:

" 'Italy's real objective in this war is not the barren mountains of Abyssinia, but to turn the British out of fruitful Egypt. Abyssinia is only the first step.'

" 'An Italian was arrested in the dockyard at Malta with a bomb in his pocket when attempting to get on board a British warship.'

" 'An automobile bearing a G.B. touring plate was overturned in Milan and its English occupants chased by an angry mob.'

" 'The Italians are a lot of cowards; remember how they ran away at Caporetto!'

"And so on, and so on."

Lovelace nodded. "Yes, I thought digging up that last business was absolutely uncalled for; a gratuitous insult to a friendly power. But I suppose their Press said the same about our troops having been nearly chivvied out of South Africa by a lot of farmers in the first year of the Boer War."

"Exactly." Barrotet leant forward earnestly. "Now these things are pinpricks only, but constantly irritating pinpricks, goading each of these naturally friendly people to distrust, fear, and hate each other. No ordinary journalist in either country is so stupid, or wantonly malicious, as to wish to influence his people to a degree of bitterness where they might force their leaders into war. Ninety per cent. of these paragraphs were inspired."

Christopher's black, unruly hair was damp about the temples, and he listened with eager, fascinated attention as the Frenchman went on softly:

"The *Millers of God* traced those paragraphs to their source. In the Bureau, from which they emanated, a certain man was receiving secret payment on a very high scale to distort facts and utilise every possible episode to aggravate bad feeling between Italy and Britain. The *Millers of God* decided to 'eliminate' that man. He is now dead."

A little shudder shook Valerie's shoulders. On her record-making flights she had had to face the fact that, if anything went wrong, she might be forced down over land or ocean and, when her frozen fingers could no longer cling to the slowly sinking plane, drown; or crash to earth where she would be consumed in a blinding sheet of flame. Yet there was something infinitely more horrible in the Frenchman's quiet statement that this man had been "eliminated." It conjured up thoughts of darkness and stealth; the unsuspecting victim taken unawares; his stark terror when he found himself cornered and cowed before the pistol barrel, knowing there was no escape.

"That's right! That's right!" Christopher whispered, and Valerie turned to look at him. His dark eyes shone with a sombre fire, two pools of blackness in the matt pallor of his handsome face. He was trembling slightly and seemed almost carried out of himself by his fanatical zeal for this secret war that was to end all wars. For the hundredth time since she had left her home on Long Island, she told herself: "It is a Crusade . . . a Crusade . . . and he needs my help. I mustn't let him down."

Her glance shifted to Lovelace. The older man was quietly puffing at his pipe. His was a stronger face, tanned to a permanent brown by years of travel in hot countries, and lined a little at the corners of the mouth and eyes. His lids were lowered and he appeared quite impassive. She would have given a lot to know what thoughts were passing behind that unrevealing mask. He had said that if, by giving his life, he could prevent another war he would endeavour to screw up his courage to it, and she had little doubt about his courage; but she did not believe that he gave his full approval to the methods of the *Millers of God*. Suddenly he spoke:

"Did you give this fellow any warning?"

Barrotet nodded. "Yes . . . and he refused to take it."

"Well, that was fair enough, I suppose. He certainly deserved death according to your standards."

"None who is sentenced by the *Millers of God* does not."

"Go ahead then. What is Penn's particular job to be?"

The Frenchman sat silent for a moment. "Do you know why this war was started?" he asked.

"I know the usual reason given. The Italian need for expansion."

"That is what the Italians believe themselves, but only because they have been made to do so by intensive propaganda. The truth is very different and known only to those behind the scenes. Abyssinia is practically the only black man's country which has so far remained closed to the white man's exploitation. It is rich in minerals and there is good reason to suppose that great quantities of oil could be obtained from a certain district of the country. For years whites of many nationalities have been pestering the Emperor to grant concessions. He has refused to do so because he considers it better that his people should remain semi-barbarous and free from work in mine gangs than flaunt the tawdry trappings of western civilisation.

"Having failed to secure concessions by arguments or temptations, those interests, which we do not need to specify, decided to force the Emperor's hand. His country is not rich by our standards. If it were compelled to sustain a war the necessary money to purchase armaments would become a vital necessity. What has Abyssinia to sell? Nothing except concessions. You follow me?"

"The devils!" Christopher snapped. "So they worked on the minds of the Italian people until they lost all sense of reason and began to clamour for a war which would revenge the defeat at Adowa. Just think of it! That happened in the time of the grandfathers of those poor wretches who're dying out there to-day. Hardly one of them could have given it a thought until they were stirred up by this vile propaganda."

Barrotet bowed. "To come now to the present situation. War has been made but those who made it have not yet secured their concession and, although they are reaping profits, the war is small. The corpse is not big enough for the vultures. They hope to secure their concession shortly now, but war is even more profitable than concessions and, if they get it, they intend to use it to bring about another general conflagration."

Lovelace shook his head. "They won't succeed. In spite of all the mud that's been slung Britain and Italy are still friendly at rock-bottom. Besides, Mussolini must realise that Italy would be bound to lose in a war against the British Empire, even if the other members of the League ratted on us."

"Perhaps, although it is admitted that the hundred-and-eighty mile stretch of sea which separates Italy from North Africa is too wide for the British Fleet to close against Italian transports. Also that Italian bombing planes have sufficient range to attack Alexandria and return to their bases on the Libyan frontier. However, that is by the way. All that I say now has application not only to the tension over Abyssinia. The war there may burn itself out. If it does, other equally grave situations are certain to be fermented and made use of for the same purpose, by the enemies of peace, in the future. Let us concede that Britain could master Italy alone. Could she, at the same time, defend herself from Germany?"

"Germany!" Lovelace exclaimed. "But for years past Germany and Britain have been drawing closer together. We can't understand her ill-treatment of her Jewish citizens, but that's about the only difference of opinion between us."

"You may think so and I, a Frenchman, agree that at heart Britain is nearer to Germany than she is to France, but there is a far more serious question between you than Germany's determination to become one hundred per cent. Aryan. Have you so soon forgotten that the whole of her Colonial Empire was taken from her after the great War, and that Britain annexed her most valued possessions?"

"Of course she'd like to have German West and Tanganyika Territory back but we're not willing to give them up—that's true."

"It is. Germany raised the question of the return of her Colonies before she left the League, but she received no satisfaction. The soulless intelligence we have to fight misses nothing. It has worked upon the minds of the German people ever since. Never for a day are they allowed to forget what they consider to be this great injustice and insult to their pride as a nation. Why have they made their country an armed camp again? Not to crush France, although they hate us. They have been preparing for the chance which will soon be given them: the opportunity to regain their lost Empire."

Lovelace showed a keener interest now. This was no longer a question of high moral principle alone. It touched in him a deeper and more primitive chord: the welfare of his own country. "How will they try to bring Germany in?" he asked quickly.

The plump Frenchman leaned forward and tapped the table. "We return now to their immediate intention. Their present plan; you understand me? If they secure this Abyssinian concession they will tempt Germany into purchasing it at a very reasonable price. An arrangement has already been made to that effect."

"But surely that would set the Germans and Italians at loggerheads?"

Barrotet smiled a little pityingly. "On the contrary,

it will bring them together. The concession is a double-edged weapon in that it will provide Abyssinia with just enough money to make things difficult for the Italians. Mussolini dare not retreat and throw in his hand. If he is forced to it he will go down fighting. His people already consider Britain to be behind the Abyssinian resistance, and that she is doing her best to hamstring Italy by the application of these, only partially successful, sanctions. Yet he is no fool, and before he allows his countrymen to force him he will seek allies."

"And then?"

"He will say to the Germans: 'These concessions which you have purchased in Abyssinia are no good until you can operate them fully. I will offer you something better. For many months Britain has been concentrating her strength in the eastern Mediterranean, Egypt and the Sudan. At home she is almost defenceless. I will attack and hold her main forces in Africa while you devastate London and her principal centres of population from the air. Afterwards we will divide the British Empire between us."

Lovelace looked up from his pipe. "How about France?"

"Dare France go to Britain's aid even if she wishes to do so? Mussolini's main army is still in Europe. Could France afford to risk a simultaneous attack by Italy in the south and the newly-equipped German armies in the north?"

"In such circumstances the British Army would be sent to your assistance."

Barrotet lifted his dark eyes to heaven. "Pardon, my friend. You naturally consider the British Army an important factor, but you forget that in recent years you have allowed it to shrink to a few divisions. Your home forces to-day may be excellent, but in numbers they are less than those of the weakest Balkan state. No army which you could place in the European field could possibly turn the scale for France against the combined might of reborn Italy and new Germany. It is for that reason France has been negotiating an alliance with Soviet Russia, and I do not say that she will not honour her obligation to the League and Great Britain. Only that, without Russia behind her, it would be suicide for her to do so. A man thinks twice before he takes his own life, however black the future may appear."

"I see your point," Lovelace admitted. "Britain is the great bulwark of Capitalism, and if the Bolsheviks thought there was a chance of her being smashed once and for all they might refuse to come in. Then, if France considered the odds against her too heavy, we might have to face the whole shooting-match on our own."

"That is so. Within a month, perhaps, if the plot to utilise the Abyssinian situation cannot be stopped. Even if we succeed in that you must still regard such a combination as a menace which you may have to face in the future, and if Russia, France, and the Little Entente did come to your assistance your case would not be very much better. Japan would immediately move against Russia, and apparently, from the recent trend of events, Poland, Austria and Hungary would join Germany and Italy in their attack on France."

Lovelace shook his head. "Either way it sounds desperately grim, but I can't think the Germans have the least wish to go to war with Britain."

"They have not. At present there is no personal hate between the two countries at all, except amongst the British Jews who are so bitter against the Nazis. But day and night the agitators are at work poisoning the minds of the German people with the delusion that because they have lost their colonies they have lost their honour. Mussolini is a very able statesman, and he will use that feeling to bring Germany in with him against Britain rather than face the collapse of Fascism through a stalemate in Abyssinia."

"And it is this Abyssinian concession which the

warmakers propose to use as their bait to involve Germany ?"

"Yes. That is their present programme. At the moment the Italian armies are steadily advancing into Abyssinia. When the rains come they must call a halt, and then the Emperor will have a breathing space in which to consider his position. The Italians will dig themselves in and, since modern weapons give natural superiority to defence over attack, even where opposing armies are equally well equipped, no Abyssinian offensive will be able even to shake the Italian line. If the Emperor can manage to hold up the Italian advance until the rains come he will have at least six months in which to equip and train many of his regiments to fit them for modern warfare in the next year's campaign. So far he has used his private fortune to purchase supplies, but now the Abyssinian war chest is exhausted. He must choose between leaving his warriors to be massacred when the Italians advance again, or selling concessions to provide them with modern equipment which will strengthen their resistance."

Valerie nodded. "And he will take the latter course as the lesser evil, because it is his only chance to escape complete defeat and the total loss of his Empire."

"Mademoiselle, you have said it." Barrotet waved a plump but muscular hand. "The matter is already agreed and a date fixed when Paxito Zarrif will be in Addis Ababa to give the credits and receive the signed concession."

"Paxito Zarrif," Lovelace murmured. "I've heard of him. He's a fabulously rich Armenian—isn't he ?"

"Yes. He is also the man who has arranged for the sale of the concession to Germany immediately he has secured it, which would give her a strong interest in Abyssinia and bring the whole question of overseas territories for her to a head."

"Unless . . ." murmured Christopher.

"Unless Paxito Zarrif fails to reach Addis Ababa."

"Penn hasn't got to go to Abyssinia after all, then," Lovelace cut in.

"No. At present Zarrif is at his home in Athens. We knew that there was reason to suppose that he would remain there for about three weeks when we sent for you. He is not due in Addis Ababa until the first of May. That is the date which has been arranged for the signing of the concession."

"He may be leaving Athens at any moment now, then," Christopher said anxiously.

"Unfortunately, that is so. Therefore the affair is doubly urgent. When you responded to our call that you would leave immediately, we naturally expected you would sail on the *Europa* and arrive six days ago. Your delay in reaching Europe has caused us grave anxiety. It shortens so much the time you have to work in."

"If time is so essential, why did you select an American?" Valerie asked.

"Because Zarrif is very carefully protected. It was decided that a wealthy young American would be less suspect than anyone on this side and would stand more chance of getting at him."

"You're wrong there," said Christopher quickly. "I was warned that they knew what I was up to before I left the States and that if I quit the country I'd be dead within a week. That's why we took the longer route via Canada and a slower boat."

Barrotet's eyebrows shot up into his broad, low forehead.

"*Mon Dieu!*" he exclaimed. "But this is difficult—perhaps you are being watched now."

"I doubt it." Christopher shook his head. "We came by Miss Lorne's plane from Rotterdam and went to earth in this hole after Lovelace had taken us seven times round Paris in seven different taxis."

"That is good, but the fact that they know you may

prove a serious handicap to your operations." Barrotet produced a sheaf of papers. "Look! Here are particulars about Paxito Zarrif, also a letter stolen from a Mr. Jeremiah Green as he lay dying of fever in the Sudan. He was on his way to Zarrif as a go-between, on behalf of the Abyssinians, but he did not know Zarrif personally. We had hoped that by presenting yourself to Zarrif as Jeremiah Green you could have found an opportunity to . . ."

"As they know Penn to be associated with the *Millers of God*, they're certain to have cabled his description," Lovelace interrupted. "He daren't adopt your plan now. He'd be rumbled at the start."

Barrotet's black, boot-button eyes fixed themselves upon the Englishman. "Does the enemy yet know that you have taken a hand in this affair?"

Lovelace shrugged. "There is no earthly reason to suppose they have ever heard of my existence."

"Then why should you not impersonate Jeremiah Green, and lure him on some pretext to a spot where . . . Penn could do the rest?"

Valerie's eyes were on Lovelace's face again. He was fingering uncertainly the small upturned moustache which decorated his upper lip.

"You are sure that if this concession goes through it means a universal smash-up?" he asked after a moment.

"Yes. We who know the inside facts are virtually certain of it."

"All right—I'll do it then."

Barrotet pushed across the papers. "I am glad that you have so decided. Please now to memorise these few names and addresses that I will tell you. They are the *Millers of God* living in the Near East upon whom you may call for assistance in case of necessity. Afterwards, when you make your escape, it is better that you should go on to Haifa or Cairo and lie low there for a time than that you should return to Europe, where the

International police will be more occupied in trying to trace Zarrif's executioner."

Ten minutes later the Frenchman left them, and his last words were: "Remember, please, that time is short. All our previous efforts to stave off war will have been wasted unless Paxito Zarrif is dead by the first of May."

CHAPTER VI

THE OPENING OF THE CAMPAIGN

SPEED! Speed! Speed! That was the essential factor which now dominated their mission, as emerged very clearly from the conference that Christopher, Valerie, and Lovelace held immediately Monsieur Paul Barrotet had departed.

The *Millers of God* had planned that Christopher should arrive in Athens a week before Paxito Zarrif was expected to start for Abyssinia. Six days had now been lost, owing to Christopher taking the longer route from the United States in order to keep his departure secret. It was imperative, therefore, that they should make every possible effort to reach the Greek capital within the next twenty-four hours.

"It's ten to eleven," said Valerie. "We've nothing to pack but our handbags. If we leave at once I can take you the best part of the way to-day."

Lovelace shook his head. "We can't have you mixed up in this horrible business any further."

"Nonsense. If you go by train you're certain to miss him, and here am I placing my perfectly good plane at your disposal."

"I know, but Christopher's as rich as Crœsus. There's nothing to stop him chartering a plane to take us."

Valerie sniffed contemptuously. "And what sort of a pilot would you get? Think of the delay, too, in making the necessary arrangements."

"That's true," Christopher agreed. "And after all, why shouldn't she fly us down to Athens—as long as we keep her out of things once we're there?"

Lovelace stared at the rash, good-looking young pair of lovers angrily. If he had been Valerie's fiancé his attitude would have been very different. Nothing would have induced him to allow her to be even remotely connected with these dubious schemes. He had promised his assistance in an affair about which he did not yet care to think for more than two moments together, and Christopher was pledged beyond retreat. Their enemies were known to be organised and on the watch for them. Even if Christopher brought his mission to a successful conclusion, it was certain that the enemy would endeavour to exact vengeance, not only on him, but on anyone known to be associated with him. How could he expose the girl to such obvious danger? Lovelace could not understand it, and yet he saw two things clearly. The boy was obsessed by his crusade to the exclusion of all reasonable thought, and *he* was the girl's fiancé. Having registered a protest, what right had an outsider to interfere further between the two of them?

"Let's go, then—shall we?" Valerie picked up her bag and hurried from the room, cutting short any further discussion as to whether they meant to let her take them, and a quarter of an hour later they were discussing flying times in a taxi on the way to the airport.

"If we can get away by midday I ought to be able to get you down to Brindisi before nightfall," Valerie said. "We'll sleep there and, all being well, be in Athens by lunch time to-morrow."

"I'm glad I've been picked for the job—glad!" Christopher's voice held a note of exaltation as he cut in. "If anyone ever deserved death this man Zarrif does."

"Don't, Christopher! Don't let's talk of it." Valerie laid a restraining hand upon his arm. Her face was pale under the chestnut hair. Much paler than usual, Lovelace noted. Her big eyes stared into his, seeking comfort and reassurance, but he had none to give her. He could only make a little shrugging gesture which was meant to convey sympathy and understanding. For the rest of the journey they bumped over the *pavé* in silence. A few moments later they were walking across the Le Bourget air-field to the hangar that housed Valerie's plane.

When they had come in that morning she had given orders for it to be looked over and prepared for further flights, so they found it all in readiness.

Owing to her reputation in the air-world quite a little crowd collected to see them start. Numerous courteous officials attended to the formalities with special dispatch, and one gallant Frenchman declared: "It is a pleasure to be of service to Mademoiselle Lorne; to meet her personally and see that she is as beautiful as she is brave."

Within an hour of Barrotet having left them they were in the air and Le Bourget fading into the grey landscape behind them.

By two-fifteen they were over Nice, the white villas on its outskirts looking like little dots among the grey-green of olive trees, and the Mediterranean appearing like a placid lake; the lapping of its waters on the curving beaches only becoming perceptible as they descended towards the airport.

The climate was considerably warmer, and they were enabled to enjoy a belated luncheon in the open. Over it they studiously avoided any mention of the reason for their journey. It was very pleasant there eating *Omelette aux Champignons* and *Poulet Vallée D'Auge*, washed down with a carafe of red Provence wine; while the idle, well-dressed crowd passed in and out, waiting for the great airliners to bring new arrivals to the coast of pleasure, and the scent of the late mimosa on the tables filled the air with fragrance.

When they set off to complete the longer part of the day's run Valerie declared the afternoon to be perfect flying weather. She climbed very high and set a course dead for Naples. As they passed over the beautiful bay, and saw the little spiral of smoke rising from Mount Vesuvius on their right, she turned east through the gap in the mountains and brought them down safely at Brindisi, on the heel of Italy, well before dusk had fallen.

Lovelace thought it safer for them to sleep at a small, unpretentious hotel in the town than at the airport; feeling that they could not be too careful. Christopher had managed to slip out of America before the enemy organisation knew he had started, but they would be on the watch for him in Europe.

No private sitting-room was available, so after dinner they sat on in the deserted *salle à manger*, and made a more careful examination of the papers Barrotet had left them.

There was the stolen letter which was to serve as an introduction to Paxito Zarrif. It was in Amharic, but a translation was attached which showed it to be a simple statement that the bearer, Mr. Jeremiah Green, was a trusted friend of the writer, and would give Zarrif the latest authentic news from Addis Ababa. It also confirmed the first of May as the date fixed for "that business of which your Excellency knows," and it was signed by "The High Noble Lord. Ras Desoum."

"He's a personal friend of the Emperor," Lovelace said. "As luck would have it, I met him when I was out there. He wasn't very popular about the Court, but the Negus liked him because he was educated in Europe."

"What're the other papers?" Valerie asked.

Christopher ran his eyes over them. "Particulars about Zarrif. The routine he follows when he's at home in Athens, a list of his servants, and all about his bodyguard. Six armed men are always in the house, apparently, and two of them on duty every hour of the night and day. This last is a plan of his house."

"Let me see that—may I?" Lovelace took the plan and studied it for a moment.

"It's a biggish place," he remarked, "and the whole of the ground-floor is given up to reception rooms; 'rarely used, kept shuttered and all windows wired with electric burglar alarms,' it says in a note in the margin. The first-floor, north side, is where the spider spins his poisonous web. Look! The first room, which runs the width of the house as you turn left off the landing, is marked 'secretary's room,' the next, larger and the whole width of the house again, is Zarrif's workroom. Beyond that there's a valet's room facing west—one of the thugs sits there all night, I expect—and bathroom, W.C., etc., facing east. Then, at the extreme end of the house, comes his bedroom. There's no way of reaching that without going through the others first. On the opposite side of the landing are the dining-room, library, and clerk's office. The top floor is only bedrooms for the staff."

They read the particulars about Zarrif's habits and employees, then Valerie yawned. "Well, we've had a long day. I've flown you from Rotterdam to Brindisi since dawn, you know, so I'm off to bed."

"You've done us darned well," Lovelace agreed quickly. "All the same, I can't help wishing you were out of this."

"Thanks, but I'm quite capable of taking care of myself." She gave him a lazy smile over her shoulder as she left the room.

"Why the hell don't you insist on her remaining in Italy?" Lovelace shot at Christopher once they were alone.

"What!" Christopher looked up vaguely from the papers he was studying. "But you heard what she said. It's true, too. Valerie's perfectly capable of taking care of herself. Besides, we need her to fly us to Athens to-morrow."

"Surely we can make other arrangements?"

"It's a bit late to try and do that now, and even if we could, no hired pilot would be so dependable as Valerie.

You see, we must be in Athens by midday to-morrow, because Zarrif's due to leave the day after. If we miss him I shall have failed the *Millers*."

Oh, damn the *Millers*," snapped Lovelace angrily.

Christopher stood up and stared at him in surprise. "What's wrong? D'you want to back out? You're quite free to do so if you like."

"No, it's not that," Lovelace shrugged impatiently. "I've promised you my help so you may rely on it for what it's worth. But the whole thing's so damnably dangerous that it's monstrously unfair to drag Valerie into it. You love her, don't you?"

"Of course I do," Christopher's smile was quite unperturbed, "and she loves me. That's why I couldn't stop her coming with us even if I wanted to. So we'd better make the best of it. Good night."

"Good night," Lovelace muttered in reply as the pale-faced young man turned away. He saw that it was useless to argue further, and settled down to spend another hour over two more rations of the pale golden Arum liqueur he always drank when in Italy, while he endeavoured to memorise every detail in the plan of Zarrif's house.

By nine-fifteen the following morning they were in the air again; the waters of the Adriatic sparkling below them in the sunshine, and seeming bluer than the Gulf of Genoa had the day before. Half an hour later they were over the tattered Greek coastline with its ragged fringe of islands. At a few minutes before twelve they landed at their destination.

"Nowhere near a record," said Valerie as she climbed out of her plane, "but better than a hired pilot would have done for you any day."

"Bless you!" One of his rare smiles lit Christopher's handsome face for a second. "This is a horrible show, but it helps a lot to have you with me."

Hand in hand they walked into the airport restaurant, and Lovelace watched them go a little grimly. While

Christopher ordered lunch Lovelace was telephoning in the name of Mr. Jeremiah Green.

When he rejoined them ten minutes later his face was even grimmer as he said:

"Paxito Zarrif is still in Athens. He's agreed to see me at four o'clock this afternoon."

CHAPTER VII

INTO THE LION'S DEN

"AND now," Lovelace insisted when they had finished their meal, "we must face facts. Even to have allowed Valerie to land us here was an abominable risk. It connects the three of us together, and if you, Christopher, succeed in what you're out to do, the police will start hunting for her directly they find out you came in on her plane. If she's determined to stay we can at least separate. She'd better take a room here in the airport hotel while we get fixed up somewhere in the city—although I'd rather she flew back to Italy this afternoon."

"How shockingly ungallant you are." The dimple in Valerie's cheek deepened as she smiled at him.

"Honestly!" he raised a grin, " 'we don't want to lose you but we think you ought to go,' as the war song had it."

"The worst the police could do is to hold me as a witness."

"Yes, the police perhaps; but you may run into far greater danger from another quarter if you remain with us."

"Well, I'm remaining until . . ." she laughed rather shakily, "until the deed is done, but I'll take a room here if you like."

She registered at the hotel and then they all drove into the town together. Athens was hot, dusty, airless. Its streets of shoddy modern shops proved disappointing to Christopher, who had never visited it before, and had always visualised it as still the Pearl of the Ægean. Nothing but the ruins of the Parthenon, dominating the city, remained to testify to its ancient glory, and the arid, treeless wastes on the outskirts of the town shattered his dream-image of a palm-decked southern capital. He was glad to get out of the sun glare into a cool courtyard at the hotel Lovelace selected for them.

Valerie dealt tactfully with him, as she always did when these moods of depression were upon him, and they agreed to remain where they were until Lovelace returned when he left them to drive out to Zarrif's house in the heat of the afternoon.

He found it to be a walled property some way outside the town, and its only entrance a pair of rusty iron gates. Telling his cabman to wait, he jerked the old-fashioned bell-pull. A dismal clang sounded inside the porter's lodge, and a surly-looking fellow came out to peer at him between the bars.

When he gave the name of Jeremiah Green the porter unlocked the big padlock that secured the gate and let him through. Having fastened the gate again behind the visitor the man accompanied him up the short drive to the house.

The garden was a dismal sight. Some withered palms, olives, and cypresses struggled for existence in the stony soil. Ragged cacti, aloes, and myrtle bushes formed a jungle on either side. There were no flowers except upon the semi-wild creepers which straggled across the grass-grown paths.

The house, by contrast, was in good repair, but all the ground-floor windows were shuttered, as Lovelace had expected. At the front door the porter rang another bell; a grille was lifted and two eyes peered out at them. Lovelace gave Green's name again and the door was unlocked, upon which the porter left him. A second man, whose hip pocket displayed a bulge which suggested a large calibre pistol, relocked the door and led the way upstairs. On the first-floor landing a third guardian sat reading a newspaper; after being given the visitor's name he opened the door which Lovelace knew led to the secretary's room.

A thin man with shiny black hair sat there behind a desk. His quick eyes searched Lovelace's face as he bowed. "Mr. Green, I was expecting you. Please to sit down."

He spoke in English, but from his accent and appearance Lovelace judged him to be French.

"You have a letter for Mr. Zarrif," he went on. "May I see it ?"

"The letter is personal, I'm afraid," Lovelace replied, settling himself in the nearest chair. "Perhaps you'd be good enough to let Mr. Zarrif know I'm here."

The dark man smiled. "Certainly—in a little moment—but first I must see the letter, please. I have knowledge of all Mr. Zarrif's affairs, and no one sees him before I have, er—what you would call—vetted them, first."

Without further argument Lovelace produced the stolen letter.

The secretary scanned it quickly and returned it with a flourish. "That is quite satisfactory. Now your passport, please, Mr. Green."

Lovelace was almost caught unawares, but he was poker-faced by habit and managed to mask his dismay as he said lightly : " 'Fraid I left that in my dispatch-box at the hotel."

The black eyes on the far side of the desk showed sudden suspicion. "How am I to know then that you are Mr. Jeremiah Green ? That letter might have been lost or stolen. You must return to your hotel and produce your passport before I can allow you to see Mr. Zarrif."

Lovelace knew he was up against it. If he once confessed that he was unable to produce the passport he would never get as far as the secretary's room again, let alone penetrate to Paxito Zarrif's sanctum.

He screwed his mouth into a rueful grin : "I'd go back with pleasure but for the fact that I'm a pretty sick man. Dysentery, you know. That's what Abyssinia does for you. I'm as weak as a rat, and the jolting of the taxi on these rotten roads gave me positive hell coming out here. A return trip to the city and back would about lay me out, I think. Isn't there any other way you can satisfy yourself about my identity?"

The secretary considered for a moment. "Tell me how you left Ras Desoum and his children," he said.

"He has none," Lovelace answered at once. He was gambling on the Ras not having married in the last few years, and his memory of him as a tall effeminate man with many vices but no love of women.

After that the secretary fired questions at him with the rapidity of a machine-gun. It was a gruelling experience, and Lovelace had to think like lightning while expecting to be caught out every moment in some hopeless blunder. He would never have come through it but for the knowledge acquired during his Abyssinian visit, and if Christopher had been in his shoes, as was originally planned, the young American would not have survived the ordeal for two minutes.

At last the man behind the desk appeared satisfied. He smiled again. "Forgive, please, the little traps I set for you, Mr. Green, but there are certain people most dangerous who seek to gain entry here. We have to be very careful of our visitors."

"So I have observed," replied Lovelace dryly.

The man on the landing was then called in to keep him silent company while the secretary disappeared into the inner room. About three minutes later he reappeared with the announcement: "Mr. Zarrif will see you now."

The curtains of the bigger room were drawn, and it was only lit by a single desk lamp, the shade of which had recently been adjusted so that the light shone full upon the visitor. Paxito Zarrif sat still and silent behind it, a presence rather than a man, almost invisible in the heavy shadows.

At first Lovelace could see nothing but his eyes, green,

searching, vital; then the presence spoke in a thin, sharp voice, and the substance of the man became clearer. He was smallish in stature with narrow shoulders; a thin-bridged, beaky nose, and a much fairer skin than Lovelace would have expected in an Armenian. His forehead was broad and lofty, his hair grey, and a little goatee beard decorated his angular chin.

He glanced at the letter Lovelace handed him and plunged at once into a series of rapid questions on the state of affairs in Addis Ababa. The secretary's cross-examination had been difficult enough to deal with, but Mr. Paxito Zarrif's was infinitely more so.

His brain moved from subject to subject with the speed of a prairie fire, yet devoured every scrap of information on each before passing to the next.

Lovelace felt his forehead grow damp as the interview progressed, from the double strain of both faking up plausible particulars about the progress of the war, of which he knew nothing except what he had learnt from the papers, and at the same time inventing an excuse which would enable him to secure a second interview. Suddenly the thought of his pretended illness gave him a line. He gasped, leaned forward, and gripped his sides with both hands.

Zarrif ceased questioning him for a moment. The perspiration on his forehead now served a useful purpose; it was obvious that he was ill. He groaned again and muttered something about having gone down with dysentery in Africa.

"You should have told me of this before." Zarrif spoke now in a softer tone; he seemed all at once to have become quite human. "Give me your arm. This way. I have suffered myself. It is an agony." He led Lovelace towards the further door beyond which lay the bath and valets' rooms.

When Lovelace returned the older man was busy with some papers. "You had best go back to your hotel now," he said kindly, "but there is much which I still wish to ask you. Do you think you will be well enough to come out here again this evening ?"

Lovelace leaned heavily on the table. "Yes. I haven't had a bout like this for some days now. It must have been something I ate for lunch, I think, that started it up again, but I'll be all right in an hour or two. What time d'you wish to see me ?"

"Nine o'clock. If you are too ill, telephone, and we will appoint a time to-morrow morning. It must not be later, as I leave here in the afternoon." Zarrif touched a bell upon his desk and the secretary appeared.

Promising to be back at nine, Lovelace gave the impression of making an effort to pull himself together. Heartily glad to escape further questioning, he allowed himself to be led downstairs and escorted off the premises.

Outside the gates he found a tall thin man talking to the porter. The man glanced at Lovelace, who noticed that he had deep, sad eyes set in a delicate, aristocratic face, which was marked by a heavy scar running from the corner of his mouth down to the left side of his chin.

Slumping into his taxi with a groan, Lovelace let himself be driven away, but after he had gone half a mile he stopped the cab, got out, and walked back to make a more careful survey of Zarrif's property. Both the porter and the tall man had disappeared.

The road curved round the garden and ran up a hill at the back of the house. Two hundred yards from it he had no difficulty in seeing over the wall and picking out the first-floor windows of the rooms he had visited. The wall was not a high one and a man could scale it easily by standing on another's shoulders, but a wire, which glinted faintly in the late afternoon sunlight, ran along it about six inches from the top ; an electric alarm evidently. If it were cut, depressed, or pulled in scrambling over, bells would rouse the guards into instant activity.

Having found out all he could about Zarrif's defences,

Lovelace walked back to his waiting taxi and was driven into the city.

On his way back he thought over the situation. If Zarrif was leaving Athens the following day, the coming night was virtually the only opportunity Christopher would have in which to get him. They must act at once, and Lovelace thought he could see a way in which the business could be done.

He visited a wireless store and then an oilshop, at both of which he made certain purchases, and packing most of these into a kitbag he had bought for the purpose, he took it to a garage near his hotel, where he arranged with the proprietor for the hire of a car. By six o'clock his preparations were completed and he rejoined his friends.

"I saw the old boy and I'm going out there again to-night," he told them. "D'you really mean to go through with this, Christopher ?"

"I do." The young American's dark eyes lit up with almost savage determination.

"All right. I think I can give you your chance. How does that ether pistol of yours work ?"

"It contains little cylinders of highly poisonous gas. They are smashed and the puff of gas ejected with tremendous force by compressed air. One breath of it is enough to kill almost instantly."

"Good. I'm glad it's to be a painless business. It must be done silently too, if you're to stand any chance at all of getting out alive yourself, because the whole place is lousy with gunmen."

"There's no chance of getting him away from the house, then ?"

"Not an earthly. I had the devil of a job even to get in. You'll have to do it in the house, or not at all—that's certain." Both of them listened intently as Lovelace told of his experiences that afternoon.

"It seems almost impossible for me to get at him at all then," Christopher said gloomily. "How d'you propose that I should set about it ?"

"Let's leave that till after dinner—shall we ?"

They dined early, and Lovelace thought he had never sat through a more trying meal. Christopher displayed alternate moods of pessimism and gaiety. Although almost a teetotaller, he ordered a magnum of champagne and began to talk of his last wishes in the event of his being caught and killed by Zarrif's men. Valerie grew paler and paler as the meal dragged on until Lovelace feared that she would faint at the table ; but with almost superhuman pluck she managed to keep her end up and laugh with Christopher during his outbursts of forced hilarity.

When at last coffee was served, Lovelace produced a small map of Athens and its environs. Passing it to Christopher, he explained to him the route he must take to reach Zarrif's house. It was not difficult, being a straight main road except for the last quarter-mile, and, as the house stood alone on the slope of the hill, Christopher agreed that he would have no trouble in finding it.

"Right, then," Lovelace went on. "I shall have to leave you in a few minutes now, to keep my appointment, but I want you to follow me in a private car which I've hired for you from the Delphic garage. It'll be handed over to you here by their man at a quarter to nine. In it there's a pair of folding steps and a kit bag containing various other things we'll need. You will drive yourself out, but you're not to stop at the house ; go straight on round the bend at the back and up the hill for about two hundred yards. Stop then, and wait until I join you there. I've ordered your car a bit early to make certain of it arriving up to time ; but don't start before nine, because I don't want you hanging about there longer than necessary. I hope to be out of the house by half-past, but in any case I'll manage to be with you, somehow, before a quarter to ten. He turned to Valerie : "Could you fly the Adriatic by night if need be ?"

"Oh, yes," she nodded; "I've done far more difficult trips than that."

"Then I want you to return to the airport when Christopher sets off. See that your plane's in readiness, then wait at the hotel. If you don't hear from us by eleven o'clock you're to leave at once for Brindisi. Is that all clear?"

As the others nodded he lifted his glass of champagne. "Well, here's lots of luck to all of us," he said briefly. Finishing his wine, he stood up and left them.

On his second visit to Zarrif's house he paid off his taxi. The guards made no difficulty about letting him through, and the secretary, who was still at work, led him at once into the inner room.

Zarrif inquired courteously if he was better, and on learning that although still shaky he was fairly fit, settled down to bombard him with a fresh series of questions. Lovelace dealt with them to the best of his ability, but one almost took him off his guard. It was a sudden inquiry. "Do you know anything about the *Millers of God*?"

For a moment he feared that his imposture had been discovered, and that Zarrif had only been playing with him; but his one hope lay in keeping up his part.

"Yes," he said slowly. "It's a sort of society, isn't it, which threatens people who speculate in currencies to such an extent that nations are forced into a corner and driven off gold."

"It threatens those and others. What more do you know of it?" Zarrif's piercing eyes seemed to probe the deepest corners of his visitor's mind.

"Nothing—only rumours picked up in travelling here and there."

"I see. You have nothing definite you can give me. Well . . ." The wizened old man's questions switched to another subject, and Lovelace breathed again.

A few moments later he pretended to be seized with

another attack. Zarrif showed no surprise, but treated him with the same consideration as before.

When Lovelace returned to the big, gloomy room he apologised and said : "If there's any more information you want I'll come out to-morrow morning. I'll be all right again by then."

Zarrif nodded. "There is still much that I wish to hear. If you are free to return to Abyssinia I should like to have you with me. It is always of great value to be able to consult a man who has been so recently at the scene of action."

Lovelace hesitated a moment.

"You will not find it necessary to work for a long time afterwards if you do as I suggest," Zarrif went on quietly. "I pay my people well, as anyone who has been in my service will tell you."

"All right—I'm game," Lovelace replied, simulating a stab of pain. "What time do we start ?"

"My secretary, Cassalis, will meet you by the bookstall at the airport at one-thirty to-morrow. We shall leave shortly after. Good night."

Zarrif pressed the bell upon his table, and three minutes later Lovelace heard the iron gates of the house clang to behind him.

He found the hired car up on the hillside. It was partly concealed by a group of cypresses. The moon had risen and showed the plain below almost as clearly as in daylight, but it showed something else as well. Valerie was seated in the driver's seat beside Christopher.

"What the hell're you doing here ?" Lovelace snapped at her angrily. "Didn't I tell you . . ."

"Never mind what you told me," she cut him short as she got out. "I'm my own mistress and I take orders from no one. I'm only here to mind the car and get you away more quickly."

For a second he was minded to call off the whole business, but Christopher was beside him now, trembling with excitement and urging him to give his orders. No such opportunity to get Zarrif might ever occur again. With sudden decision he gripped Christopher by the arm.

"You see the left end of the house. The last three windows on the first floor are those of Zarrif's bedroom. The next is the bathroom, and the fifth the lavatory. If you look carefully you'll see a dark streak running down from it. That's the two ends of a rope I bought this afternoon, took in round my waist, and threw out of the window a few minutes ago after passing it behind the pipe that runs up to the cistern. It'll bear you easily and it's not difficult to climb.

"Yes!" breathed Christopher. "Yes!"

Lovelace pulled the step-ladder and bag out of the back of the car. "Come on," he said, and led the way off the road down the rocky slope.

Christopher had Valerie in his arms. With feverish lips he was kissing her all over her face. Suddenly he thrust her from him and scrambled after Lovelace down to the wall.

Lovelace was already getting his kit out of the big bag. It consisted of a large screw-hook, a pair of rubber gloves, a length of electric wire, a roll of insulating tape, a pair of wire cutters, and another length of rope.

Propping the steps against a near-by tree, he screwed the hook into the trunk about ten feet up, level with the wall top, then, passing the length of wire through it, he drew on his rubber gloves and, moving the steps, attached one end of it to the alarm wire above the wall. Next, he shifted the steps fifteen feet along, drew the loose wire taut through the hook, and performed the even more delicate operation of attaching its free end so that it would carry the current round the V and take the strain without sounding the alarm. Moving the steps again, he set them up half-way between the two joins.

"Be ready to run," he whispered, glancing over his shoulder. With a set face he cut the alarm wire where it now formed the base of the triangle he had erected.

They held their breath for a second, fearing to hear the electric gongs shatter the silent night, but no sound broke the stillness.

"It's all right," Lovelace muttered. "Pass me the rope."

When Christopher handed it to him he threw one end of it over the wall in the centre of the gap where the wire had been a moment before, ran down the steps, and attached the other to the lower portion of the tree.

Christopher already had one foot on the steps. Lovelace caught him by the elbow. "Go canny when you reach the sill in case they've spotted the rope and are waiting for you. If they are, you'll have to drop and run. If all goes well, pull the rope by one end when you reach the ground again and bring it back with you. If you can do that they'll never know how you got in. We'll be waiting for you at the car. Up you go now and good luck to you!"

"Thanks," Christopher gasped, "thanks," and running up the steps he slipped noiselessly over the top of the wall into the garden.

Lovelace turned and scrambled up the hill. He found Valerie leaning against the car.

"Why did you come?" he panted. "Why the devil couldn't you keep out of this?"

"How—how could I leave him to come alone?" she whispered. Then he realised that she had given way at last and was weeping unrestrainedly.

He put his arm round her shoulders, muttering little phrases of comfort and encouragement as he fought to regain his breath. Her sobbing became a little less passionate. It faded to a whisper of quick-drawn gasps. All his anger with her for adding to his responsibilities by appearing on the scene had evaporated. She was in love with Christopher, that insane—or was he terribly sane?—idealist who was now struggling through the bushes towards the house. Lovelace's heart ached for her, but he could do nothing; only hold her closer and watch the section of the moonlit garden that he could see across the wall.

"Anthony, I'm frightened," she gasped suddenly. "I wish—I wish I hadn't come."

She had never before called him by his first name. "I wish to God I'd succeeded in persuading you not to," he said huskily.

"You're all against this, really, aren't you? It may be justice in the sight of God—as Christopher says—but actually its horrible to think about."

"Yes," he said slowly, "and whatever misery Zarrif may be plotting to bring on the world, he seems a decent sort. He was darned decent to me when I shammed illness so that I could fix that rope for Christopher to get into the house. I've never hated anything quite so much as giving him this chance to-night."

"Oh, Anthony, Anthony, I feel just the same—but what else could we do?" She suddenly pressed against him and he held her tighter yet while her shoulders shook with a fresh burst of sobs.

"I ought to have gone in with him, although I never promised that," he muttered. "He's such a boy. I had half a mind to, but—well, as you turned up I felt I couldn't leave you—in case things go wrong."

"I'm glad I came, then—after all. This isn't your show. He must see it through himself . . ." She broke off suddenly. "Look! There he is, going up the rope. He's nearly reached the window."

Christopher was swarming up the double rope hand over hand. Another moment and he gripped the window-sill. Cautiously he raised his head. The moon gave sufficient light for him to see that the room was empty. Heaving himself up, he wormed his way over.

Once inside the house he paused only long enough to get his pistol out of his pocket. He gripped the butt firmly in his right hand and advanced on tiptoe; his left hand outstretched to grasp the shadowy protuberance of the door knob. It turned noiselessly under his touch;

the door swung open and he stepped cautiously through it. From the plan of the house he knew that he was now in the small hallway. The valet's room must be opposite him, a few paces away, and Zarrif's bedroom to his left. The moonlight which silvered the bathroom behind him hardly penetrated sufficiently to lessen the close, heavy darkness. The gloom was only broken by a thin pale ribbon of light on the floor to the right; indicating the door of the room in which Lovelace had faced the grey, elderly Armenian less than a quarter of an hour before. Christopher passed his tongue over his dry lips and tried to still his breathing. It sounded like a rushing wind, which must alarm the household if he could not control it, as he stood there with the sweat streaming down his forehead. Nerving himself for the final effort, he ran his finger-tips lightly down the door until he found the handle, gave it a sudden twist, and flung it open.

Zarrif was seated quietly writing at his desk. As Christopher entered he swung round; his hand shot out towards his desk bell; but Christopher was quicker, and Zarrif withdrew his arm at the whispered caution when he saw the big black pistol, with its thick attachment like a silencer, pointed at his head.

"What do you want?" he challenged huskily, coming to his feet. "What do you want?"

"Your life!" whispered Christopher, his black eyes blazing in his thin, dead-white face. He stepped forward and thrust his weapon to within a yard of Zarrif's mouth. "You've forfeited it by your proved attempts to promote mass-murder. I am a *Miller of God*, sent to execute justice upon you."

For a second Paxito Zarrif's green eyes flickered towards his bell again; but now it was beyond his reach. He drew himself up and his voice held a contemptuous ring as he answered "I have had a long life and an interesting one. Shoot, then, if you wish—*assassin*!"

CHAPTER VIII

LOVE AND LOYALTIES

THE car sped at a furious pace back down the hill towards Athens.

"I couldn't do it," Christopher sobbed, his head on Valerie's breast. "I couldn't do it! He was an old man and quite defenceless. He stood there waiting for me to kill him and my courage failed me."

"Darling!" She sought to comfort him as they rocked together in the back of the car over the bumpy road. "I understand. Please, please, don't give way so. I think I'm glad."

"Glad? But you don't understand!" he exclaimed angrily. "Paxito Zarrif deserved death. The *Millers of God* appointed me to be his executioner, and Lovelace took a big risk to give me a perfect opportunity. Then, just because I found Zarrif to be frail and old, and he stood up to me, I chucked my hand in and ran away."

Lovelace, in the driver's seat, threw a quick glance over his shoulder. The alarm gongs were still ringing in his ears and he expected to see a car crammed with Zarrif's gunmen hot on their trail; but only the empty silver road showed bright in the moonlight behind them. "Didn't you even take the precaution of knocking him out?" he asked curtly.

"No," Christopher admitted shamefacedly, "as I hadn't the heart to kill him I just bolted and skedaddled down the rope from the window. Directly I turned my back he must have roused the house. I was lucky to get over the wall and reach you so quickly."

"Have you got the rope, or did you leave it dangling?" Lovelace shot out as he jammed down the accelerator.

Christopher sat up. "I remembered what you told

me about pulling one end of it instinctively, I think, and it came running down all over me. It's here in the car. I left the short one over the wall, though."

"That doesn't matter. I don't know that anything does now; but at all events they won't know how you got into the house. You might have been hiding in his bedroom for hours."

As they swerved round the corner into the main road Lovelace looked back again. No car was following. Evidently Paxito Zarrif was satisfied to have got rid of his murderous visitor without ordering his henchmen to give chase. Those tense moments when the alarm bells had shrilled out their warning and Christopher was scrambling breathlessly up the hill towards the car were still fresh in his memory, but he eased the car down as they came into the suburban traffic.

When they reached the heart of the city he pulled up on a corner two hundred yards from their hotel.

"You'd better get out here, Christopher," he said. "I know you don't care about drink in the ordinary way, but if you could manage a nightcap, make it a stiff one and get to bed. I'll be back later—when I've returned this hired car—but first I'll take Valerie out to the airport in it."

"Good night, darling." Valerie kissed her fiancé again before he scrambled out.

Christopher came round to the front of the car. His dark eyes looked larger than ever and his face paler as he said hesitantly: "Good night, Lovelace. I'm so sorry I let you down."

"Good Lord, you didn't let *me* down." Lovelace laughed now that the abortive affair was over. "I did no more than pave the way for you. I'm not a *Miller* myself, remember, and I never promised to do more than stand by because the opposition crowd had threatened to do you in."

"You ran a big risk getting into Zarrif's house to spy out the land under the pretence of being Jeremiah

Green; and an even greater one when you faked illness to fix that rope for me."

"Oh, forget it." Lovelace grinned again. "You get to bed and in the morning I'll probably persuade you to join the relief organisation which I was going out to when we first met. That's all above-board, and the poor devils behind the lines in Abyssinia need all the help they can be given."

Christopher threw back his head. "You'll do fine work, I know, but that's only bandaging the wound after it's been made. Someone has *got* to get at the root of this thing and stop the wounds ever being inflicted. I failed the *Millers* to-night, but I won't fail the second time. Even if you refuse to help me further, I've *got* to find another opportunity."

"So you mean to have another go at it," Lovelace said slowly.

"Yes. I pledged myself to kill Zarrif, and if I don't I'll never be able to respect myself again."

Valerie leaned out of the back of the car. "Please go in now, darling, and get to bed. You're so terribly overwrought. We'll talk it over quietly to-morrow."

"You angel!" He smiled suddenly and, seizing her hand, kissed it. "What should I do without you? Sleep well, my sweet."

Lovelace drove Valerie out to the airport hotel, but it was still early, only a quarter-past ten, and her nerves were so strung up that she did not wish to go to bed.

"Park the car and stay with me for a little," she said.

"All right," he agreed. "We'll get a drink in the lounge and, God knows! I need one."

They had their drinks, but the lounge was stuffy and overheated, and a too attentive waiter hovered within earshot, so Valerie suggested that they should go outside where they could talk freely.

There was no wind, so the air was clear of the dust that fought a daily battle with the struggling vegetation in the arid garden. The moon was now high in the heavens, bathing the plain in its brilliant light, yet softening the modern contours of the distant city so that it seemed a fairy town illustrating some old romance. The Acropolis, its ruined state no longer perceptible, and seeming as magnificent as when it was first built, dominated the scene upon its rocky crag. For an hour or two ancient Athens lived again, clothed in the still warmth of the southern night with all the splendour of the past.

"Mind if I smoke my pipe ?" he asked, producing it from his pocket as they sat down on a bench.

"No, you love it, don't you ? I've noticed you always smoke it in preference to cigarettes when you want to think."

"Yes, and I've got some pretty hard thinking to do at the moment." He offered his cigarette case.

"Thanks." She took one. "About Christopher, you mean, and his determination to go on with—this ?"

He nodded. "That's it. I want to think up some really telling arguments against his attempting another cut at Zarrif to-morrow. If Christopher's left to his own devices it's a hundred to one on his bungling it."

"You—you don't mean to give him any further help, then ?"

"No. I've done all I promised, so now I'm through. I don't see the fun of risking my neck in some wild scheme that would probably end in the deaths of both of us, and for all our sakes I'd give a lot to prevent him attempting Zarrif's assassination on his own. D'you think there's any chance of my being able to persuade him to chuck his hand in and sever his connection with the *Millers* ?"

"Not a hope. As I told you once before, Christopher Penn is Christopher Penn, the most pig-headed, quixotic darling ever born between Panama and Alaska. No one can make him change his mind once it's made up."

"Except yourself. He's in love with you, so he'd

stop this murder game if you asked him to for your sake."

"Perhaps. I don't know. But I'm not certain that I want him to."

"I see," he hesitated; "you still think of it as a sort of Crusade, then?"

She drew slowly on her cigarette. "The cause of the *Millers of God* is a just cause. Their systematic execution of the men behind the scenes, the war-makers who deliberately manipulate the Press and national feeling for their own profit, is the only practical scheme ever devised which may in the end stamp out war altogether."

"It's murder all the same—you can't get away from that."

"No, it's justice. Nothing has ever been more just than the secret execution of these men who are responsible for limitless human suffering."

"You won't try and dissuade Christopher from going on, then?"

"I can't. It's a matter of his conscience. Besides, I know he's right, you see. If he loses his own life in another attempt on Zarrif he will deserve a martyr's crown as much as any Christian saint who suffered death for an equally high principle."

"I agree with the principles of the *Millers* all right—in theory," Lovelace fidgeted with his pipe, "but I hate the whole business when it comes down to brass tacks."

She turned to him quickly. "So do I. The personal side of it is horrible—horrible. Yet you'd do a lot to stop the criminal stupidity of war once and for all—wouldn't you?"

"Yes. I once formulated a plan which entailed death for certain people in the event of war. Wrote an article on it called 'Pills of Honour,' but, of course, none of the papers I sent it to would publish it."

"What was your idea? Tell me about it."

"Well, it would sound quite mad to many people, but it won't sound mad to you. The statesmen of Great

Britain are always talking of setting an example to the world and I wanted either to call their bluff or give them a real opportunity to do so. The people as a whole are dead against war and, if they liked to agitate enough, they could force their Members of Parliament to push a Bill through the House of Commons. There's no reason why the Members should object either since it would not affect them—only the Cabinet. My Bill would make it law that the Chief Government Analyst should be in waiting at any Cabinet meeting when the question of plunging the country into war was under discussion. With him he'd have a little box of pills—one for each member of the Government."

"If they decided that no other possible course was open to them than the step which would ensure certain death for hundreds of thousands of their countrymen, and misery for millions more, the Government Analyst would hand round his little box of pills and the Ministers would endorse the absolute necessity for their decision by their own rapid and quite painless death. . . ."

"I see," she nodded, "but wouldn't that be robbing the country of all its natural leaders at one fell swoop ?"

"I don't think so. If someone dropped a bomb in Downing Street while the meeting was on and the Cabinet was blotted out the very greatest sympathy would be extended to their relations; but it wouldn't stop the British Empire from functioning for one moment Equally able men with the possible advantage of better health, from being just a little younger, are available to fill their places immediately. Most Cabinet Ministers are men of a certain age who have the best part of their lives behind them. They've been fortunate too in achieving success and fame. If they're ready to send young men, with all their lives before them, to be torn to pieces by high explosives or choke out their hearts from poison gas, because they find it vital to their country's welfare, surely they shouldn't flinch from sacrificing their few remaining years as an endorsement of their absolute belief in the rightness of their decision."

Valerie smiled. "That would be a great step. If your Bill went through your Government would do some very hard thinking before they pledged their country to any more dangerous pacts. It would have the advantage too that if war had to go on and they did commit this mass *hara-kiri* to save the honour of their nation it would be such stupendous evidence of their conviction that there was no alternative that the whole country would rise, as one man, to destroy the aggressors. Anyhow, there would never be any more fear of your Cabinet plunging you into some wholesale slaughter because a Ruritanian had shot a Graustark frontier guard."

"Exactly! And I believe any Government which had the courage to pass that Bill would go down to posterity as having made the greatest contributions to permanent peace in history. Once it'd gone through the British Parliament other States would force it on their rulers too, because the masses in other countries don't want war any more than we do."

"I wonder." Valerie lit another cigarette. "Your dream moves in the right direction but there's one big snag in it. The *final* responsibility for starting a war may rest with National leaders but nearly always they're forced to it by the pressure of public opinion. The poisoning of a national mind is as necessary to the creation of war as the murder of millions of deluded people is to its fulfilment. The way of the *Millers* is terrible but sane. There can't be any lasting peace until the concessionaires, the armament racketeers, and all those soulless ghouls who deliberately foment trouble for their own gain, are wiped out."

For a moment they sat in silence. "How long have you been engaged to Christopher?" Lovelace asked suddenly.

"Three, no, four months; but our friendship goes

back much further. We've known each other since we were children. Our homes on Long Island lie side by side and neither of us had any brothers or sisters."

"Yes," Lovelace murmured, "he told me that."

"I worshipped him when he was little," she went on slowly. "He wasn't rough like the other boys, but gentle and idealistic. Yet he could fight like a tiger when he was roused. He did once—for me. A bigger boy had teased me over some stupid thing till, like a little fool, I began to cry. Christopher found us like that and half-murdered him. That was when I was nine."

"Later, in our teens, I came to think him just the handsomest boy that ever walked. His dark, curly hair and pale skin, and those wonderful eyes, you know. Lots of other girls thought the same, of course, but he never gave them a look. I honestly don't think he's ever kissed a girl in his life except me. He was more dreamy, more impractical than ever, and it was then I began to mother him."

"We had to part to go through college, but it was already an understood thing that we should marry when we were older, and our first thought when vacations came round was always to be together again. When he was twenty-one all his great business interests were handed over to him formally. For a few years he worked terribly conscientiously on the boards of his companies and travelled all over the States to make a thorough personal investigation of his affairs. That was when I took up flying and began breaking records because, you see, we were separated for a bit. He wasn't very successful as a business man. He wasn't practical enough and he placed the well-being of his work-people before the piling up of profits. That couldn't go on indefinitely; his companies began to suffer; his shareholders began to kick. Eventually his co-directors combined against him and he was practically forced into retirement. He came back to me as handsome and attractive as ever but—well, just a bit shattered. He needed me more than ever and he took it for granted that we were to carry out our boy-and-girl understanding. One night he just said, 'Isn't it about time we thought of getting married?' and I agreed that it was."

"Did nothing occur before then to make you feel that one day you might prefer someone else?" Lovelace asked slowly.

She turned to him sharply. "Why do you ask that?"

"I don't know," he shrugged. "Your flying must have taken you about the world a bit—I only wondered."

"I'll be quite truthful," she confessed after a moment. "There was just one episode, years ago, when I was travelling in Europe with my father and mother—before I went to college. That changed me from a child into a woman, I think. It haunted me for a long time but it was only a sort of schoolgirl dream."

"Have you ever met the man again?"

"Yes, but he didn't even know me. After the first shock I wasn't really surprised either. It was only a silly incident that happened to make a tremendous impression on a little girl but could have had no significance at all for a grown man."

"How strange—life is strange, isn't it?"

She nodded. "Anyhow, that's all over. It never happened except for the things my imagination built round it. Nothing has ever really come between Christopher and myself—and I'm glad. I've never realised until these last few weeks quite how desperately he needed me. He needs you too."

"Valerie." He placed a hand gently on her shoulder and turned her towards him. "Where did we meet before? Why do you make such a mystery of it? I know we did—won't you tell me?"

The bright moonlight glinted on her smooth chestnut hair as she shook her head. "It was in the land of dreams perhaps, but this is Athens and Zarrif is leaving here to-morrow to obtain his Abyssinian concession. If he succeeds we know that it will be used to bring about another European war. Christopher means to try to stop him, but what chance will he have unaided? Poor, flame-like, impractical Christopher is standing alone as the sole defence of the peace and happiness of ten million homes. He needs us, Anthony—both of us—and we can't let him down."

"No," said Lovelace slowly. "We can't let him down."

CHAPTER IX

A SUICIDAL PLAN

AT six-thirty the following morning Christopher invaded Lovelace's room and shook him gently by the shoulder.

"Lovelace!" he said in a low voice. "Lovelace, wake up, I want to talk to you."

The sleeping man turned over and blinked his eyes. "What's the matter?" he muttered. "What's the time?"

"I don't know, something after six, I think," Christopher said vaguely.

"Then you can go to hell," Lovelace grunted. "I never talk to anyone before nine," and he buried his head firmly in the pillow.

He was furious at being wakened in the middle of a very pleasant dream. In it, he was a young man again and back at Fronds, the lovely old place in Yorkshire that had been in his family since Charles II's time. He knew that he was not much over twenty because the gardens were beautifully kept, just as they had been before he succeeded to the title and heavy death duties had compelled him to close the place down. It was high summer and the sun made dazzling patches of light and shade upon the neatly trimmed yew hedges of the famous Maze. Lovelace had known every turn and twist of it from his earliest boyhood and he was only strolling through its high-walled alleys to its centre because he wanted to think something out and be alone. Why he should have found it necessary to seek refuge there when he could have sat in the far more lovely pond garden or paced the long, walled border with its multitude of flowers, he could not recall. Suddenly the peace of the place had been disturbed by running feet and a pleading voice had cried, "Please! please! show me the way out of here." The dream had become confused then and he felt himself rocking as though in a ship at sea while someone was saying, "Lovelace, Lovelace, wake up!"

He tried to recapture it as Christopher tiptoed from the room, but he could only see the gardens, now overgrown and uncared for, as they had been since straitened circumstances had necessitated his living on the few hundreds a year which was all his father had been able to leave him with the place.

For the hundredth time he wondered if it wouldn't really be wisest to sell Fronds. It was a very gracious house, a little larger perhaps than most people wanted these days, but a moderately rich man could keep it up quite easily and close one of the wings if he found it too big for him. The gardens were famous and could soon be put to rights again with a little money. The roofs were sound and there were plenty of bathrooms since it had been modernised, when his over-generous father had spent far more than he could afford running it, free of all charges to the country, as a hospital during the war. He hadn't known then, of course, how a grateful Government would repay his patriotism by taxing him so highly, when the war was over, that he could no longer live there without making inroads on his capital, and that death duties would prove the final blow which would make a mockery of his son Anthony's inheritance.

It was saleable enough, Lovelace knew. He was often getting letters from Mount Street house agents asking him to allow them to offer it and holding out the prospect of interested parties who would be pleased to enter into negotiations. The place and contents, which included a few good pictures and a fairly valuable library, would bring him enough to turn his eight-hundred-

and fifty a year income into the best part of three thousand a year. That would make life a far more pleasant affair and enable him to spend a good portion of his time at the more expensive places where most of his friends congregated when they were abroad, or to keep his end up among them in London if he wished, instead of being forced to trek from one remote portion of the globe to another by the cheapest means of travel because living was reasonable and the places of some interest when he got there.

Yet he could never bring himself to sign the letter that would place Fronds on the market. He knew that he would never make enough money himself to live there again. Long ago he had come to accept the fact that he was not the type of man who makes money and that he lacked all aptitude for business. But he had various fairly wealthy aunts and cousins who might possibly remember him substantially in their wills, although he had no real reason to expect it, and if that did happen he knew that he would never be able to forgive himself if he had parted with Fronds. Besides, he had always felt that one day he might marry and have a son. How that would improve the situation, he did not see, unless his wife happened to be an heiress. Still, as long as a son remained even a remote possibility he did not feel that it would be fair to the boy to rob him of the chance of living in the old place which had been the home of his forefathers for so many centuries, if times were better then.

With these well-worn thoughts passing vaguely through his mind he dropped off to sleep again; but not for long. At half-past seven Christopher roused him out once more; this time to say that Valerie was downstairs and anxious to talk to him.

Grumbling, but resigned now to the fact that further sleep was impossible, Lovelace tumbled out of bed, wrestled with the indifferent plumbing which had been installed two generations before in the small Greek hotel, and made his way down to the lounge a little after eight.

Valerie was seated in a basket chair under an old fig tree that grew in the centre of the courtyard. Her face was pale and her big eyes unnaturally sunken in the hollows beneath her level brows.

"Sorry to get you up so early," she apologised at once, "but I simply couldn't sleep."

Lovelace was feeling better now he was bathed, shaved and dressed. He looked at her with grave concern. "Don't worry about me, please. What about some breakfast ? I'll bet you haven't had any yet."

She shook her head. "Thanks. I've had some coffee, but I couldn't eat a thing."

"That's nonsense," he said firmly. "You don't go on a starvation diet when you're in the middle of one of your flying stunts, do you ? You know how vital it is to keep up your strength."

"You're right," she admitted with a wan little smile. "It's a bit unfair that I'm not supposed to have nerves like any ordinary woman but I've got myself to blame for that. I'll do what I can with some rolls and butter and some fruit while you're feeding, if you like."

"Good, come on then."

Christopher laid a hand on his arm as he was about to move in the direction of the little dining-room. "If you must eat, why not do it at the airport restaurant while they're getting Valerie's plane ready ?"

They both looked at him in surprise as he hurried on : "I didn't sleep much last night, either, so I had a chance to think the whole thing out. I've behaved abominably in dragging the two of you into this. I suppose I've become obsessed by it in a way, otherwise I'd have realised before the danger you were running on my account. It's a bit late to apologise for that now, but I meant what I said last night about going on with it, and before I take the next step I want both of you to be safely out of Athens. That's what I came to tell you, Lovelace, when I roused you out early this morning."

Lovelace hesitated a moment. It struck him as grimly humorous that after Valerie had persuaded him, the night before, to give his further assistance by stressing Christopher's absolute dependence on their help in carrying out the task to which his mystic idealism impelled him, they should now find a new and determined Christopher who told them politely but firmly that he meant to complete his mission on his own.

"I see," he said slowly. "Well, I'm all for Valerie clearing out. Have been from the beginning, as you know, but I don't feel at all happy at the idea of leaving you myself."

Christopher shrugged impatiently. "This isn't your show any longer. I mean, you've done all you promised in providing me with a perfect opportunity—more—as you fixed things so that I could have got away safely afterwards, and I'm very grateful to you. But I mucked it and Zarrif's leaving Athens at midday. There's no time now to prepare another fool-proof chance and I naturally don't expect you to risk your life in the attempt I've decided to make on him before he gets away."

"Now look here!" Lovelace pushed him back into his chair and sat down himself. "Let's hear what you intend to do before we go any further."

Christopher bent forward and spoke in a low voice although the courtyard was deserted. "Zarrif's going to Addis Ababa, isn't he, although we haven't the faintest idea which route he means to take. It's only the 13th to-day so that gives him eighteen days for his journey as he's not due there till the 1st of May. He probably intends to transact all sorts of other business on the way out, but where, we haven't the faintest notion. Once he's left Athens in his plane we're stuck. It's clear therefore that I've got to get him before he starts—within the next five hours. We know already that it's impossible for me to get into his house and, seeing the sort of bird he is, he'll probably drive to the airport in a bullet-proof car, so it's not much good my standing at the gate to have a pot at him. I'd only get shot myself to no purpose by one of his gunmen. But he's got to leave his car to walk over to his plane, hasn't he? Well, that's my opportunity and I mean to take it."

"But, Christopher!" Valerie gasped. "That's suicide! Even if you succeeded his bodyguard would shoot you down."

Lovelace looked thoughtful. "Your reasoning's sound enough about the odds against your ever being able to trace him once he's left Athens, and about the airport being the only place that gives you any hope of doing the job here, but as Valerie says, there's not a chance in a million of your getting away afterwards."

Christopher stood up again. "I know, but I've brought that on myself. It's the price I've to pay for acting like a squeamish fool when the going was good. I think I'd best say good-bye to you both now. You'll read about what happens in the papers, I expect."

"Sit down, you young idiot," Lovelace snapped. "It's revolting to see you dramatise yourself like this." He had caught Valerie's glance beseeching him to prevent the insane plan and went on more quietly.

"How can you talk so glibly of us reading about your being riddled with bullets. We both know you're doing the heroic thing—sacrificing yourself for an ideal—and all that. But is it necessary? Can't we think of another way."

"There is no other way," Christopher stated with a mulish look.

"Maybe you're right; but at least you might give us the chance to exercise any brains we've got on it before you go rushing out to die."

"Yes, please, Christopher, please," Valerie added imploringly. "At least listen to what Anthony has to say."

After that the discussion became heated. Valerie denounced the scheme as sheer madness, entailing Christopher's certain death, while Lovelace backed her up with every argument he could think of, realising now that it was Valerie, not Christopher, whom he would be letting down by withdrawing from the affair unless he could turn the pale-faced young fanatic from his purpose. From becoming a reluctant accomplice he found himself pressing the younger man to accept his further help, for it only needed Christopher's change of front and new desire to have them both safely out of it to spur him into a determination to save the boy from committing such a crazy action, whatever the risk might be himself.

At last, after wrangling for nearly a quarter of an hour, Christopher agreed to postpone any definite decision until after breakfast and they moved into the dining-room of the hotel. Valerie continued the discussion with him there on a lower note, using obscure phrases so that the garlic-breathing waiter should not understand what they were talking about even if he knew English. Lovelace, meanwhile, despatched a hearty breakfast almost in silence while he cudgelled his brains for some way out of the impasse.

By nine o'clock they were back in the deserted courtyard; Christopher still grimly determined to carry out his suicidal plan, and Valerie very near to tears at the ill-success of her attempts to turn him from it, when Lovelace suddenly intervened.

"Look here," he said. "It's quite true you were supposed to do the job in Athens, but as long as the job's done before Zarrif reaches Addis Ababa that's all that really matters. As there is still the best part of three weeks to go before he's due there he's bound to be stopping off somewhere. Why shouldn't we follow? Then another chance may present itself where Christopher won't have to run this insane risk."

"That's all very well," Christopher muttered, "but

once he's left Athens what chance have we got of ever finding him again? His business may take him to any one of half a hundred places at the eastern end of the Mediterranean."

"True, but you'll remember that Barrotet gave us the names of several of the *Millers* who live in that part of the world. There was that Italian in Cairo, and the Dane in Haifa, and the German in Alex. If Zarrif fetches up in any of those places these lads are almost certain to hear of it and be able to tip us off."

Christopher shook his head. "We've only got eighteen days, remember. Even if we got in touch with them all by cable, by the time one of them reported that Zarrif had turned up in his area, and we managed to get there, the chances are that Zarrif would have moved on again. It's no good arguing; I've made up my mind and I'm going to do it when he leaves his car at the airport to-day."

Lovelace knew that his next suggestion would entail a damnable risk to himself. He had thought of it at breakfast but dismissed it in the hope that some other way might be found. Now he saw that the time had come when he must play his last card if Valerie's young man was to be prevented from occupying a slab in the Athens morgue that evening.

"I don't think I told you," he said, "that when I saw Zarrif last night he offered me a job, believing me to be Mr. Jeremiah Green, of course, and that I could give him all the latest dope about what's been going on in Abyssinia. He asked me to report to his secretary, Cassalis, at the airport at one-thirty to-day so that I could go with them and be on hand if Zarrif wants to consult me. I agreed, imagining then that the old devil would be dead within an hour."

Valerie's face lighted up with sudden hope. "Then—then, if you kept the appointment, you'd be able to leave Athens in Zarrif's party and let us know where he is directly he arrives at his destination."

"That's the idea," Lovelace nodded. "What about it?"

"I don't like it," Christopher shook his head. "It means your running the most ghastly risk the whole time you're with them. If they found out you're not Jeremiah Green that bunch of thugs would be capable of killing you without the slightest compunction."

"They might have done that yesterday," Lovelace shrugged, "but I got away with it. And now they've really accepted me as the unfortunate Mr. Green, the situation's far less dangerous. Anyhow, the risk is mine and I'm taking it with my eyes open. So that settles the matter."

Valerie threw him a glance in which gratitude was mingled with a new fear. "I hate the thought of your doing this for us. Oh, Christopher! won't you please let Barrotet know that you haven't been able to manage the job, and get him to put one of the other *Millers* in the Near East on to tackling Zarrif when they pick him up again?"

Christopher shook his head. "No; it's now or never. Lovelace's scheme is sound enough, but I see no earthly reason why he should risk his neck for me. It's best for all of us that I should stick to my original plan."

"You'll do nothing of the kind," Lovelace said with quiet finality. "You agree that my scheme's all right, so we'll adopt it; otherwise I shall come with you to the airport and take the far bigger risk of getting myself shot down when you do your heroics. You don't want that, do you?"

Christopher smiled. "You're a grand chap, Lovelace, and you've put me in a corner. I couldn't possibly let you do that, and you know it, so I'll accept this scheme of your going with Zarrif as Mr. Green if that's the only alternative."

"There's one big snag to it," Valerie remarked. "You may find it impossible to communicate with us."

"That's true," Lovelace nodded. "But if I can't I'll manage to get in touch with one of the *Millers* whose address we have and you'll learn my whereabouts from him."

"But time . . . " insisted Christopher, leaning forward, ". . . is the essential factor. By the time we learn where you are Zarrif may have moved on again."

Suddenly Valerie laughed. "There's only one thing for it then. We must all be ready to leave the airport at the same time as Zarrif, so that Christopher and I can follow you in the plane."

"Good Lord!" Lovelace exclaimed. "I thought we'd ruled you out at last. It's Christopher's wish as well as mine now that you should take no further hand in the affair."

Another hectic argument ensued but Christopher was obsessed again with his mission. Valerie could help him to accomplish it far better than any hired pilot, he knew, and in his mind he minimised the risk which she might run by his old belief that she would have no hand in the actual business and was perfectly capable of taking care of herself wherever they might land and whatever might happen to himself and Lovelace. In the end the two of them over-ruled Lovelace's objection and it was agreed that Valerie should have her way.

They spent an hour with their heads bent over an old atlas and a number of guide books which they borrowed from the manager of the hotel, marking out all the principal cities in which it was likely Zarrif might stop on his way out to Addis Ababa. In each they agreed upon a small hotel where Valerie and Christopher should stay. Then Lovelace memorised the addresses in order that he might get in touch with them as rapidly as possible.

They had an early lunch and parted with subdued farewells, not knowing in what place or country they might meet again; it having been decided that it would be better for Lovelace to drive out to the airport independently.

At a little before one-thirty he arrived at the bookstall to keep his appointment with Cassalis. It was only then that he realised he would have to show his passport before leaving.

If Cassalis asked to see it, or even caught sight of it when he produced it at the barrier, there would be an abrupt end to the fiction that he was Jeremiah Green, Ras Desoum's messenger to Zarrif from Abyssinia. With confused and miserable misgivings he stood there waiting for the secretary's arrival.

CHAPTER X

THE HOUSE ON THE EDGE OF THE DESERT

DURING the minutes Lovelace spent waiting by the bookstall he felt irritable and anxious. Irritable on account of the long wrangle he had had with Christopher that morning and anxious because, quite apart from any difficulties which might arise if he had to produce his passport, he saw, now he had a chance to think things over alone, that, even though there was no actual evidence to go on, Zarrif might well suspect some connection between the two visits Mr. Jeremiah Green had made him the day before and Christopher's attempt to murder him later. If Zarrif did suspect anything the fat would be in the fire with a vengeance.

In the distance Lovelace caught sight of Christopher and Valerie sauntering, side by side, across the aerodrome towards her plane. The sun was gleaming on her chestnut hair as she stepped out to keep pace with him. He too was bareheaded and, even so far away, his matt-white face under the short, dark, curling hair looked like the profile of some young Greek God who had just come to life again. Lovelace was conscious of a warm glow of satisfaction at the thought that he had certainly saved him from a martyr's crown, at all events for the moment, but when they were safely embarked and ready to take the air his forebodings about his own situation returned with renewed vigour.

'Cassalis' arrival put an end to his gloomy speculations and concealing his anxiety he gave the Frenchman a friendly smile.

"You are punctual, *mon ami,*" Cassalis remarked

cheerfully. "That is good. Monsieur Zarrif much dislikes to be kept waiting."

Lovelace felt a little secret thrill of elation. It seemed that at least he was not suspected of any connection with Zarrif's unwelcome visitor. "Mr. Zarrif has not turned up yet," he said, "at least I haven't seen him."

"You would not," the dapper secretary replied quickly. "Mr. Zarrif is a very extraordinary man and has many unusual privileges. He keeps his private plane here for convenience but no formalities are required when he and his entourage come or go in it. I left his car only this moment. It has driven straight on to the landing-ground. I meet you so you have no delay in passing the officials. Come, let us proceed."

An ill-assorted pair, they walked over to the barrier. Cassalis slim, effeminate, quick stepping and conscious of his own importance, his dark eyes shining like polished jet in his sallow face; the Englishman a good head taller, slower of gait owing to his longer stride, his limbs moving easily with a hidden power, his healthily tanned face an unrevealing mask and his partly lowered lids half concealing his lazy glance.

At the *guichet* the passport officer greeted Cassalis with a friendly nod and the two exchanged flowery compliments in Greek.

The critical moment had come and Lovelace knew that somehow he had got to divert Cassalis' attention. Putting his hand in his breast pocket he drew out his passport and with it a dozen bank-notes which, with apparent clumsiness, he allowed to flutter to the ground.

Murmuring an apology he thrust his passport through the *guichet* before stooping to pick up his money. Cassalis was already busy collecting some of the scattered notes. It took only a matter of seconds but, when they rose again, the officer had already given the passport the cursory glance which was sufficient to satisfy himself in the case of Cassalis' friend. With a smile of thanks to the official Lovelace slipped the document back in his pocket. As he turned towards the flying-field he gave a secret sigh of relief. He was safely over the first fence, at all events.

Zarrif's plane was a great, grey, four-engined monster. Three cars stood near it but he and his suite were already on board when Lovelace and Cassalis went up the gangway.

The machine was divided into four compartments. A kitchenette in the tail; a biggish saloon which accommodated the bodyguard—six tough-looking customers—two of whom Lovelace had seen the day before; a combined dining-room and office, and, adjoining the cockpit, Zarrif's own sanctum.

Lovelace was taken through to him at once. He looked smaller and more narrow-shouldered than ever in the daylight yet his green eyes showed him to be a dynamo of mental activity and Lovelace was struck again by the unusual fairness of his skin for an Armenian.

Zarrif pulled at his little goatee beard as he inquired kindly after his new employee's health. On learning that the night's rest had restored him after the previous day's attack he dismissed him with orders that he should remain in the middle cabin with Cassalis.

As the plane moved off Cassalis unlocked a low steel cupboard and Lovelace saw that it contained four machine-guns, equipment for fixing them, and several boxes of ammunition. The bodyguards were called in and, obviously following a well-established routine, they disappeared with two guns aft and two forward to place them in position. Within ten minutes of leaving Athens the plane had been converted from a private airliner into a powerful fighting machine.

Lovelace forebore to comment but Cassalis gave him a knowing grin. "It is well to be prepared—eh, Mr. Green?"

"Yes rather, but er—what on earth for?" Lovelace fingered his little upturned moustache and his brown eyes were open wide in bland inquiry.

"Ah, who can tell!" The Frenchman shrugged mysteriously. "But there are strange people about these days and some of them perhaps use aeroplanes. There are no witnesses in the sky to see what happens and if we were all picked up drowned people would say 'this is an accident!' Mr. Zarrif is one who has a great aversion to accidents."

Opening a satchel, Cassalis took out a sheaf of papers, but after a moment he thrust them back again having apparently decided not to start work at once. Instead he settled himself more comfortably and said:

"Tell me, Mr. Green, about Abyssinia. As you will have assured yourself from my questions yesterday I know much of the Emperor and his principal ministers. It is my business to do so, but I have never been there."

"I was only there myself . . . " Lovelace caught himself just in time. Lulled into a false security by Cassalis' friendly acceptance of him as a colleague he had forgotten momentarily that he was impersonating the messenger who had been struck down by fever in the Sudan. He had been about to say quite truthfully, "on a visit to see the Emperor's coronation in 1930." The slip would have cost him his life. With a hardly perceptible hesitation he managed to substitute " . . . for a few months this winter. What d'you want to know about the place?"

"Of the people, the customs, the country?" Cassalis made an airy gesture; evidently having noticed nothing.

"All three vary tremendously. The ruling caste are the Amhara. They're quite light skinned and have nothing negroid about them except their fuzzy hair and they don't think of themselves as blacks at all. In fact they regard negroes with more contempt than most white people do. They've a culture of their own which was probably quite a high one in pre-Roman times but they've been isolated for so many centuries that it became sterile and decadent long ago. They're such snobs that they look down on whites almost as much as they do on negroes. Altogether there's only about two and a half million of them—that's roughly a fourth of the total population—but they hold all the important posts and are thoroughly hated by the other races of greater Abyssinia; the races they ruled in the dark ages but have only reconquered in quite recent times, I mean."

"Who are these other races?"

"Well, the Gallas are the largest; they're about four million strong. Then there are the Guragis; a mysterious race said to be descended from white slaves brought out of Egypt three thousand years ago. They're the workers of the country. The others despise men who labour and particularly anyone who has anything to do with commerce. The deserts of the east and south are inhabited by the Danakils and Somalis; blood-thirsty, uncivilised savages. In the mountains to the north on the borders of Eritrea live the Tigres who're not much better. In the west there's a backward race of negroes called Shankalis, and round Harar you find the more cultured Hararis who come from Arab stock. Then a race of black Jews called Fallashas occupy the neighbourhood of Gondar. None of them agrees about a single thing except in their hatred of their overlords, the Amhara."

Cassalis nodded. "It is a country of many nations then; like Austria-Hungary before the Great War? Held together only by the strength of its ruler."

"Exactly. The fact that it might break up at any time, even without pressure from outside, is the worst problem the Emperor has to face, and what makes things even more difficult for him is that he daren't do a thing without the sanction of the Church."

"They are Christians of a sort—is it not so?"

"Yes. The people of the four mountain kingdoms, Amhara, Shoa, Tigre, and Gojjam, which compose true Abyssinia, are Coptic Christians. The Abuna, their chief priest, is under the jurisdiction of the Archbishop of Cairo. He's really the most powerful man in the country because every third Christian in Abyssinia is also a priest and takes his orders from him. The Emperor's big trouble is that the Church is dead against any sort of progress. They put every possible obstacle in the path of his reforms and if he seriously offended the priests they could push him off his throne to-morrow. He'd give anything to get rid of them, I think, but he's not strong enough and, even with a war on his hands, he has to keep in with them by attending service four times a week. Services which start at six in the morning and go on until past midday."

"He is much handicapped then; more than I had thought."

"He is," Lovelace agreed. "Abyssinia's in the state now that England was in under the Plantagenets. The people are lousy, diseased, ridden to death with religion, and only acknowledge allegiance to their own feudal overlords. The great nobles are greedy, fierce and resentful of any central authority. Many of them were independent kings themselves only a few years ago and would revolt again on the most flimsy pretext. The Emperor can only keep them in check by retaining the goodwill of the Church and playing them off one against the other."

"How do they live—the better class I mean?"

"The Emperor lives like a cultured European now, but that's quite an innovation. When he was younger he used habitually to sleep in vermin-infested beds. Most of the nobles do still, and their so-called palaces are little more than two-roomed houses with a collection of squalid huts clustered round them. Their favourite food is raw meat to this day and they eat it with their fingers."

"*Nom de dieu*, what a country!" The Frenchman threw up his hands.

Lovelace smiled. "You'll get used to it. They're a lazy, ignorant, verminous lot, and their favourite word is *Ishi-naga*, which means 'all right—but to-morrow.' Still, Europeans manage to survive somehow and think how tremendously you'll appreciate civilisation when you do get back to it again."

"Thank you, Monsieur Green. I have heard enough of this abominable country to which we go. Fortunately we stay there at most a day or two. You will forgive me now please if I work." Cassalis picked up his satchel again and began to spread his papers out on the dining-table.

Having told nothing but the truth Lovelace was mildly amused at its effect on the effeminate Frenchman, but soon he turned his thoughts to more serious things. One point had emerged from the conversation. Zarrif only intended to spend a day or two in Addis Ababa. That meant he had business to transact and would make a prolonged halt on the way out. But where? Lovelace wondered if the production of his hideously dangerous passport would be necessary again on landing and how he would be able to communicate with Valerie and Christopher. These questions, and the danger of his situation, troubled him acutely as they flew on through the golden afternoon, leaving the eastern end of Crete below them on their right and ploughing steadily towards the south-eastward.

At five-thirty they sighted land again and began to descend in circling spirals. A large town was visible some miles away on their left along a narrow strip of sea-coast. Inland, behind it, spread a big lake but they were coming down on a deserted shore. A river, winding away to the inland lake, showed below them. On its bank, a few hundred yards only from the sea, a solitary white building set among gardens was visible. The plane tilted at what seemed a horribly risky angle, dropped in a great curve towards the earth, then straightened, bounced along a stretch of sand, and halted within fifty yards of a white villa surrounded by palm trees.

As they disembarked Lovelace saw that a great khaki hangar waited to house the plane near one wall of the property. A dusty track bordered by ragged palms led towards its gate where a little group of native servants in tarbooshes and white clothing stood ready to welcome Zarrif. Preceded by two of his gunmen he trudged through the sand, a small, bent figure, towards them. They salaamed as he approached but he never gave them a word or a glance and walked straight on up to the house.

Lovelace, thanking his gods that Zarrif's privileges apparently included the right of making an unofficial landing which rendered the production of passports unnecessary, followed with Cassalis and the remainder of the bodyguard.

By pausing for a moment to fiddle with his shoe-lace Lovelace managed to drop a few paces behind the others and was able to snatch a quick lock round without being observed. The city he had seen from the air was some miles along the coast and no longer visible. A stony track, just wide enough to accommodate a single car, ran from the villa towards it but disappeared among the sand-dunes which were partially covered with coarse grass. No other house or building except the hangar, into which Zarrif's pilot was now taxi-ing the big plane, broke the scorched monotonous landscape. Far away, in the direction of the city, a tiny speck moved in the cloudless sky.

It was that for which Lovelace had been looking. At so great a distance it was impossible to identify it as Valerie's plane, and he knew that it might well be one of the Royal Air Force machines with which the British were said to be filling Egypt, or a civilian flyer, but the sight of it cheered him. There was a decent possibility of it being Valerie which increased his hope that she had managed to keep on Zariff's tail as they crossed the Mediterranean and would have seen them come down at the villa. He broke into a trot and caught up the others just as they were entering the garden.

Inside, the villa proved cool and commodious. A gallery ran round the tiled hall on a level with the first floor. Cassalis escorted Lovelace to a room opening off it, then left him with the suggestion that he would doubtless like to rest until dinner for which he would be called at eight o'clock.

He had no desire to rest at all but, courteously as the suggestion was made, the tone in which it was given warned him that he was not expected to wander about the house uninvited.

The room contained a large double bed, draped in mosquito netting, and was furnished in the ornate French style of the early nineteen hundreds. A partly open door in one wall disclosed a bathroom. He unpacked his scant belongings, undressed, enjoyed a shower, and then sat down to consider the situation.

He felt certain that the big town he had seen further along the coast, when the plane was landing, must be Alexandria. Christopher and Valerie would just be arriving at the Gordon Pasha Hotel there for, even if they had lost sight of Zarrif's plane when crossing the Mediterranean, that had been agreed upon as their first port of call if he headed towards Egypt.

Yet Lovelace, not having foreseen that Zarrif might stop at a house of his own miles outside a town, had no way of communicating with them. There was no telephone in the room and he would not have dared to use it if there had been. He made up his mind that somehow or other he must get out of the house and in to Alexandria that night. It would be a long and tiring walk but he could get a car to bring him out again and, having made fresh arrangements with Christopher, he should be safely back in his bedroom again before dawn. In the meantime his position would continue difficult and dangerous. The only comforting thought was that neither Zarrif nor Cassalis could have any possible suspicion that he was not Mr. Jeremiah Green.

He dined alone with the Frenchman, who proved an amusing enough companion and seemed glad to have his company. After the meal he seized the opportunity, when they were studying some old prints on the walls, to push his tobacco pouch behind an ornament and then, without protest, he allowed himself to be shepherded upstairs again to his room. Cassalis indicated a long shelf of books and expressed the hope that he would find something there to interest him before wishing him good night with courteous but unmistakable finality.

Knowing he had several hours to wait before he dared attempt anything Lovelace took the hint and settled down to read. He was patient by nature and the time slipped past quickly. By midnight, as far as he could judge, all the lights in the house were out, and, when he listened intently for any sound or movement, the place was so still that he could hear his own breathing.

He dared not remove his shoes ; to have been caught carrying them would reveal a guilty intention and, if he ran into one of the gunmen, he meant to excuse his midnight prowling by saying that he had left his tobacco pouch downstairs in the dining-room. However he was banking on the man on duty being safely out of the way at some permanent post in the neighbourhood of Zarrif's bedroom. He put out the light, quietly turned the handle of his door, and pulled. It did not yield a fraction. Someone had locked it.

That gave him cause for anxious thought but he came to the conclusion that, since they could have no grounds for suspecting him, they were only treating him as a new-comer to the establishment and exercising a precautionary measure by keeping him a prisoner.

He moved over to the window and peered out. It was not a long drop to the ground and somehow he would manage to scramble up again. The garden was still and moonlit. Only the faint howling of a jackal out in the desert broke the stillness. He threw one leg over the balcony; then paused. A shadow had moved at the foot of one of the palm trees. It was a big dog. It lifted its head, barked once, and subsided into a menacing growl. Lovelace withdrew behind the curtains of the window. As he did so a figure came round the corner of the house. One of the gun-men was on duty in the garden.

Mr. Zarrif apparently made it as difficult for his guests to get out of his establishments as for unwelcome visitors to get in and Lovelace felt there was no alternative but to abandon his attempt for that night at least. As he climbed into bed he recalled Cassalis' statement that "Mr. Zarrif was one who had a great aversion to accidents."

Next morning a light breakfast was served to him in bed. He had scarcely finished it when Cassalis arrived to say that Zarrif would like to see him at ten o'clock. By the appointed time he was dressed and ready to wait upon the elderly Armenian. For an hour they talked Abyssinia together. Lovelace found it a little easier to sustain the ordeal now that he had had some practice at it and, when the interview was over, asked if there was any objection to his spending the afternoon in Alexandria.

Zarrif looked at him in cold surprise. "My staff are sufficiently well paid to take their recreation only when they have left my service," he said quietly. "I fear that I may need you at any time."

For a moment Lovelace thought of mentioning Otto Klinger, whose name Barrotet had given as an associate of the *Millers of God* resident in Alexandria, and saying that he wished to see him on business; but that would have meant compromising Klinger with Zarrif if anything went wrong later. His only course was to accept the situation with outward cheerfulness.

After the interview he was given the run of a small sitting-room at the back of the house which had a large selection of books in it. From the window he could see over the garden wall and glimpse the slope running down to the turgid, muddy river; a native felucca with a large, triangular sail was tacking up stream, but it was too far off for him to contemplate attempting to use the river traffic as a means of communication with his friends.

He began to study the titles of the books and decided to use one of them for a matter that had been troubling him ever since the previous evening. If he slipped up, as he feared he might from hour to hour, and they searched him, the discovery of his passport would damn him utterly; yet he was loath to destroy it, as its loss might prove a serious handicap if he wished to leave the country at an hour's notice later on. Now, making certain that he was unobserved from the garden, he pulled a heavy volume of Natural History from a lower shelf, jammed the passport well home between the leaves, and replaced the volume in its set.

That done, he felt a trifle easier in his mind. He could always swear he had lost it, and at least they could not now secure any proof of his real identity.

He had rescued his tobacco pouch from the dining-room after seeing Zarrif. Filling his pipe, he lit up and sat down to think; to try and plan some way of leaving the house without arousing suspicion. If only the party had stopped at some hotel, as he had naturally assumed they would, there would not have been the least difficulty in his getting in touch with his friends. A carefully worded note slipped into the hand of one of the hotel servants with an adequate tip, when no one was looking, and Christopher would have known the place that Zarrif had selected for his headquarters during his stay in Alex. within an hour.

As it was, Lovelace dared not risk bribing Zarrif's own servants to take a message, because he knew that if they betrayed him he would pay for his indiscretion with his life, and in the face of Zarrif's refusal to allow him to go into Alex. it would have been madness to attempt to leave the house in broad daylight.

Sitting there in the quiet room all through the morning, he was aware, although he could not see them, that, from time to time, visitors arrived; presumably to see Zarrif. While he puzzled his brains for a way out of his dilemma, Lovelace wondered upon what strange errands, fraught, perhaps, with far-reaching consequences for countless innocent people, these mysterious visitors came.

He could not bring himself to hate Zarrif as a person. The elderly Armenian had shown him every courtesy—more, he had even momentarily put aside important business to show concern over his new employee's health. Yet Lovelace knew that the man was ruthless, evil, completely callous about everything outside his own personal interests, and engaged in plotting a thing which would bring about incalculable human suffering through a mad lust for power and monetary gain.

By lunch-time he had reached no decision. The meal was brought to him on a tray, and deft, silent-footed native servants waited on him.

When he was alone again he confessed to himself that for the moment he was powerless, and decided he must postpone any further action until the coming night. Selecting a book from the shelves he sat down to read, and remained immersed in the adventures of a man in far less delicate situations than he was himself until the shadows drew a veil over the garden and he could no longer see the sails of the native boats upon the river in the near distance.

That evening he dined again with Cassalis. Afterwards Zarrif sent for him, but detained him only ten minutes. When he was free he went up to his room and read till midnight. Once more, after the house had gone to rest, he made a cautious investigation. His door was locked; the dog and watcher occupied the garden. In an evil temper after his long worrying day, and really anxious now, he went to bed.

On the following morning he was escorted to the back sitting-room and left there undisturbed. The staff were as polite as ever, so he came to accept the fact that he was kept a virtual prisoner only as part of a cautious routine: simply to ensure that he should learn nothing of Zarrif's business.

He attempted to occupy himself with books and papers, but as hour after hour slipped by he became more and more concerned with the apparent impossibility of getting in touch with his friends. Before they left Athens it had been arranged that if Christopher and Valerie succeeded in keeping track of Zarrif's plane they should remain for five days at a prearranged address in any town at which they saw him land. If Lovelace failed to communicate with them during that time they would then proceed a stage further south; on the assumption that Lovelace was too closely watched to send a message and that Zarrif would most probably move, without their being able to witness his departure, towards Abyssinia as the date of his appointment in Addis Ababa drew nearer.

After a little Lovelace flung down his book. His eyes were reading the printed lines, but his brain was not taking in their meaning. He realised, quite suddenly, that he had not the faintest idea what the last chapter he had read had been about. His mind was solely occupied with the knowledge that two of the days during which Christopher and Valerie would remain in Alex. were already gone and that there seemed no more likelihood of his being able to communicate with them during the next three than in those which had passed.

As the brief twilight fell, heralding his third night in Egypt, his nerves were becoming a little jumpy from having to keep so strict a watch upon his tongue at every meal; and wondering what sinister business brought those visitors whose footfalls he could hear, but whom he could not see, to this mysterious house on the edge of the desert; yet he had no premonition of coming trouble when Cassalis arrived to say that Zarrif wished to see him. He walked across the tiled hall without the least suspicion that anything had gone wrong.

His first intimation of the unusual was the sight of two of the bodyguard standing behind Zarrif's desk with their automatics drawn ready in their hands.

A big, flashily-dressed negro, his face shiny with perspiration, stood in front of the desk. His arms hung loosely at his sides and he seemed to have shrunk a little so that he no longer fitted his smart, white suit of European design.

Lovelace took in the scene at a glance. A second later he felt something prod him in the back. Turning he saw that Cassalis, his shiny jet-black eyes gone hard and soulless, was holding a pistol to his spine.

With a smile which it took a very considerable effort to produce he looked at Zarrif and asked: "What is all this—what's the trouble?"

Zarrif's green eyes fixed him like those of a snake about to strike. "The trouble is," he said icily, waving a hand towards the big negro, "that I don't know who you are but *this* is Mr. Jeremiah Green."

CHAPTER XI

THE BLUFF THAT FAILED

LOVELACE stared dumbly at the negro for a moment. He saw that his only chance lay in bluff and stepping forward he thrust out his jaw. "Who is this fellow?" he demanded hotly. "He's lying anyhow!"

"No sah!" protested the black man with an emphatic shake of his head. "I'se Jeremiah Green of Gainesville, Fla.; a citizen of de United States of America. Pastor Donovan gives me dat name in de sight o' de Lawd toirty nine year ago as I kin prove."

"Perhaps there's some mistake then," suggested Lovelace. "The name of Green is not uncommon; nor Jeremiah for that matter."

"He comes from Abyssinia and my agent in Cairo is quite satisfied that he is Ras Desoum's messenger," Zarrif said sharply, "otherwise he would not have been sent on here to me."

"Then your agent doesn't know his business," Lovelace snapped. He knew he was fighting for his life now and must use every possible weapon. "D'you think that an Amhara noble, one of the Emperor's personal friends, would stoop to make a confidant of a nigger?"

Mr. Green of Gainesville, Fla., drew himself up. "For all I'se a coloured man I hopes one day to sit upon de right hand o' de Throne. As de Lawd am ma witness I speak de truth."

"You claim to be the friend and messenger of Ras Desoum? Next I suppose you'll ask us to believe that you dined every night with the Emperor?" Lovelace inquired sarcastically.

"No, sah! I never saw de Emperor no time tho' I

tried mighty hard. I'se an educated man an' dat's why I were chosen by de Brudderhood to take de goodwill o' one Christian people to anudder in de day of dair poisicution by de ungodly. Dem Abyssinian quality may be Christian but dey's a long way from de Baptist Church what sint me over de ocean. Dey wouldn' even shake me by de hand; all 'cept Ras Desoum who do believe in de Lawd jes' de same way as I does. W'en I tells him I'se gwine back home he says to me, 'Mr. Green, yo'se jes' de very pusson to be ma hon'ble messenger to Mr. Zarrif on yo' way back thru' Eurupp.' Yessah! dat's de truth."

Lovelace had no doubt whatever that it was. He knew that coloured people all over the world were watching the war with a flaming partisanship for the Abyssinians, and that their organisations were sending the most varied offers of help, in complete ignorance of the Abyssinians' utter contempt for negroes. In happier circumstances he would have felt sorry for the earnest Mr. Green, who had travelled some five thousand miles, only to be treated as a recently released slave, at the end of his long journey, instead of as a brother who had found the Light. As it was Mr. Green had to be discredited at all costs otherwise Lovelace stood very little chance of getting out of that villa alive. He saw that from the cold glitter of Zarrif's eyes and the business-like way in which the gunmen held their pistols pointing at his midriff.

"I suppose you've got a letter from Ras Desoum to Mr. Zarrif, proving your identity?" he asked acidly.

"No sah," the negro spread out his black hands with their pale palms uppermost. "De Lawd see'd fit to strike his servant in de valley an' po' Jeremiah Green were a mighty sick man. It looked like he were booked fo' Kingdom Come an' dem heathen people stole his letter off him while his eyes were fixed on Heaven. But de Lawd raised his servant up again so he come on heah, jes' de same."

"They left him his passport." Zarrif tapped the document which lay in front of him on the desk. "It is all in order. I wish to see yours."

"It's in my room," Lovelace lied, thanking his gods that he had had the sense to hide that damning piece of evidence. "I'll go and get it."

"Stand still!" Zarrif rapped. "Cassalis—you go. Make a thorough search and bring any other papers which you can find down with you."

The pressure of the pistol was withdrawn from Lovelace's spine and Cassalis left them. Zarrif returned to his work and for the next ten minutes appeared quite oblivious of the fact that anyone else was in the room, but his two men kept their eyes riveted on Lovelace who felt quite certain that if he raised a hand they would shoot him down.

Having entrusted Valerie with any papers which might prove his identity before leaving Athens he knew that Cassalis would find nothing, but that was poor comfort. The sudden disappearance of his passport would turn their present belief that he was not Jeremiah Green into a certainty. His nerve was good but he felt it going now. His hands were twitching slightly as he strove to think of a way out of this horrible impasse. What would they do to him when they had satisfied themselves that he was an impostor? This was a secret war and one in which prisoners would not be allowed to live so that they could fight again another day. He had entered it knowing that, yet he had never quite faced the fact that he might be called on to pay the final penalty in person. Would the gunmen take him out and shoot him, he wondered, or had they some other way which would save them the inconvenience entailed by the disposal of a bullet-riddled body? He strove desperately to think of a plan by which he might save himself but he could not. His brain seemed to have seized up like a motor engine that is white-hot from overwork and lack of oil.

Cassalis returned and with him he brought two more

of the bodyguard. "Search him," he told the men, and then, turning to Zarrif: "Upstairs there is nothing, Monsieur. No passport or papers of any kind."

Lovelace was seized from behind and his pockets emptied out on to Zarrif's desk while he cried hotly: "My passport was in my bag this morning. I saw it! Someone's taken it! They must have . . . "

"No one takes anything in this house without my orders," Zarrif said quietly. "You have destroyed or hidden it since we left Athens. You are a spy and we have only one sentence for spies—death."

Lovelace shrugged. "Prove it!" he cried, and, swinging round as the gunmen released him he suddenly caught sight of the negro's face. From black it had turned to greeny-grey, the white-rimmed eyeballs were starting from their sockets, the thick-lipped mouth hung open, and his long arms, dangling at his sides, trembled as though he were suffering from a fit of ague. The man had been badly scared when Lovelace first saw him and was obviously panicky at finding himself in a place where the master of the house kept armed retainers; now, he was frankly terrified, horror-struck at the thought that the gunmen might commit murder before his eyes at any moment.

In a second Lovelace saw that he must involve him too. It was unfair, a rotten thing to do, but if Zarrif could be made to suspect them equally it was unthinkable that he would kill them both. They would be locked up under guard until further investigations could be made and one or other of them proved innocent. A bad enough look-out for him, the guilty party, but it meant time—time in which to think—a few more hours of life—perhaps a chance to escape—anything, anything, was better than being wiped out immediately.

"Listen," he said firmly, "listen, Mr. Zarrif. My passport's gone—disappeared—I don't know where. But I had it in Athens, didn't I? Cassalis saw me show it at the airport barrier."

"I suppose that was so?" Zarrif looked at his secretary interrogatively.

"He showed *a* passport," the Frenchman said slowly, "but the inside of it I did not see."

"No matter," insisted Lovelace. "I *had* a passport then. If I were not Jeremiah Green I would never have dared to produce it with Cassalis at my elbow. That would have been too great a risk for any spy to take. Another thing; it was I who brought you the letter from Ras Desoum. You can't deny that, and you've been questioning me for days about the situation in Abyssinia. If I wasn't Jeremiah Green how could I have told you so many things you wanted to know? I had a passport, I had the letter, and I've given you all the information for which you asked."

Before Zarrif could speak Lovelace drew a breath and jerked his head towards the wretched negro. "Now, what about him? He's got a passport but he's got nothing else. He's only spun you some yarn about having his letter stolen—and another about his being Ras Desoum's envoy. You *can't* be such a fool as to believe that. You know Abyssinia. Is it likely that the Ras would entrust his secret business to a nigger? He's an impostor. He hasn't got a single thing to stand on except that passport and it's faked—I'll bet a thousand pounds to a halfpenny that it's faked."

"No sah, no sah!" the black man gibbered. "I couldn't go fakin' no passport in a hundred years. I call de good Lawd to . . . "

"Silence!" snapped Zarrif and his eyes fixed themselves on Lovelace's drawn face. "One of you is lying and I believe it is you. There are many matters which might interest a European if he could obtain access to my house, but what could this coloured man stand to gain?"

"God knows!" Lovelace burst out, but he added, his voice suddenly sinking to a whisper, "unless—unless he's one of those people you spoke to me about—the *Millers of God*!"

"I ain't don' nothin' and I ain't nobody," wailed the miserable Mr. Green, but Lovelace saw the very faintest tremor run through Zarrif's frail body.

Next moment Zarrif's hand was raised in a swift gesture towards the negro. "Seize him" he cried to the two men behind his desk and before the quivering wretch could get out another word the gunmen had him by the arms.

Zarrif sat back again with a little sigh. His quick eyes flickered from one to the other of his prisoners and he seemed to be considering his next step. At last he spoke quietly to Cassalis: "Take them away. It would be best to put them both in the cistern, I think."

"Mercy boss, mercy! I ain't don' nothin' an' de Lawd am ma witness," screamed the black man, now utterly frantic with terror at the thought that they meant to drown him, but Lovelace allowed himself to be led away quietly. He knew something about eastern houses. In a place outside the town like this there would be no water-mains so the basement would be used to store an adequate water-supply. They were to be imprisoned in the cellar, or cistern, as it was called in all the older houses which had no tanks in their roofs. It was certain to be full of rats, and probably leeches, but it was doubtful if there would be more than a couple of feet of water in it. Whatever the discomfort it was better than death. There might even be a way out to the river if he could find it. At all events it meant a temporary respite and now the worst had been avoided he sagged with unutterable relief as his captors lugged him out into the hall and along a corridor.

In the servants' quarters at the back of the house one of them lifted a heavy trap in the flooring while the other held him covered with his pistol.

A flight of wooden steps was revealed, leading down to still, glassy water which dully reflected the patch of light. Something scurried in it, rippling the surface for a second. Lovelace was given a push and, with a sigh of resignation, he stumbled down the steep steps. When his feet reached the water level he went cautiously but he touched the bottom after another couple of steps. As he had suspected it was only about eighteen inches deep.

The sound of shouts, curses, prayers, came from above. Suddenly the square of light was obscured by a falling body. Lovelace stepped quickly aside and Mr. Green came hurtling down beside him with a resounding splash. The water did little to break the negro's fall. He lay there groaning, gasping, sobbing. Lovelace picked him up and propped his quivering body against the steps as the trap descended with a thud and they were plunged in total darkness.

The place was silent as the grave and pitch black. He spent the next few moments trying to restore his companion to some degree of sanity. At last, although still inarticulate, the negro recovered sufficiently to prop himself up without being supported. Then Lovelace left him to make a tour of inspection.

Wading slowly through the water he advanced with his hands outstretched before him into the Stygian blackness. After he had gone a couple of yards he found a pillar. Leaving it on his right he proceeded a few more steps and ran into another. They were the supports of the house and he guessed the place to be full of them, knowing that the majority of these subterranean cisterns were constructed on similar lines.

Another moment and he came up against the wall. It was smooth and slimy. Moving sideways step by step he kept touching the damp stones here and there so as not to miss a foot of their surface up to the highest level that he could reach. He came to a corner and passed on, another, another and another. Eventually he was at the place where he had started. There was no opening, such as he had hoped to find, connecting the cistern with the river.

By the sound of Green's incoherent prayers, which

had now become a continuous muttered whispering, he made his way back to the steps. He was frightened—now—just a little. There was no way out? How long would Zarrif keep them there? The dank still darkness . . . the rats . . . the heavy silence! But, of course, they were only being kept there as prisoners. Just until Zarrif could satisfy himself as to which of them was really Jeremiah Green. All sorts of things might happen before that. He fought to reassure himself and began to consider the possibility of bribing their guards.

It was then that he noticed a new sound. A low steady rhythmic beat coming faintly from above.

"Stop that!" he exclaimed sharply, giving Green's shoulder a push. "Listen! Is that an electric pump?"

The negro ceased his whimpering. Lovelace stood stock still, almost up to his knees in water. The thud, thud, thud, of the engine was perceptibly louder.

He remained motionless, a new terror gradually forming in his mind—and then he knew. He knew that the water was rising. An engine had been turned on which was pumping it up into the cistern from the river. It would rise and rise until it reached their thighs, their waists, their armpits, until their gasping mouths were pressed against the ceiling.

Zarrif believed *him* to be the spy, but what was the life of a wretched nigger to a man like the Armenian, whose golden harvest depended on the death of millions? Mr. Zarrif was one who had a great aversion to accidents. He meant to take no chances. Lovelace knew now that both he and the wretched Green had been condemned to die there in the close, black darkness.

CHAPTER XII

IN THE CISTERN

THE water in the cellar was only rising very gradually but the rhythmic thud, thud, thud, of the electric pump sounded with inexorable regularity. There was no way, other than the trap-door, out of that underground cistern and Lovelace knew that, as it filled, he might keep floating until his head was forced against the roof but then he must surely drown.

The negro began to mutter huskily again.

"Oh Lawd, Lawd! Oh Lawd Jesus heah ma prayer! I'se a po' sinner. I knows I done wrong. I knows it. But git me out o' this. Oh Lawd Jesus git me out o' heah!"

With an impatient shove Lovelace thrust his fellow-prisoner aside and stumbled up the steep ladder. In the pitch darkness he misjudged the height and hit his head a stunning crack against the trap-door, slipped, slid, and fell into the knee-deep water.

For a moment he lay there unconscious; his head resting on one of the slimy steps just above the waterline. When he raised it again he did not realise for a few seconds where he was and in that brief span of time a dozen scenes from his past life flashed through his disordered mind.

He saw again the green lawns of his house in England and the beauty of the well-kept gardens as he had known them when a boy. Old Beetle, the butler, was welcoming him home, when he had returned after his father's death, and addressing him for the first time as Sir Anthony. He was the tenth Baronet; and his next of kin was a distant girl cousin whom he scarcely knew. Fronds would be sold, under his present will, when he died. Suddenly he regretted intensely that he had never married and had a son.

As he moved his head a stabbing pain shot through it and he thought himself back in India, just coming round after a murderous struggle he had had years before with a dacoit. Other memories of his travels flickered before his mental eyes. The poor little Chinese girl who had had both her legs blown off at the knee when he was doing relief work behind the lines in Manchukuo. The human devil who was selling water by its weight in silver to the refugees dying of thirst in a Bolivian forest when he had turned up there with his ambulance. The drunken crowd of white-clad savages who had yelled their heads off with excitement when Haile Selassie was crowned Emperor of Abyssinia in 1930.

Abyssinia! Something clicked in his brain and the reason for his present desperate plight flooded back to him. The fanatical Christopher's association with the *Millers of God* and their abortive attempt to assassinate Paxito Zarrif in Athens. The *Millers* were madmen or were they all terribly sane? Anyhow, it was murder and he would never have lent them his help unless—yes, unless Valerie Lorne had overcome his better judgment—and she was Christopher's fiancée.

Now they were in Egypt; the other two half a dozen miles away in Alexandria without the least idea where he was, and he himself at Zarrif's lonely villa on the fringe of the desert; caught out, captured, and flung down into this underground cistern to die.

At the thought he staggered to his feet, dashed up the steps again, and began to batter on the underside of the trap with his clenched fists. Yet, even as he bruised his knuckles on the unyielding wood until they bled, he realised the childish futility of his effort. It was impossible to break out and, even if he could, Zarrif's gunmen would promptly throw him back again.

He rested for a moment, panting slightly. Below

him the negro's supplications had risen to a more exalted note. "Oh, Lawd, Lawd . . . I ain't nobody . . . I ain't don' nothin' . . . Oh, Lawd Jesus git me out o' heah—git me out o' heah."

In spite of the heavy darkness which wrapped them round like a black velvet cloak, Lovelace could picture the unfortunate Mr. Jeremiah Green. The smart white linen lounge suit, which had doubtless been the envy and admiration of his Baptist Brotherhood in Gainesville, Fla., now soiled and sodden from his having been flung, head foremost, down into the rat-infested water.

Suddenly the white man was filled with a monstrous impatience at the black's snivelling prayers and ordered him to be silent.

Green's voice came again, whimpering now, "Oh, Mister. I ain't harmed nobody an' I wouldn't be heah if yo' hadn't said yo' was me. Let me pray, Boss—let me pray. Dere ain't no hope for us 'cept in de Lawd!"

Instantly Lovelace was smitten with a terrible feeling of guilt and pity. It was true enough. He had said he was Jeremiah Green in order to get into Zarrif's house. Then, when the rightful owner of the name had turned up so unexpectedly, he had accused the poor wretch of being an impostor. Worse, he had even suggested that the black might be a *Miller* about to make an attempt on Zarrif's life. Only to confuse the issue and gain time in which to think, of course, and never imagining for one moment that Zarrif, unable to make certain which of them was the enemy within his gates, might decide to do away with them both.

"All right," he said. "I'm sorry—terribly sorry. Pray if it helps. I only wish I could."

As he spoke he came down the steps. He felt he could not possibly stay still waiting for death to creep up to him with the rising waters. Instead he splashed through them to make a more thorough examination of their prison.

The darkness was a heavy handicap. His own matches

had been taken when Zarrif's men had searched his pockets and if Jeremiah Green had any on him they must have been soaked and rendered useless.

For nearly half an hour he searched feverishly among the slimy stone pillars ; hoping to find some contraption by which the water was drawn up from the cistern to the rooms above and which might be utilised as a way out. By the time he had satisfied himself there was nothing of the kind, and that it must be pulled up through the trap-door in a bucket to be filtered in the kitchen, the water had risen to his thighs.

Jeremiah's prayers now alternated with psalms. He chanted them in a deep, musical voice which quavered now and then as his faith was nearly overcome by terror.

Lovelace wished fervently that he would stop. That endless monologue made it almost impossible to think; and think he must unless he was prepared to die.

Suddenly it occurred to him that if he could locate the spot where the water was being pumped into the cellar they might be able to stop its rising by plugging the inlet with their clothes. With renewed hope he began another tour of the walls fumbling hastily about below the water line. At last he found the place but, instead of it being a small round hole, as he had hoped, it was a four-foot-long iron grating through which the flood was filtering at a steady pressure. The space was too big to stop up, even if they had been able to get up the grating, so he had to abandon the idea. When he returned to the steps the water was eddying round his waist.

"I won't drown," he told himself fiercely. "I can't. I'm not even middle-aged yet. I've got years of life to look forward to. I won't choke my life out like a rat in a trap." Yet, even as he fought to reassure himself, he knew that he would, unless he could think of some way to save himself.

Jeremiah was babbling away quite incoherently. His muttering was the only sound perceptible in the chill, dank darkness, and as Lovelace listened involuntarily to his ravings he realised that the negro was making his supplication in Bambara or something like it : anyhow a dialect used on the west coast of Africa. Evidently he had deserted the Christian God for Voodoo incantations in the tongue handed down to him by his forebears of a few generations back when they had been shipped as naked slaves to the American plantations.

Lovelace wiped the sweat out of his eyes and went up the steps once more. With his finger-tips he made a minute examination of the trap. It was evidently bolted on the upper side since it would not shift a fraction to the utmost pressure of his shoulder. The hinges too were on the upper side, although, even if they had been on the lower, he had no means of unscrewing them. The trap consisted of three solid planks and between them he could just make out faint ribbons of light by applying his eye to the cracks.

Cursing the negro into silence he held his ear to the wider of the two apertures and listened intently. The murmur of muffled voices came faintly from above. By their tone, more than any actual words which he could catch, he judged them to be those of the Egyptian servants rather than Zarrif's gunmen.

After a little he abandoned the attempt to hear what was happening in the room above and sat, his head buried in his hands, crouched on the top step of the ladder, his brain whirling wildly.

He tried to think sanely but he couldn't. The unceasing pulsation of the electric pump and the knowledge that with every throb it gave the water below him was creeping upward seemed to blunt his wits and shatter every attempt at concentration.

An hour had passed, or perhaps an hour and a quarter, since they had been flung into the cellar, when he raised himself and again listened at the crack in the planks above. He could hear no voices this time but, between the beats of the pump, a steady droning sound. After a moment it began to fade but before it ceased entirely he had recognised it as the distant roar of an aeroplane engine.

It must be Zarrif's plane; no other was likely to be in the neighbourhood. That meant he had left the villa then. The blood began to pulse through Lovelace's veins at greater speed. A fierce new hope suddenly animated him to fresh action. If Zarrif had gone, his gunmen would have gone with him. Only the servants would remain and perhaps they would prove merciful or bribable. He began to shout loudly for help and beat his fists upon the trap once more.

Soon he heard voices overhead. Those of the Egyptian servants undoubtedly. If he could hear them they must be able to hear him. He redoubled the strength of his cries before pausing to listen. To his unutterable dismay he distinctly heard them laughing. Of course! They were Zarrif's men, highly paid, keepers of his secrets for fear of their lives, and utterly dependable. They would have had their orders to wait until the cistern was full, remove the drowned bodies, carry them down to the river and throw them in under cover of night. Very probably they had been privy to other such slayings and regarded their part in this only as a matter of routine.

Lovelace sank down again and rocked from side to side; a prey now to fearful imaginings about the coming moments of his death and compelled at last to acknowledge the utter hopelessness of his situation.

Jeremiah had crept close up beside him and now burst into renewed supplications: "Oh Lawd, who did deliver Daniel from de lions' den! Who did lead Moses by de hand when he were in de Wilderness—hearken to ma prayer."

Almost instinctively Lovelace found himself praying too. "Please God let me get out. Help me. Help me think of something. Or—if I've got to die—give me the strength to die courageously."

He tried to pull himself together and stretched down his leg to test the height of the water with the toe of his shoe. It had risen a lot since he was standing in it and he judged its depth now to be about five feet.

There was nothing to be done. Nothing but wait in the grim darkness and fight to keep control of his nerves up to the last horrible moment.

Dully he wondered where Christopher and Valerie were. It must be eight o'clock or later. They were probably dining quietly at their hotel in Alexandria. Perhaps they were even speculating when they would hear from him, but they would not be worried. He had told them that it might prove difficult for him to keep in touch with them while he was with Zarrif but that he would get a message through somehow. The arrangement was that they should remain in Alexandria for another three days unless they received instructions from him to the contrary. They would go to bed confidently expecting to hear from him to-morrow or the day after; but by the time they were asleep to-night he would be dead.

Jeremiah had fallen silent at last and, as Lovelace realised it, he remembered what a missionary had once told him of the African negro's fundamental attitude towards God. "It seems strange," he had said, "that they should worship sticks and stones since they all believe in the Great Creator; but this is what they tell you, 'God made the world and all that is in it including the spirits of the forests and rivers. We pray to them because when God had finished his work he went away and left us. How could anyone expect the Great God, who has other worlds to make and the Sun and the Stars and the Moon to care for, to remain here, just to listen to the prayers of insignificant people like ourselves?'"

At the time Lovelace had felt how well that had explained the patient humility of the negro races and that many white people might be better for considering their little personal woes less important in the sight of Almighty God.

Now, he understood Jeremiah's silence. The negro's thin veneer of Christianity had fallen from him and he had even abandoned as useless the deeper rooted Bambara incantations to the old familiar spirits of his tribe. He had reverted to that philosophic belief basic in his people and crouched there silent, like a trapped animal, waiting for the end.

Lovelace envied him his new-found calm. His own more agile brain was still racked with regrets over the things that he must lose by death. Valerie came again and again into his mind. She was Christopher's of course, had been apparently from childhood up: still, that did not matter now and the image of her gave him more satisfaction than that of any human being he had ever dwelt upon. He wished desperately that she had not made such a mystery of their first meeting. He was more certain than ever that he had met her somewhere years ago and he would have liked to have known where before he went out.

The water crept over their feet and up to their ankles as they perched huddled together on the upper steps of the ladder with their heads pressed against the trapdoor. A rat scuttled past below them yet they hardly noticed it. Both were sunk in a heavy torpor; only the steady rhythmic beat of the engine now penetrated to their dulled senses.

Suddenly the crack of a pistol sounded in the house above. It was followed by another and another, dull but distinct, then came a muffled cry of pain.

They both roused instantly. Lovelace began to batter upon the trap door again and to yell for help with all the strength of his lungs.

He heard shouting, another fusillade of shots, trampling feet, a scream as somebody was hit; but he never ceased his frantic cries for help and violent pounding on the wooden trap.

Next moment it was drawn up. Gasping for breath he staggered out and turned to pull up the half-fainting Jeremiah.

After the darkness of the cellar he was temporarily blinded by the light but, in a moment, he saw that Valerie was helping him with the black and that Christopher stood behind her, his pale face tense, his black eyes gleaming as he clutched a smoking automatic in each of his hands, covering their escape.

CHAPTER XIII

THE ENEMY STRIKES BACK

"NOW! I really must know what's been happening," Lovelace declared as he took his first sip at a welcome glass of hot grog.

Half an hour had sped by during which questions were hardly possible. Every moment had been occupied by their flight from Zarrif's villa, the race back to Alexandria in a hired car with a strange driver and Lovelace getting out of his wet clothes at Valerie's orders to roll up in warm blankets on the sofa of a dingy hotel sitting-room.

She smiled and patted the cushions into a more comfortable position behind his shoulders. "I really ought to wait until Christopher comes back; then we could both hear how you got caught."

"Never mind about that. I'll tell you later. What's happened to Christopher though? Where's he gone rushing off to at this time of night?"

"To try and find Otto Klinger."

"What, the member of the *Millers* who lives here?"

"Yes. Zarrif has gone and you say you have no idea where he is making for so Christopher thought Klinger might possibly be able to help us to get on his track again. He didn't like to leave it till the morning."

"It must be getting on that way already."

Valerie laughed. "My dear, you've lost count of time. It's only a little after nine o'clock. As soon as you're feeling fitter I'm going to order a belated dinner to be sent up to us."

"Good Lord!" he passed a hand quickly over his eyes. "And I thought it must be well past midnight. Every moment I spent in that hellish cistern seemed an eternity. But how the devil did you find out what had happened to me?"

"We didn't, and you wouldn't be here now if one of the enemy hadn't had a shot at murdering Christopher this afternoon."

Lovelace raised his eyebrows and whistled. "Phew, they've got on to the fact that he's here then?"

"Not here—I hope." She glanced at the carefully curtained windows. "This isn't the Gordon Pasha Hotel, where we agreed to stay, you know. We quit that in double-quick time, after the attempt had failed, and picked on this as another unpretentious little place where we might hope for a few hours' grace before they ran us to earth again. It was our forced change of address which made us decide to go out to Zarrif's villa on the chance of being able to let you know about it."

"You knew I was out there then? Saw us landing, I suppose."

"Yes. I lost Zarrif's plane in the cloud banks over the eastern end of Crete, but I held on my course as it looked as if he was heading for Alex. and I managed to pick him up again just as we sighted land. There was no mistaking that great, four-engined machine of his. That night Christopher and I went out to have a snoop round the villa. We knew you must be somewhere inside it unless they had dropped you overboard and that was hardly likely."

Lovelace frowned. "I'm afraid I'm awfully dense but I still don't see how you knew they'd caught me and chucked me into that filthy cellar."

"We didn't," she shook her sleek chestnut head, "but once we'd left the Gordon Pasha we realised you wouldn't know where on earth we'd got to, and we felt it would be far too risky to go back there and inquire for letters, so we went out to the villa in the hope of getting a message through to you about our change of address."

"And then?"

"Well, we left the car with the chauffeur about half a mile down the road, walked up to within a couple of hundred yards of the house, and installed ourselves behind a sand-dune. The heat was simply grilling there but we stuck it and watched the place all through the afternoon, hoping you'd appear at one of the windows or come out for a stroll in the garden, because we thought it absolutely vital to let you know we'd had to leave the Gordon Pasha. We'd printed the name of this hotel in large, black letters on a big sheet of white cardboard that we meant to hold up for you to see if only you showed yourself and we could attract your attention while no one else was about. We saw Jeremiah Green drive up with one of Zarrif's men but there wasn't a sign of you."

Lovelace nodded. "I was in a ground floor sitting-room at the back of the house all the afternoon; more or less confined there although not actually a prisoner. But go on; what happened then?"

"We had almost decided to chuck it up and come out again to-morrow morning when Zarrif's pilots appeared and ran his plane out of its hangar. Twilight had fallen by then but the place was lit up by the hangar arc lights and as it looked as if something interesting was going to happen we stayed on. Zarrif appeared with Cassalis and the whole bodyguard about three-quarters of an hour later. They all went aboard the plane and she sailed away to the south-westward. As you weren't with them it was obvious you had either remained behind on purpose or that something had gone wrong."

"So you came in to see?"

"That's it. We waited a good bit longer to see if you'd come out and take the road to Alexandria but as you didn't we made up our minds to go in and get you."

"Jove! That was plucky of you."

Valerie's grey eyes danced. "Christopher did all the heavy stuff; but I must say I enjoyed it."

"Did the servants put up much of a fight ?"

She shook her head. "One took a pot at us but Christopher shot him in the thigh. He chivvied the others along the hall, firing over their heads, till we got into the kitchen. We could hear you shouting by that time, fit to wake the dead, and the blacks were tumbling over each other out of the window."

"What a bit of luck for me you came in when you did." Lovelace sighed. "But tell me about the attempt to murder Christopher this afternoon."

"It was quite well planned," she said slowly. "You know there are lots of these students' riots going on in Egypt. They don't seem to care a bit for you British."

He nodded. "That's Ben Jelhoull, unless I'm much mistaken. He's behind all this anti-British trouble."

"Who ?" She raised her straight eyebrows in a puzzled frown.

"Ben Jelhoull," he repeated. "Haven't you ever heard of him ? He is known as the Hitler of Algeria, and runs a sort of Nazi movement there for the blacks—or Arabs, I suppose one should call them—anyhow, the Mohammedans ; and he's become a real thorn in the side of the French."

"What's that to do with Egypt ?"

"A lot. Ben Jelhoull's followers are known as the Young Turbans. The movement has spread until it's so powerful to-day that it controls the coloured population of the whole of North Africa from Morocco to the Red Sea. It's no longer anti-French, but anti-white ; and if there's a general blow-up the Young Turbans will prove a very big factor to reckon with. They'll start a *Jehad*, a Holy War, and that won't be much fun to have on our hands if we're up against Italy, Germany and Japan at the same time."

"It's more vital than ever, then, for us to stop Zarrif getting that concession which may set fire to the powder magazine." Valerie's eyes were very earnest.

"Yes, but tell me what happened to Christopher."

"Well, one of these riots occurred outside the Gordon Pasha this morning. It wasn't anything serious, but the police had to fire a few rounds over the heads of the crowd before they would disperse. Our sitting-room was on the second floor, so Christopher and I watched the trouble from our window. Some of the mob were hurling brickbats, and a few, who had revolvers, were firing wild, but there didn't seem the least danger of our being hit at that height, because they were aiming at the police in the street."

Valerie paused for a moment. "What made me look up I don't know, but I did, just when the riot was in full swing, and at a second floor window on the opposite side of the street I saw a man aiming a rifle dead at Christopher. I just had time to pull him down as the man fired. The bullet whizzed over our heads and smashed the mirror of an old bureau. Of course, if Christopher had been killed it would have been put down to a stray shot from the street."

"That's about it." Lovelace nodded. "Jove! what a narrow squeak. I wouldn't mind betting that riot was engineered specially to cover the attempt. The devils. I suppose they've been on the look-out for him in every likely town since he left Long Island. I wonder how they managed to get on to him when he was staying under an assumed name at a little place like the Gordon Pasha, though."

"Simple, my dear," Valerie laughed. "Yesterday we ran into a delightful idiot called Bob Tucker just outside the Museum, where we'd been putting in an hour to kill time while waiting for news of you. Bob's one of the nicest bad hats I've ever known. We had drinks together at a near-by café, and he took a snap of Christopher and me sitting at one of the tables. It was only afterwards he told us he'd turned journalist and persuaded some daft editor back home to send him out as war correspondent to Abyssinia. It never occurred to us at the time, but I'm news, of course, wherever I go, and there was the picture in Alexandria's leading news sheet this morning with, 'World's richest flying girl, Valerie Lorne, and her millionaire fiancé, Christopher Penn, now on vacation in Alex.,' in nice large letters underneath."

Lovelace gave a rueful grin. "I see. That's what gave you away. Naturally, the moment the enemy saw that they dragged every hotel in the place until they found your description tallied with two people staying at the Gordon Pasha. It would be easy enough for such an influential bunch as they must be to fix up a riot for the purpose of having a shot at Christopher afterwards. I didn't know you were particularly rich, Valerie."

"I'm not, compared with Christopher's standard, but I'm close on a millionaire in dollars. I'm an orphan and an only child, too, you know, so I live with an aunt—when I'm at home, that is, which isn't often. Bob Tucker was interesting about Abyssinia."

"He's been there and come back, then?"

"Yes. He clung on until his paper refused to send him any more funds. Apparently the Abyssinian censorship is so stringent that the correspondents couldn't get a thing worth sending to their papers so the people at home got fed up with paying good money out for nothing, and recalled nearly all of them. He says it's a lousy country, and God alone knows why the Italians want it."

"It'll be a very different place when they've been in occupation for half a dozen years."

"Well, Bob says there's no question about their winning. It's only a matter of time. The climate, lack of roads, and their distance from their bases are the only serious obstacles they have to contend with. Troops of filthy ruffians are still pouring into Addis on their way to the front, though, and if only the Emperor can provide them with enough rifles and cartridges they may hold the Italians up until next year; especially as the rains are due in a few weeks' time."

Lovelace nodded. "Mobilisation takes months in a place like Abyssinia where communications are almost confined to goat-tracks and every petty chieftain has to be bribed and flattered before he'll consent to bring his followers along to take a hand. Had this chap Tucker any genuine information about the progress of the war ?"

"No. He didn't know a thing about it until he got back to Jibuti and saw the European papers. The Italians are said to have reached Lake Tana the day we arrived in Alex., and Badoglio's motorised columns are pushing on, but how long he'll stick the pace nobody has any idea."

"Lake Tana's only just half-way from the Eritrean frontier to Addis, so he's got the worst half of the journey to make yet, and if they get too far ahead of the main army they may get cut off. What had Tucker to say about conditions in the capital ?"

Valerie smiled. "Bob says it's in an unholy mess. The Emperor's somewhere on the battle front, at Dessye, they think, and as nobody has any power to do anything without him the whole machinery of government, such as it was, has seized up. The Press bureau ceased to issue anything, except wild statements that ten thousand Italians had been cut to pieces every day, so the correspondents had to rely on bribing spies to get some sort of news ; and since they didn't really know anything either, but just provided any sort of lie they thought might earn them a few thalers, their information became equally unreliable and stupidly fantastic, after a bit. The nobles, who ought to be supporting the Emperor, are drunk most of the time. They laze about, boasting of what they or their fathers did at Adowa in 1896, and how they mean to drive the Italians into the sea. Bob says he had no idea until he went there that any race of blacks could possibly regard white men as their inferiors ; but the Abyssinians do, apparently.

"That's hardly to be wondered at," Lovelace shrugged.

"Comparatively few of them had ever seen a white until about nine months ago, and look at the specimens who have been crowding into the place since: every sort of shady character who thought he might make a bit out of their war. Concessionaires like Zarrif who'd see the whole lot of them slaughtered without a qualm if it happened to suit their book. Armament racketeers who'd sell them dud cartridges, so as to make a bigger profit, if they had the chance. Cashiered officers from half the armies in Europe willing to drive them into battle with machine-guns at their backs if they're paid well enough for the job. Phoney Red Cross men laying for a chance to steal the funds, and every other sort of trickster playing half a hundred different games to do the poor devils down."

"You'd have to get up early in the morning to trick an Abyssinian," chuckled Valerie. "At least, that's what Bob says. And as for graft, well, he told us that sort of thing wasn't understood in the States at all. Compared with their fuzzy-haired officials our tough eggs back home are still in the kindergarten class. He'd hoped to save a bit on his expenses, although I'll admit that's a grand laugh coming from Bob, but he passed up every dime he had in bribery—even to get himself allowed to walk round. He's come back dead broke, and I suppose that's why he thought he'd make the price of a few drinks by selling our picture to the local daily."

Lovelace frowned. "You know, that young man's let us in for a packet of trouble, and I'm afraid we haven't had the last of it yet. D'you realise that from now on half the population of Alex. may recognise you and Christopher the moment you set foot in the streets? I expect that nebulous group of thugs we vaguely call the enemy have been questioning the reception clerks in all the hotels with a copy of that paper in their hands ever since they learned that you'd cleared out of the Gordon Pasha. They're bound to run you to earth here before long. If you ask me, we're up against it, Valerie."

Her face went suddenly grave. "You—you're not thinking of backing out now—after—after what happened to you this evening, are you?"

"Good God, no!" He drank off the rest of his grog and smiled at her. "I was never keen on this murder game, as you know, and I wouldn't have come in at the beginning if Christopher's life hadn't been threatened. Then, after the mess up in Athens, I'd certainly have chucked in my hand if it hadn't been for you. But now the thing has become really personal. That cold-blooded swine Zarrif did his best to murder me to-day. Worse, he ordered the death of that poor innocent negro, the real Jeremiah Green, without the slightest compunction. I've got a score to settle with Mr. Paxito Zarrif, and I mean to move heaven and earth to see he gets his deserts."

Valerie laid her hand on his for a second. "I'm so glad, Anthony—so glad."

He looked away, concealing under the mask of his tanned face the sudden emotion her touch had roused in him, and asked abruptly: "How is he—Jeremiah, I mean?"

She smiled. "When you went up to Christopher's room to get your clothes off, and I was booking another for you at the desk, I wanted to get one for him too; but he wouldn't have it. He was inquiring about sailings for the States. When they told him there was nothing for the next two days, he said he'd take a passage anywhere provided he could sleep on board a British or American boat to-night."

"Poor Jeremiah," Lovelace laughed. "At least he has the sense to know he'll be safe under the Stars and Stripes or the Union Jack. He's had a filthy trip, and he won't feel really good again until he's back in Gainesville. Still, think what a story he'll have to tell all the coloured girls when he does get home. Can't you see their eyes rolling?"

"Tell me about him—and yourself. You must know

I'm dying to hear what happened to you; yet you've been making me talk about Abyssinia all this time."

"Let's order dinner first, shall we. Christopher may be back by the time they bring it up. Then I'll give you a full and true account of how Jeremiah and I very nearly found a watery grave."

Christopher was back in time to join them at the scratch meal the little cosmopolitan hotel provided, and over it he listened with Valerie to Lovelace's unpleasant experiences while a member of Zarrif's household.

"What luck did you have with Klinger?" Lovelace asked when he had concluded his narrative.

"I was fortunate to find him in," Christopher replied promptly, "but he's performing at a concert to-morrow night, so he was practising in his flat this evening. He's a Heidelberg graduate and has a job in a private German bank here. I found him a nice fellow; about my own age. He's a diehard Nazi, as far as Germany's internal politics are concerned, but he swears that Hitler doesn't want war and that all the younger generation, like himself, are out to stop it at any price."

"Could he tell you anything about Zarrif?" Lovelace inquired.

"As a *Miller* he knew him, of course. It's up to each one of us to watch the enemy and find out as much about them as we can. Klinger knew Zarrif had a villa here; he's been out to it in Zarrif's absence, and actually has a plan of the place. He knew Zarrif had been in residence there for the last couple of days, too, but he had no idea where Zarrif's gone to now."

"You're determined to follow him, then?" Lovelace asked. "Even to Addis Ababa if need be?"

Christopher gave a vigorous nod. "Even if I have to walk there."

"In that case, perhaps, we'd better go straight to Addis Ababa and wait there till he turns up," suggested Valerie. "He's bound to arrive there some time before the first of May."

"To-morrow's only the 16th," said Christopher, "and he's travelling by plane, remember. It's hardly likely he means to arrive there nearly a fortnight before he's due. He must be stopping off for a day or two somewhere on the way to transact further business. It would mean another chance for us to get him if we could only find out where."

Lovelace shrugged. "That's all very well, but we haven't got time to go chasing half over Africa, and we don't know if he means to go down the Nile to Khartoum, then over the mountains, or if he'll take the Red Sea route to Jibuti and follow the course of the railway inland from there."

"I favour the Red Sea route," said Valerie. "It's inhabited most of the way, and at least there's the railway to guide us when we have to cross Abyssinia. I'm as good a pilot as most people, but frankly I'd rather not attempt flying over those trackless mountains east of the Sudan."

"I don't think you ought . . ." Lovelace began, but she cut him short.

"For goodness' sake don't start that argument again. Remember what I told you in Athens."

Lovelace remembered clearly enough—that Christopher needed them both, and they must not let him down—but, more than ever now, he hated the thought that she should be exposed to such very real dangers as they had already encountered.

Christopher caught the meaning of their quick exchange and looked across at him. "I tried to persuade Valerie to leave us to it again this afternoon, but she won't. She says she is of age and her own mistress, and that having come so far she intends to fly her plane down to Addis Ababa anyhow. If she won't listen to me, her fiancé, I don't suppose she'll hear reason from anybody else, so we can only accept the situation and, at least, we'll be able to look after her if we all go together."

"All right, then," Lovelace sighed, "and we take the Red Sea route, eh?"

"Yes. I should have suggested that anyhow, because Klinger did give me one piece of information. It seems that Zarrif's hand in glove with a bird called Abu Ben Ibrim, whose headquarters are in Jibuti. Ben Ibrim is the big noise in every sort of dirty work that goes on along the Red Sea. Slave trading's his special racket, but he deals in smuggled ammunition, hashish, and all sorts of other things as well. It's more than likely Zarrif will go via Jibuti to have a word with him, and I thought that if we did too we might manage to get on Zarrif's track again."

"What, visit the Arab and try to pump him? But is it likely he'll have anything to do with us without an introduction?"

"I haven't got that, but Klinger said that if we pretended we were friends of a Jewish oil refiner here in Alexandria, named Melchisedek, Ben Ibrim would be almost certain to receive us."

Lovelace nodded. "I see, Melchisedek's another of the bunch, and it is up to us to think out a good story for Ben Ibrim. Well, when do we start?"

"The earlier we get off to-morrow morning the better," said Valerie decisively. "The thugs who tried to do Christopher in to-day may find out our new address at any time."

"I wouldn't mind betting they know it already." Lovelace grinned ruefully. "As likely as not that handsome chauffeur who drove us back from Zarrif's is a Young Turban; if so, he'll have reported his day's work as a matter of routine by now. It's a good thing our rooms are adjoining. We'd better sleep with the connecting doors ajar. In fact, we'll have to sleep with our eyes open and our guns handy every night from now on."

CHAPTER XIV

OUT OF THE PAST

VALERIE mopped the perspiration from her face. She had given up trying to keep it powdered hours before. It was eight o'clock at night, and they had only arrived at Jibuti at ten o'clock that morning, yet she felt as limp and washed-out as if she had lived for a month under the blazing, fiery sun that burnt up the capital of French Somaliland.

Their journey had not proved too fortunate. With previous records in her mind and a supreme confidence in her abilities as an air-woman, she had attempted the seventeen-hundred-and-fifty-mile flight from Alexandria in one hop, but on the previous afternoon her plane had developed engine trouble over the Red Sea and she had been forced to come down at Massawa.

The Eritrean capital had been literally crawling with Italian troops and all the auxiliaries who infest the principal base of a big military campaign. The harbour, if you could call it that, was packed with transport, hospital ships, cruisers and submarines, which stretched along the coast as far as the eye could see. Thousands of men, looking in the distance like a swarm of ants, worked frantically upon the new mole which would protect the anchorage. Innumerable engines puffed and snorted as they drew their loads over the intricate network of light railways. Legions of blacks were unloading munitions and supplies from countless lighters at every wharf. The town itself was a positive hive of activity. Italian soldiers thronged the pavements of all the principal streets, and every one of them seemed to be hurrying somewhere. Thousands of Askaris, lithe, smartly turned-out native troops, the coloured tassels in their tarbooshes lending a note of colour to the scene, marched, drilled and manœuvred in every available open space.

Beds were not to be obtained at any price, and they had been compelled to sleep with their clothes on in the plane.

Valerie had located the trouble, and, first thing next morning, they had set off on their last four hundred miles to the south.

After Massawa, Jibuti seemed a quiet backwater yet, as the headquarters of all the neutral hangers-on in the war, it was crowded to capacity.

Christopher's money and Lovelace's method of dealing with cosmopolitan innkeepers secured them two rooms in a small hotel. They at once made inquiries about Abu Ben Ibrim, and found that every guttersnipe in Jibuti knew the house of the powerful Arab. Lovelace wrote a letter mentioning Melchisedek of Alexandria and requesting an interview. It was dispatched by hand, and a reply came back that Ben Ibrim would receive them, in the cool of the evening, at nine o'clock. Through most of the day they had remained sweltering in the hotel while the inhabitants of the town apparently slept.

Owing to the intense heat, Government offices and most business houses opened at five in the morning, closed at nine, and did not open again until eight in the evening, as Lovelace told his friends, but, new to this slice of tropical Africa, Christopher and Valerie had refused to lie down during the broiling hours, and were now feeling the fatigue consequent upon their ill-advised activity.

Lovelace was still upstairs dozing on his bed when, at last, the sun set and they moved out on to the terrace. For a little while they sat there sucking down iced drinks and panting for a breath of air in the close hot darkness.

Behind them the big bar which was also the only lounge of the hotel had just commenced its nightly traffic. As in other French Colonies, no colour bar was exercised, and all who could pay were welcome. The place was of the middle grade, as Lovelace had thought it imprudent to advertise their presence by attempting to secure better accommodation. A wireless had been switched on which drowned the buzz of the big refrigerator behind the bar; some couples had already started dancing; black, brown, yellow, and white men were drifting in. A few coffee-coloured Eurasian girls in European clothes were present, but no white women. The honours of the house were being done by a brigade of black Somalis, who, naked to the waist, displayed fine shoulders and beautiful breasts. They twitched their hips and shook their short silk skirts provocatively as they moved among the tables, but there was nothing sordid about the spectacle. Their shrill chatter in the dialect of the port was like that of a crowd of happy children.

The only other occupant of the terrace was a tall, thin man, seated alone, at a table near by. After glancing at them once or twice he rose, bowed courteously and, introducing himself as Baron Foldvar, asked if they would take pity on his loneliness by allowing him to offer them a drink.

Valerie smiled an acceptance and motioned to a vacant chair beside her. The stranger possessed a delicate aristocratic countenance with sad, grey eyes set deep under heavy brows. A scar, running from the corner of his mouth to the left side of his chin, marked his face but did not mar it.

After the Somali waiter had been summoned and a fresh round of drinks ordered Baron Foldvar inquired suavely, "Do you go to Addis Ababa, or have you just come down the line?"

"We only arrived in Jibuti this morning," Christopher told him, "and we're hoping to be able to transact our business here so that it won't be necessary for us to go up into the interior."

"Indeed!" The older man raised his eyebrows. "Your case is unusual. Nine out of every ten white people in Jibuti are either coming or going from Addis in these days. The tenth only remains here because he cannot beg, borrow, or steal enough money for his ticket."

"Are you just back or on your way up?" Valerie asked.

"I go up on to-morrow's train. An abominable trip; so I'm informed. Insolent native officials from whose persecution there is no escape except by bribery; the most disgusting food; and even the water offered in the buffets of the wayside stations quite undrinkable so that one must go with a private supply of Vichy if one would escape enteric. I have travelled much but I confess that I find the prospects of this journey particularly unalluring."

Christopher sipped the orange juice that the waiter had just set down before him. "It sounds beastly. Thank goodness we'll be travelling by plane if we do have to go. Have you heard anything fresh about the war?"

"The vanguard of the Italian columns are reported to have entered Dessye, the Emperor's battle headquarters."

"Is that so? If it's true, they're moving mighty rapidly. D'you think they can keep it up?"

Baron Foldvar shrugged. "It is impossible to say. Anything might happen in such a crazy war as this. When the Italians opened their campaign I am quite certain they never dreamed of achieving the swift progress they have made in the last fortnight. Now that they have initiated this lightning thrust who shall predict how far it may penetrate?"

"The Italians have changed their policy then." Valerie leaned forward. "We know practically nothing about the actual war but you seem very well informed. Do tell us what's been going on."

"I know very little," their new friend replied gravely, "but at one time I was an officer on the Imperial Austrian General Staff. Before the Great War I was for some time Assistant Military Attaché to the Austrian Embassy in London. That is why, pardon me if I seem to boast, many people have been kind enough to say that I speak very good English."

"You do indeed," Valerie agreed. "But you were saying . . . "

"That as a Staff Officer it was my duty to study all problems which might give rise to future wars. Particularly with reference to Italy because, in those days, although they were both members of the Triple Alliance, the interests of Austria-Hungary and Italy differed upon so many points."

"The last twenty years have altered all that," Christopher remarked.

"Yes, Mussolini has changed the Italian mentality a great deal. Under Fascism the national self-confidence has increased out of all recognition but his influence has not been sufficient to eradicate the Italian army's memory of their defeat at Adowa in 1896. That defeat has been much exaggerated. It was largely due to the parsimonious attitude of the Government in Rome who refused to grant even one tenth of the money for the Italian expedition against Menelik that the British had voted for their General Napier when he marched against the Emperor Theodore and penetrated as far as Magdala in the previous decade.

"In actual fact, they lost less than a thousand white troops and between three and four thousand Askaris; while both performed prodigies of valour during that disastrous retreat fighting against overwhelming odds. Yet they've never been able to get rid of the idea that they were badly beaten. Perhaps that is not altogether surprising as, almost unsuspected by them, Menelik gathered together over a hundred thousand warriors secretly in the mountains and fell upon them when they were still in the initial stages of their retirement.

"In any case, that memory still dominated De Bono's policy at the opening of the present campaign. He was terrified of pushing his outposts forward even another mile unless he could support them with masses of troops. Yet he could not advance his main forces until roads were made behind them at every step to ensure the delivery to them of adequate ammunition and supplies. Hence the extraordinary slowness of the Italians' initial operations. The war opened on October 3rd; by the 6th they had already avenged Adowa and a few days later they took the sacred city of Aksum, both less than twenty-five miles from the Eritrean frontier. Then they stuck. It took them over a month to advance another sixty miles to Makale because they were proceeding with such extreme caution.

"Even when Marshal Badoglio took over at the end of November he failed at first to draw the best results from his General Staff's appreciation of the situation, and the policy of a creeping advance in mass was continued. But the Abyssinians played into his hands. Instead of waiting, as they should have done, to ambush his columns in the precipitous gorges of the Tigre, they massed to attack him in the open.

"It was child's-play, with his modern armaments, to defeat and scatter them. Once the main bodies of the enemy had been met and routed he had little to fear in the way of hordes of fanatical warriors suddenly appearing from nowhere. Being a first-class soldier he altered his policy completely and began to push his flying columns forward.

"They are still advancing. His aeroplanes spray the heights on either side of his columns, as they thrust their way onward, with mustard gas. Not to kill the miserable natives, but to make the heights untenable. A humane form of warfare if one regards it soberly since it prevents continued skirmishes which would otherwise entail death and many casualties on both sides.

"The Italians still have a long way to go and every dusty mile they cover carries them farther from their bases. If the Emperor will succeed in checking them with the masses of new troops he is still assembling, or the Italians will achieve their main objective, Addis Ababa, before the rains come, remains to be seen."

"That's the most interesting résumé of the campaign I've heard so far," Christopher acknowledged handsomely. "I take it you were through the European war, Baron?"

"Yes. I fought in it, of course," the older man sighed. "A hideous tragedy which few of my generation can ever forget."

"Did you fight against the Russians or the Italians?" Valerie asked.

"The Russians, in the early days; then I was taken prisoner. On that account I was also compelled to witness many of the horrors of the Russian Revolution."

"But how interesting," Valerie exclaimed, "actually to have lived through history in the making. Won't you tell us what it was really like?"

Baron Foldvar spread out his thin, elegant hands. "It is a long story and a sad one. For many people, the profiteers and so on, the war was a glorious opportunity. Even for some young men who fought it was only a marvellous adventure, but for me, it was the end of everything. If you wish I will tell . . . but no. The private tragedy of a stranger would only bore you."

"No, please?" Valerie insisted. "I was only a baby at the time of the Great War but it affected all my generation tremendously and so few of us really know anything about it. Please tell us, unless speaking of your memories pains you too much."

The Austrian smiled for the first time. "How I envy you both your youth and eagerness to hear even of terrible things if it may serve to increase your knowledge. Ah well, my own youth, at least, was unimpaired by tragedy. Twenty-two years ago I was a Captain of Huzzars in Vienna.

"What a city it was in those days! It is still beautiful although only the empty shell remains now that it is no longer the capital of an Empire but only of a Province. Then, it was the gayest, the most romantic city in the world; a perfect paradise for lovers. To drive up the hill to Grinzing in the evening and dine there, with a pretty girl, in one of the wine-gardens while the musicians played Strauss beside your table and the fairy lamps twinkled in the trees above. For poor and rich alike what more had life to offer? I suppose I should be grateful that my early years were set in pleasant places and that I lived them during a peaceful well-ordered epoch. How right the British statesman, Sir Edward Grey, was when on the eve of the Great War he said: 'One by one the lights of Europe are going out.' There is no nation where youth has been privileged to have its fling with the same carefree happiness and security since.

"But I digress. In the autumn of 1913 I met the lady who was afterwards to be my wife. All through the winter I wooed her. Love-affairs did not reach their climaxes so swiftly then because young girls of good family were very carefully chaperoned. It was at first an affair of hesitant greetings and shy confidences when we met at big gatherings in the houses of our mutual friends. Then of smuggled notes; apparently chance but, actually, carefully arranged meetings when we were riding in the Prater and stolen half-hours at dusk when I clambered over the high wall of her garden.

"The Viennese women are notoriously the most beautiful in the world, perhaps through the admixture of races in the old Austro-Hungarian Empire since the upper classes of them all frequented the capital; but among all those superbly beautiful women the lady of my heart was surely the most beautiful. At least I thought so and, although you may find it difficult to believe now, I was considered a very handsome young man in those days; also as a Cavalry Officer in one of the crack regiments who had been transferred to the General Staff I was naturally much sought after, so I had ample opportunity to meet all the loveliest girls in Vienna.

"Fortunately our families were much of the same standing so the obstacles to be overcome before we could marry were mostly the products of our own imaginations. In the spring of 1914, when I screwed up my courage to ask her father for an interview, he listened to my proposals with the utmost kindness and a few days later our engagement was announced.

"In June we were married; having received the blessings of both our families and the good wishes of a host of friends. I had obtained long leave from my military duties for the honeymoon and we settled down to enjoy two utterly carefree months in the country on an estate which formed part of my patrimony.

"Five weeks later I was recalled by telegram. We had been shocked and distressed by the assassination of the Archduke Ferdinand but, in our bliss, we had not bothered our heads about the quarrel with Servia which followed. Indeed, we had hardly seen a paper. We were utterly absorbed in the supreme joy of possessing each other. That I should wake each morning beside my beautiful young wife seemed a miracle. The new way in which she dressed her hair seemed infinitely more important than the threatening note drafted by some elderly diplomat in our foreign office.

"I left at once for Vienna. Few of us had the power to realise it then, but one by one the lights of Europe *were* going out, a civilisation and free intercourse between free people which it had taken centuries to build was to be destroyed in one mad hour, and it does not look as if it will ever come again in our lifetime. Ten million men, at least, were earmarked for death within the next few years, although they could not know it; most of them young, healthy, happy people like myself, and not a fraction of them had the least interest in the quarrel for which they died.

"I resigned my Staff appointment in order to be with my regiment. Any young man would have done the same. But my resignation was not accepted. Instead, I was sent to a Divisional Headquarters not far from the Russian frontier. The Division was composed of Czechish soldiers. The Czechs were a subject people who had always hated Austrian rule, much as the Irish have always been resentful of English domination. Perhaps we should have been wiser to have given them some form of home rule when their Deputies pressed for it before the war. Of course, they have their own republic now, but when the war broke out they were in a ferment of discontent, and they welcomed it as a chance to gain their liberty.

"Instead of fighting for us, whole battalions of them, led by their own officers, marched over to the Russians, with all their equipment and their bands playing. We did what we could to stem the tide of desertion, but in a few hours Austrian machine-guns and Austrian bullets were being used to massacre the handfuls of loyal troops with which we attempted to hold the frontier. Within three days of the opening of the war I was taken prisoner by the Russians."

The Baron paused to drink from his glass of lager, in which the ice had long since melted. Valerie eased her position a little; even now the sultry night had come her garments were still sticking to her. After a moment the Austrian went on:

"It was not so bad at first. Some sense of chivalry still existed between the officers on both sides. The normal feelings of decency and humanity inherent in most men of every nation had not then been destroyed by the hideous hate propaganda which later turned honourable opponents into savages.

"The Russians sent me under escort with a number of other prisoners to Kiev. There I endeavoured to get news of my young wife. I could learn nothing definite, but from prisoners who were captured later I heard rumours that, in the national emergency, she had become a nurse and was tending the wounded on the Polish front.

"During those awful empty weeks of dull prison routine the one overwhelming craving which obsessed me was to get back to her. The war had not settled down sufficiently for a regular service of prisoners' letters and parcels to be established. She wrote to me, I don't doubt, but I never received any of her letters. In those early days of the war everything was chaotic. Our only news was hearsay ; rumours that the German drive on Paris had been checked, but that the Russian steam-roller was lumbering down towards Berlin ; rumours of our friends fighting on many fronts and that this or that relation had taken up some kind of national work. I could not stand the uncertainty and inaction, so I determined to escape.

"I will not weary you with details of those feverish days of preparation for the attempt, or the excitement of the actual dash for liberty, which I made with two other officers. We got away, but we were caught again two days later.

"As a punishment we were separated and each of us transferred to a harsher form of captivity. I was sent to Omsk in Siberia ; a little ugly town that, although it was the centre of a Government controlling thousands of square miles of territory, seemed to be composed only of many hundred shoddy, wooden buildings scattered over a great area.

"It always seemed to be raining there, except when it was snowing, and in winter the cold was intense. To appreciate the torture that cold can be you must not think of winter in Switzerland, where you are well fed and wrapped in warm furs, but of a bleak plain where the wind cuts like a knife, through garments worn paper-thin, to an ill-nourished body.

"Month after month dragged by. There was hardly a soul in the prison who could speak more than a few words of my language. I learnt Russian, but my spirit grew numb from continuous physical discomfort and the knowledge that I was many thousands of miles from home. In that remote place no post ever reached me, and news of the war itself was of the vaguest. All one could do was to cling to life and hope on that the war would soon be over. I could learn nothing of my wife, but all through those dark days the thought of her warm loveliness and our eventual reunion was the one thing which sustained me.

"The revolution in St. Petersburg, when it came, had no effect upon us prisoners. We heard tell of it, of course, but the Whites, who represented the old regime, dominated an area as big as Austria-Hungary, of which Omsk was nearly in the centre. The Ural Mountains and vast tracts of unmapped forest lay between it and the cities where the Reds had their first successes. The dreary round of prison life went on much as before.

"When the news of the peace of Brest-Litovsk filtered through we appealed to be sent home ; but in the meantime spasmodic outbreaks had been taking place from one end of Russia to the other. The Red virus was spreading. Every town and village had its secret committee. The White officers were wholly occupied with their attempts to check the Revolution ; they had no time to spare for the repatriation of prisoners or the means to send them home even if they had wished to do so.

"Within six months we had half a dozen different Governors. They could do nothing but tell us that, for the time being, we must stay where we were. There was a revolt among the prisoners, engineered in secret by the Bolsheviks, who were out to make any sort of trouble for the Whites. Realising the root from which the mutiny sprang, the authorities acted with the utmost brutality. Scores of the prisoners were shot down and the rest of us were herded into kennels so that a handful of troops could keep us covered with machine-guns and prevent a repetition of the outbreak.

"Shortly afterwards fighting began in the streets of Omsk itself. For several days it was indecisive, but in the end the Reds gained the upper hand. All my fellow prisoners were then released except the officers. As representatives of the old order we were condemned to die.

"Those ruffians shot down my friends in batches. I dropped before they fired and feigned death. I allowed myself to be carted off and buried alive in a hastily dug trench with the bodies of the others. I nearly died of suffocation, but, when the murderers had gone, I clawed my way out through the thin layer of earth they had shovelled on top of us. Then I started to walk home.

"I found the whole country in a ferment. The hand of every man was raised against his brother. I dared not go near a town of any size, because, by that time, the Reds were in possession of all the railways.

"I took to the forests, living on berries and roots and the occasional charity of solitary peasants that I encountered who seemed as utterly bewildered as myself. No one knew what was happening outside his immediate area. Everyone was terrified of strangers. The accepted policy was to shoot first and ask questions afterwards. Reds and Whites were hated with equal intensity, and both were murdered by the country people on every possible occasion when they thought they would be able to escape reprisals. I lived in a nightmare from which it seemed that I should never waken as, week after week, I progressed a few miles farther south.

"Often I had to make detours which delayed me many days. Once I built a raft to float myself across a broad river, but of its name I have no idea. Countless hours were wasted in hiding from ragged bands of desperate-looking men. Sometimes sheer starvation compelled me to go into villages, and the sights I saw then do not bear a full description. Wholesale massacre seemed to have depopulated the land. Every hamlet had its quota of naked corpses rotting where they lay, and the survivors must have fled to the forests or the mountains. I saw women with their breasts cut off and bayonets left sticking in their swollen stomachs. Men with their eyes gouged out and their finger-nails torn away. Little children who had been clubbed to death or impaled upon wooden stakes. If there is a God in Heaven He will call the Bolsheviks to account for the unbelievable barbarities they perpetrated during those years in order to achieve a political idea. Liberal-minded theorists in every country are seeking to excuse them now. The human memory is short, atrocities are soon forgotten, but the blood and tortured agony of countless thousands of their own people still cry out against them, and any country which tolerates their disciples lays itself open to the possibility of similar horrors. They are at work in India to-day, and Spain. At any time there . . ."

The Baron broke off and passed his hand across his eyes. "Forgive me. It is all years ago now ; but when I was in Russia I saw such terrible sights with my own eyes that I am apt to get over-excited when I think of what may be in store for other countries. Where was I ?"

"You were telling us of your journey home," Valerie said almost in a whisper.

"Ah, yes ! Well, I lived as a wild beast, and, like an animal, I shunned all contact with men, convinced that the whole race had degenerated into packs of bloodthirsty hunters. I was still over five hundred miles from the old Austrian frontier when I sickened and was stricken down with cholera.

"I was wrong to think that charity was dead in the

hearts of all men. I owe my life to a *moujhik* who found me and carried me to his shack. He and his family nursed me through the crisis of the fever. I recovered, but every one of them caught the cholera from me and died. I was so weak that, after I had buried them, I had to lie up there for a long time before I could begin to stagger south again. The adventures which befell me and the hardships I encountered would take a dozen nights to tell, but the one thought which braced me up was that if only I could keep going I should eventually get home and find my beautiful young wife again. At last, a lean, starved skeleton, I crept out of Russia.

"But the country that I entered was not a part of Austria as it used to be. It was a new Republic where the people were hostile to Austrians and refused to speak German or succour a German-speaking stranger. The war was long since over, but the whole of Central Europe was still in a turmoil and racial feeling was running high. The peasantry were little better off than those I had left on the other side of the frontier. True, their homes were not being burnt over their heads by merciless Commissars who accused them of giving help to the Whites, but their barns were empty, thousands of them were dying from the influenza plague which ravaged Europe after the war, the breasts of the nursing mothers were bone-dry, their feverish eyes buried deep in their emaciated faces, while the children who survived on starvation rations were twisted with rickets and prematurely old. The people had the same wolfish look that I had grown to know so well in Russia, yet they were too weak and apathetic to do much work upon their farms. It seemed as if they were just waiting for death to take them ; convinced that things had gone too far for the world ever to right itself again.

"When I reached Austria, a filthy, broken-down, penniless tramp, no one to whom I spoke would believe my story and lend me money for a train-fare. Starvation was rampant there also, work at a standstill, and everybody bankrupt. I had to tramp even the last hundred miles until I entered Vienna.

"I went straight to my house. It was empty, shut up, and to let. For a little I just walked about the streets, not knowing what to do. In spite of all that I had seen while begging my way through the country, I had somehow expected my house and servants to be ready to receive me if I could only reach the end of my journey. The blow was a terrible one and I almost lost the last remnant of sanity which lingered in my brain; already half-crazed from years of acute privation. Then I thought of Sacher's Hotel.

"Old Madame Sacher, who owned the place, was a great character. Every member of the Austrian nobility before the war was known to her, and many of us counted her a dear friend. She is dead now, but her hotel is still, I think, the most comfortable in Vienna. Its cuisine has a European reputation, and there is that personality about the place which makes it far more attractive than some of its larger rivals. I went to Sacher's and, before the waiter could stop me, slipped through the bar, which adjoins the street, to her private office on the ground floor.

"Dear soul, she knew me, once I gave my name, in spite of my ragged beard and tattered, mud-soiled clothing. I can see her now as she wept over me and sought to comfort me. When I had told her my story I collapsed from strain and weakness. She had me bathed and put to bed, then sent for my friends. For some days I was delirious and for weeks I hovered between life and death. At last I was fit to be moved, but she would not allow me to talk about my bill. Before the war she had amassed a great fortune; afterwards she gave it all away in credit to old clients like myself whom the war had ruined. She was a great woman whom I am very proud to have known.

"When I was fit to go about again, I found that everything was changed. It was a new world that I did not understand. Little by little my exhausted brain began to take in all that had happened in my long absence and some aspects of the almost unbelievable situation. I was still Baron Foldvar, but I had no money, no estates. My family had believed me dead ; a cousin had succeeded to my properties for a time. Later, when the Exchange collapsed, he had sold them all for the price of a ticket to America. He was living there in the most desperate poverty, so rumour said, barely supporting life by giving German lessons.

There was nothing to be done. Old friends that I met were in a similarly unhappy situation. Some had become professional dancing partners, others guides. They were glad to take any job which would secure them one square meal a day. Their women—I shudder to think of it, but more than half of those delicately nurtured girls I had known as a young man were living as *cocottes* ; often to keep destitute parents or husbands and brothers disabled in the war who could not find employment at any price. That was what the war did for my beloved Austria.

"Naturally, even during my illness, the thought uppermost in my mind had been my wife. Nobody had seen or heard of her for years. My friends either would not or could not tell me what had become of her. At last I traced her. She was in the paupers' ward of a public asylum.

"I went at once to see her. It was very terrible. She did not know me. I did not know her. She was about twenty-six then, but she had the appearance of a woman of sixty. Her head was covered with bedraggled wisps of grey-white hair ; her face was lined and shrunken like that of an old crone. She spat at me. They told me that she spat all the time at any man who came near her. That little, old, shrunken thing who, only a few years before, had been a lovely girl in the first flush of her beauty, reviled me in the most foul and abominable language. Her mind was utterly gone. She was dead ;

as dead as any living creature could ever be. Only the ill-kept shrivelled husk of her remained, and that was quite unrecognizable.

Later, they told me her history. In the Russian break-through during the first winter of the war, when a large section of our front gave way, she, and the inmates of the hospital to which she was attached, had been captured. She fell into the hands of the Cossacks. They looted the stores and got drunk on the brandy. Their officers could not restrain them. She was only twenty, more beautiful than words can say, and our marriage six months before had brought her beauty to its zenith.

"How many of them there were I, mercifully, shall never know. She lived through it; but when our troops advanced again and drove the Russians back they found her stark naked on the floor of the hospital canteen, unconscious. Her hair had gone white in a single night and her brain had given way. When she came round she was a raving lunatic."

As the Baron ceased speaking, Valerie shuddered. "It just doesn't bear thinking about," she said softly, "that such things are possible in our vaunted civilisation. Poor dear—and you. I just can't say any more. It's too utterly terrible."

The Baron shrugged. "Please do not distress yourself. It all happened so long ago and mine was only one of a hundred thousand tragedies which occurred when you were a little, laughing child playing with your dolls."

"Good God!" exclaimed Christopher. "But don't you see that the same horrors may engulf us again at any time."

"Of course," the Austrian laughed and finished up his beer. "Life goes on much as it always did. The dictators and the politicians of every country continue to make fresh promises which do not mean a thing. The nonsense talked at the League has caused this miserable population of blacks to defy the power of modern Italy Mussolini was quite willing to leave the Emperor on his throne providing he would accept Italian advisers and allow the country to be properly policed and civilised. The Abyssinians would never have fought unless they had believed that Britain was coming to their aid. She won't, of course, and in consequence countless hideous tragedies which could have been avoided are being enacted as we sit here. But the politicians will dine no less well to-night in London, Paris and Geneva."

"You're a cynic," remarked Christopher. "In view of what you've been through one can't blame you, but it seems strange that you should be able to laugh about the wickedness and stupidity which initiate such ghastliness."

"Why? Laughter, even though it be hollow, is the only thing left for people like myself. When I go up to Addis Ababa to-morow . . ." The Baron broke off as Lovelace suddenly appeared beside their table.

The two men were introduced. The elderly Austrian bowed courteously and pressed the Englishman to name any drink he would care to take with them.

"Sorry," Lovelace replied rather curtly. "Another time perhaps. I'm afraid, too, that I have to break up the party. Valerie, my dear, I overslept a little and it's a quarter to nine already. We must be off."

They said good-bye to the sad-faced Baron and, directly they were out of earshot, Lovelace snapped at Christopher: "Did that fellow tell you anything about himself?"

"Yes, the history of his war days. He was a prisoner in Russia and had the most ghastly time. I wish all the people we're up against could be forced to go through those six years of his life."

"The poor dear," Valerie added. "I could hardly keep from crying openly when he told us about his wife."

Lovelace laughed angrily. "Lies, all of it, I'll bet a monkey. He was telling the tale to gain your sympathy and get in with you so that he could learn our plans. You couldn't know it, but we've been run to earth again. The last time I saw that chap he was talking to the porter at the gate of a house you've good cause to remember just outside Athens. He's one of Zarrif's men."

CHAPTER XV

ABU BEN IBRIM ENTERTAINS

IN the narrow hallway beyond the bar Lovelace pulled up the others and spoke in a low voice. "Now Zarrif's friend, the Baron, knows where we are, it's too big a risk to stay here any longer. We'd best collect our things, pay the bill, and get out while the going's good; otherwise we may be dead before the morning."

"But where are we going to sleep?" asked Christopher.

"Lord knows! If we can't get rooms anywhere else we'll have to shake down in the plane again. I'm sorry, Valerie, but, honestly, after what happened in Alex. we should be mad to take any chances."

She squeezed his arm. "Don't worry about me. I'd rather spend the night in an open field than have any more marksmen taking pot shots at Christopher through a window. I'll slip up and get my oddments packed. It won't take me five minutes. I'll pack for both of you, too."

Leaving the two men to wrangle with the Levantine hotel proprietor and compensate him for their sudden departure, she ran swiftly upstairs. She had only just finished ramming the few belongings with which they travelled into their respective bags when Christopher joined her.

Two minutes later they were scrambling into one of the smart modern taxis that are Jibuti's pride, which Lovelace had secured in the meantime. He told the man to drive to Menelik Square, the centre of the town, and jumped in after them.

"Where do we go from there? We must find somewhere to park our bags before we visit old Ben Ibrim."

He spoke more to himself than to the others, but Christopher answered: "Why not the police station? It's open all night and our things'll be safe there. I expect we can find a friendly policeman who'll keep an eye on them if we make it worth his while."

"Good for you," Lovelace agreed, and gave fresh instructions to the driver.

The town had now stirred to movement, and the main boulevard swarmed with a motley throng. Turbaned, befezzed, topee'd, felt-hatted representatives of fifty different nations jostled each other on the sidewalks. Taxis bearing Europeans, half-breeds, and Japanese honked their way through the mob; skinny natives, clad only in coarse white cotton nightgowns, led strings of camels and heavily-laden donkeys were being pushed, cursed and bludgeoned upon their slow-footed ways by small, foul-mouthed black boys.

At the police-station a French sergeant with a little waxed moustache and a strong provincial accent, who breathed dense clouds of garlic at them, proved amenable to their request. When Christopher began to rustle a useful-looking note between his fingers the man became as suave as a born hotel-keeper, and one might have assumed that his principal function was the reception and care of strangers' luggage. At any hour they returned they would find it waiting, he said; more, for such distinguished visitors something must be done about accommodation for the night. True, the hotels were full, but the honour of France was impeached. He lived with his aunt, a widowed lady. She had one spare room and, as he was on duty all night, his own would also be vacant. If *Messieurs* could make do in a double bed the affair would arrange itself. He would telephone instantly.

The proposal suited them far better than the sergeant knew. The fact that they had temporarily escaped the attentions of the doubtless spurious Baron did not exclude the possibility that every hotel in Jibuti would be scoured for them that night; but the chances were all against their being traced to the abode of the policeman's aunt, and, if they were, Zarrif's associates would doubtless think twice before risking an attempt upon them if it was believed that they were more or less under police protection.

The offer was accepted. The sergeant would send one of his native police with them when they returned to collect their luggage so that they should have no difficulty in finding his aunt's house. In the meantime he would take steps at once to inform his aunt of their coming.

"That fellow's missed his vocation," Christopher said when they got outside.

"He'll find it yet," Lovelace laughed. "Most French Colonial officials live only for the day when they can return to France. You can always find a dozen of them sitting outside the principal café in any provincial town. When this chap's saved a bit he'll retire and, like as not, run a pub of his own. But I think it unwise, Christopher, to bribe quite so heavily. I know it's not necessary for you to save your pennies, but those big notes that you keep handing out might make some people too inquisitive about us."

Lovelace gave the taxi-man Abu Ben Ibrim's name, and he drove them to the old part of the town where he drew up before a barred gateway in a high, windowless wall. They got out and paid him off.

"I suppose it's all right to take Valerie into a place like this," Christopher inquired a little doubtfully as he surveyed the ancient fortress-like building which rose high above the others in the mean twisting street. "I take it the old rogue's a Mohammedan and their views differ from ours a good bit on the question of women."

"It's rather unusual," Lovelace admitted. "They would never bring a woman if they came to call on us, of course, and I shouldn't have dreamed of bringing

Valerie if we were just ordinary tourists in Jibuti and this was a social visit. The trouble is that ever since that attack on you in Alex. I've felt the three of us should stick together as far as we possibly can. He may think it a little strange that Valerie should be with us, but he'll probably take it as a great compliment and mark of friendliness. I don't think there's the least likelihood of her being subjected to any unpleasantness, and, in any case, all three of us are armed."

"I wouldn't miss seeing the inside of this place for worlds," Valerie declared.

Lovelace's plan was a simple one. When they saw Ben Ibrim he meant to pretend that they were friends of Zarrif's and hoped to find him in Jibuti. It would be sheer bluff. Zarrif might be in Cairo or Khartoum for all they knew, but if Ben Ibrim were hand in glove with him, as was reported to be the case, they might be fortunate enough to trick the Arab into giving them some useful information.

"We're a bit late for our appointment owing to having to collect our baggage and our chat with the sergeant," Lovelace remarked, "but fortunately time is the last thing that matters in the East. The old boy will probably keep us waiting, anyhow." He knocked loudly upon the great double gates with his clenched fist, and a strapping negro opened a small door set in them.

Lovelace spoke to him in French and they were led through to an open courtyard where an Arab, whose teeth displayed more gold fillings than ivory, received them. His master, he said, welcomed their coming and would be happy to see them in one moment. In the meantime—would they be seated?

A few moments later the Arab returned. As they had honoured his master's house, he said, by bringing a pearl of beauty, who was doubtless the wife of one of them, would not the lady deign to follow him to the women's apartments where his master's wives would derive great pleasure from entertaining her?

"They want you to go to the harem. The women there are all agog to see a white girl, I expect," Lovelace said rapidly to Valerie in English. "There's nothing behind the invitation—it's only a courtesy—but I'd rather you remained with us."

He turned back to the Arab. "The lady thanks your master and His Excellency's wives, but as she has never travelled in the East before, she begs permission to meet so powerful a Sheik. Later, she would be honoured to wait upon his ladies."

With a flashing smile from the gold-filled teeth and a low obeisance the servant withdrew.

Lovelace translated what he had said to Valerie, and added, "When the interview is over I shall start scratching my left ear. That's the signal for you to feign illness; but don't faint, otherwise they'll want to carry you into the women's quarters. If you're just ill it'll provide an excuse for us to get you away quickly without your having to go there."

"But I want to," Valerie protested. "It'd be terribly interesting to see what those legendary houris, who're said to be kept in rich Orientals' harems, are really like."

He shook his head. "In the ordinary way it'd be perfectly safe for you to do so, but for all we know Ben Ibrim has been warned to keep a look-out for us. If he has you'd find yourself a prisoner there, and that'd be far from funny. This is a ticklish business, and I don't want you out of my sight, even for a moment."

The "one moment" the Arab servant had first mentioned expanded itself into an hour and a quarter, but they were not impatient. After the burning streets, and the noisome perfumes which pervaded the hotel bar, the courtyard was a paradise.

A fountain played in it, moistening the overheated air as it splashed into a white-tiled basin. Only a man of immense wealth, as Lovelace remarked, could possibly have afforded such a luxury in Jibuti. Palm trees planted in vast tubs stood at the four corners of the courtyard, and a black boy worked like an automaton at a punkah which wafted the refreshing air towards them. Above, as from the bottom of a great square well, they saw the myriad stars twinkling in a black velvet sky; alive, near and brilliant, in a way which is unbelievable to those who have seen them only from a northern latitude. The peace and beauty of the place revived Christopher and Valerie from their fatigue as nothing else could have done.

At last the man with the gold-filled teeth appeared again. He led them through an ancient, brass-studded door to an inner courtyard, bowed gravely, and left them.

The inner court was smaller, but even more magnificent. Four fountains played in its corners; their basins and the twisted pillars of the surrounding arcades were made of marble; ancient lamps of beaten silver, burning perfumed oil, swung on chains between the arches. Its sole occupant was a man of vast proportions. Bearded, hook-nosed, eagle-eyed, his massive limbs concealed by a loose silken robe, he sat cross-legged upon a great pile of carpets.

As they went forward Abu Ben Ibrim greeted them in Arabic. Lovelace responded in the same tongue, so the conversation that followed was entirely lost on Valerie and Christopher.

With a wave of a big hand, half-covered with heavy rings, the Arab motioned his guests to take places on the cushions which made a semicircle in front of his divan. Clapping his hands loudly together, he summoned servants who brought in refreshments for them: fresh fruit, candied sweetmeats, sherbets and coffee.

For some moments the formalities were duly observed by a grave exchange of meaningless compliments, after which the huge Arab began to thaw. He was a jovial fellow with an enormous appetite for laughter; as easily amused as a child and delighting in a bawdy jest as the natural medium for humour in his race. Knowing that Valerie could not understand a word he said, he did not scruple to give full licence to his taste.

Lovelace, who had often dealt with Arabs, knew the type and played up to him accordingly, being well aware that half an hour or more might elapse before they could get down to business. Little by little he turned the conversation towards the local situation, inferred that he knew Ben Ibrim to be a slave trader and illicit armament dealer ; was in the latter racket himself, in fact, and inquired courteously how the Arab's affairs prospered.

Ben Ibrim spread out his strong, jewel-laden hands, shrugged his great shoulders, and smiled beatifically. "Was there ever such a time in the history of mankind ?" he asked happily. Allah in his wisdom had sown confusion among the ignorant that the more intelligent of his children might profit by it. Blessing upon His Holy Name. The British and Italian gunboats were so busy watching each other that they had no longer time to practise their surveillance upon the ships of honest traders that crossed the Red Sea each night. Those dogs of Abyssinians had been fooled into freeing their slaves to please the stupid League. The slaves were starving and would sell themselves again for halfpence. What easier than to transport them across the Straight of Bab el Mandeb to Arabia ? In French Somaliland one had to use a certain care still, of course, but the authorities were busy with other matters. They were very strict about the illegal import of munitions, but risks were worth running, were they not, with dynamite worth nearly its weight in gold-dust. The big man chuckled throatily in his wiry black beard.

Valerie was sipping her third little gilded cup of coffee, and she remarked to Lovelace that never in her life had she tasted better.

He translated what she said, and Ben Ibrim beamed upon her. "That may well be so," he replied in Arabic. "It comes from the finest plantation in Abyssinia, and it was there that the berry was first cultivated. I will send Madame a bale of beans if she will leave me her address."

Valerie smiled her thanks as Lovelace translated. He then turned the conversation to Zarrif. He inferred that he knew him well, spoke casually of having stayed at his house in Athens, and went on to say that Melchisedek of Alexandria had told him that he might run into Zarrif in Jibuti. He had hoped to do so. While he talked his lazy glance took in the Arab's reactions to his story with extreme carefulness.

At one point in his fabrication he feared that he had blundered. Ben Ibrim's eyes suddenly flickered; but he was smiling again so cheerfully next second that Lovelace was reassured and felt that he could only have imagined the change of expression.

"My good friend Zarrif is gone from here," Ben Ibrim said after a moment. "He flew on to Addis Ababa only this morning."

Lovelace heaved a mental sigh of relief. Zarrif would arrive in Addis Ababa much earlier than they had expected, but there were still fourteen days before the date fixed for the signing of the concession, and, now that they knew where he was, ample time to prepare a coup in the Abyssinian capital.

For another twenty minutes he talked and laughed with Ben Ibrim, but Valerie suddenly noticed that he had begun to scratch his left ear.

She closed her eyes and swayed from side to side a little, putting her right hand up to her throat.

Christopher asked if she were ill, and the two acted a little pantomime together, in which she pretended that she would be quite all right in a moment, while he expressed grave concern.

Ben Ibrim asked Lovelace in what way she was suffering and placed his household at her disposal. Lovelace replied that it was mainly fatigue and the great heat of Jibuti, to which she was not accustomed. If they left at once she would not be in bed much before midnight, and she had had a long and tiring day. He begged, therefore, that His Excellency would excuse them and allow her to wait upon his wives the following day.

The Arab stood up and they rose with him as he clapped his hands to summon his servants. "Women and horses are delicate creatures," he remarked to Lovelace, "but Allah has provided both for the joy of man, and timely care of them enables the two species to give us the maximum of pleasure. It is sad that you should have so soon to go. I still have some lovely stories I would have liked to tell you, but to-morrow is yet a day."

A few moments later, after bowing their thanks to Ben Ibrim for his hospitality, they were escorted to the outer court.

When they reached the street, Lovelace chuckled. "I've got what we wanted," he told his friends. "Zarrif was here but he left this morning by plane for Addis."

He would not have been quite so pleased with himself had he known that the moment they were out of the house Abu Ben Ibrim had picked up a telephone which was concealed behind his pile of rugs, and was even then giving an account of their visit, over it, to Paxito Zarrif, who was actually still in Jibuti.

CHAPTER XVI

THE HAWK AND THE SPARROW

NEXT morning, to the surprise and distress of the sergeant's aunt, they were up long before dawn. At four o'clock, in the comparative cool which still lasted with darkness, they drove out to the aerodrome.

Valerie made a particularly careful examination of her engine, as she knew that it might prove extremely awkward if they had to make a forced landing before completing their seven-hundred-mile journey, but by five o'clock they were in the air and heading for Addis Ababa.

They did not notice a great four-engined machine that was run out of a hangar and left the Jibuti airfield ten minutes after them. If they had it would have appeared only as a tiny speck in the distance to their rear.

The rising sun seemed to come up all at once out of the ocean behind them. It shattered the brief twilight and painted the hills beyond Jibuti in unbelievably fantastic colours. The white salt mountains, which they had seen in the distance the day before, turned orange, gold, and rose, like a magnificent sunset spread out below. Then the colours faded and hard, brilliant, clear, every feature of the land lay naked in the glare, exposed to another day of blistering sun.

Valerie followed the railway line, a tiny, string-like track across the surface of the wild, in which French fortunes had been sunk for over thirty years. No trains were visible upon it. The express to Addis Ababa still ran only twice a week, although there was a war on, yet freight and fares at scandalously high rates were now bringing fine profits to the railway company. The bi-weekly train due out that day which might, or might not, carry Baron Foldvar up into the interior was not scheduled to leave Jibuti until some hours later.

Plantations of cotton and coffee, interspersed with great areas of dense jungle which made the country appear green and fertile, fringed the railway on either side for several miles. At a quarter to six they were over the frontier and above Douelne, the first Abyssinian town, if the little cluster of buildings below them could be dignified by that name.

By seven they were over a place where the railway took a great curve to the south and then swung round to the north again, almost forming a horseshoe bend. The land in the Bight was a greenish-yellow, pock-marked surface looking as though it was pitted with innumerable small craters and, towards its centre, speckled with little dabs of white.

From the map they saw that the place half a mile below them was Diredawa, the most important city on the line between Jibuti and Addis, where it was necessary to leave the train for the great southern metropolis of Harar which lay some twenty-five miles to the south-east.

Valerie circled once, bringing her plane down to a thousand feet so that they could get a better view of the town. The few whitish dabs were brick-walled, tin-roofed buildings; the countless pock-marks *tuculs*—round, thatched native huts. Patches of blue-gum trees were now apparent, tilled fields and, in the middle of the town, some larger buildings; churches and Rases' palaces perhaps. The town had no plan as far as could be seen; no main streets or squares. It just straggled outwards from the denser cluster of hutments grouped round the bigger buildings.

As they flew on again the fertile plain on their left, to the south of the railway, dropped away towards Harar and the fruitful province of Ogaden, while to the north lay a brown, barren land which soon overlapped the line and filled the horizon on both sides as far as they could see.

It was a nightmare country of almost unbelievable desolation. In the far distance range upon range of fiercely jagged mountains pierced the sky. Out of the trackless deserts below rose steep, flat-topped kopjes like those seen in the waterless South African Karoo. No single sign of life appeared upon the inhospitable, boulder-strewn, volcanic soil. The country might have been created by Satan in a fit of diabolical hate against mankind.

The sun was now making a furnace of the earth and already objects on it were becoming indistinct from the shimmering heat haze that quivered over the sandy wastes. Instinctively, almost, Valerie mounted to a higher altitude.

It was half an hour after passing over Diredawa that Lovelace caught sight of the following plane. At first he hardly took conscious notice of it but it was gaining on them and, as the distance between the planes decreased, something about the lines of the other machine struck him as familiar. Suddenly he realised that it was Zarrif's.

The knowledge worried him as he dismissed at once the idea of coincidence. Abu Ben Ibrim had admitted that Zarrif had been in Jibuti two days before but said that he had left on the previous morning. Ben Ibrim had lied then. But why? Because something had been said which had given away the fact that they were not really Zarrif's friends. Zarrif must still have been in Jibuti the previous night then and, having got rid of them by sending them on to Addis, Ben Ibrim had warned him about them. But why was Zarrif following them now? Lovelace felt a sudden chill of apprehension and he told Christopher that it was Zarrif's plane behind them.

Christopher shrugged. "What's it matter? As long

as Zarrif *is* on his way to Addis Ababa it's immaterial which of us arrives there first."

Lovelace said no more. No useful purpose could have been served by doing so now and he endeavoured to conceal his anxiety. Having travelled in Zarrif's plane he knew that for each trip it was converted from a luxury air-liner into a fighter carrying four machine-guns. He had a ghastly feeling that those machine guns might be manned at the moment and that Zarrif was following Valerie's plane intent upon its destruction.

They were half-way across the long, desolate stretch between Diredawa and Mojjo when Lovelace's fears were confirmed all too fully. The machine-guns in their rear suddenly began to stutter.

A cold perspiration broke out on his forehead. They were unarmed; they could not fight. Zarrif meant to shoot them down and finish them once and for all, out there in the desert, where there would be no troublesome witnesses. He gripped Valerie by the shoulder.

"I'm sorry—Ben Ibrim's fooled us. Make north—towards French Somaliland—try and get clear. If you see a good stretch, land, and we'll run for it."

At the first staccato rattle Valerie had glanced over her shoulder and realised the meaning of it.

"We're done!" she gasped. "Their plane's faster than mine—and it's higher. We can't shoot back—they'll do us in for certain." But as she spoke she flung the joystick over and they curved into a sickening dive to the right of the railway.

Zarrif's plane followed. Lovelace could picture him in his forward cabin, cold and impassive, submitting with bleak resignation to this momentary interruption of his work while his gunmen carried out his orders.

A few hundred feet above the desert Valerie flattened out and zoomed up again; heading north as Lovelace had told her.

The enemy, realising that the manœuvre was a trick, banked steeply and came roaring after them. The shadows of the two planes, black and clear-cut like two huge birds, raced at two hundred miles an hour across the desert.

Valerie was climbing again which caused her to lose pace. The bigger machine swooped suddenly, diving at them with both its forward guns blazing. Valerie flicked her plane over so that it almost turned turtle; righted it again and shot skywards. The two planes seemed to miss each other only by inches but she had escaped the hail of bullets and now had the greater altitude.

Christopher lurched to his feet, his pistol drawn, his black eyes staring, waiting for a chance to open fire upon their overwhelmingly more powerful enemy.

Lovelace pulled his arm. "That's no good," he yelled, "you couldn't hit them in a month of Sundays. Save your bullets—we'll need them if we can only land."

Both planes were climbing again now; straining for height: Valerie, that she might get clear for a breakneck dive to attempt a landing on a patch of even ground she could see ahead, and Zarrif's pilot so that he might swoop at her again. For three breathless moments there was silence.

Suddenly the attack opened once more. The chatter of the machine-guns was louder now. A spate of bullets tore through the fuselage of the smaller plane. Valerie swerved; then dropped like a stone. Christopher was flung off his feet. Lovelace gasped as his heart seemed to rise up into his throat. Yet even in that moment, as they flashed out of the bullet-spattered area, he realised what a superb pilot they had in the white-faced girl beside him.

Before they knew what was happening she had righted the plane again and was heading north once more. They had dropped a thousand feet but the desert was still over two thousand feet below them.

Zarrif's plane was after them, heavier but as fast, two streams of bullets zipping from its forward guns.

A control wire snapped with a loud ping as a shot cut through it, a dozen more made a line of punctures in the metal-work of the cabin only a few inches behind Christopher's shoulders.

Valerie threw back her head. She was not looking at Christopher but at Lovelace. Her glance held no fear but distress and apology. She had done her best to get clear but it was impossible.

His grimace was meant to be a smile of thanks, admiration, understanding. He nodded once, pulled the rip cord of the emergency exit in the roof of the cabin, and shouted: "Land! Anywhere! It's our only chance."

Next second she had thrown the plane into a spin. Gyrating madly they plunged down, down, down, while the spinning earth rushed up to meet them.

Lovelace held his breath; waiting for the terrific impact which he knew must come before oblivion. Suddenly they came out of the spin and seemed to flash along the surface of the ground at breakneck speed, almost scraping it. There was a frightful jolt; they bounded into the air again with the ground still racing away beneath them until a wing-tip caught upon a giant boulder. The plane swerved violently. With the scream of tearing fabric and twisted metal it turned right round, lurched sideways, and came to a standstill.

For a moment they were too dazed to move. Christopher recovered first and began to scramble out through the roof of the cabin. "Come on!" he called, stretching down a hand to grab Valerie's arm. "Come on! They're still shooting at us."

Lovelace thrust her up and followed her through the aperture. They saw Zarrif's plane, far above them now, circling in the wide blue sky. Its guns still flashed and a hail of bullets was tearing the left wing of Valerie's machine to pieces.

As they jumped to the ground the fierce heat of the stones struck up to their feet through the soles of their shoes but they did not heed it as they dashed for cover.

Instinctively they headed for a natural arch formed by two big rocks, about a hundred yards away, and flung themselves down beneath it.

For a few moments bullets continued to clatter on the stones about them; then there fell a sudden silence broken only by the drone of the plane above. It grew fainter and Lovelace peered out. The enemy were apparently content with having shot them down; for the plane had turned and was heading away towards Addis Ababa.

He wondered that Zarrif should be satisfied to leave them still alive when, by expending a little more time and ammunition, he could have descended to a closer range and massacred them in spite of their scant cover. Yet they must be thirty, if not fifty, miles now from the railway line and a hundred from a village that contained a white man. They would die of thirst and starvation in that blistering desert before they could cover half such a distance. All the same it was strange that Zarrif should have left them even so slender a chance of life.

Suddenly he saw something move behind a boulder. Through the shimmering heat haze a savage, brown face, surmounted by fuzzy, black hair, was peering at him.

Valerie gave a cry and gripped Christopher's arm. She was looking in a different direction and had seen another. The whole region seemed to come to life and there were scores of dark, shiny faces glaring at them.

Lovelace understood then why Zarrif had left them. He had seen the tribesmen from above. This was Danakil country where whites were first terribly mutilated and then murdered. He had gone on to Addis Ababa, quite satisfied that there was not the slightest chance of their ever troubling him again.

There was only one thing for it, Lovelace knew. He had got to shoot Valerie first and himself afterwards.

CHAPTER XVII

THE LAND OF SATAN'S CHILDREN

LOVELACE stared out into the heat haze. The blistering sun was already scorching his back and shoulders through his thin tunic. The yellow-brown rocks danced and shimmered. Above them, no more than twenty yards away, peered the brutal faces of the savage Danakils. It was no nightmare, but reality. This was Abyssinia, and an end to their mad venture before they had been two hours over the frontier of the country. A swarm of the fuzzy-haired warriors were already looting the wrecked plane.

"Speak to them!" Valerie's voice came low-pitched and urgent at his side. "Speak to them and tell them we're not Italians."

He shook his head helplessly. Even if he could have said in the dialect of the tribe: "We are neutrals on our way to Addis Ababa to stop war—not to make it," he doubted if it would have made the least difference.

These barbarous Danakils were killers of unprotected travellers in normal times, as even then the Emperor's writ was so much waste paper more than fifty miles from his capital. He had to collect his taxes by a series of armed forays each year, and the townships of his so-called Ethiopian Empire, which was six times the size of Abyssinia proper, were only kept in subjection by garrisons of Amhara soldiery. Lovelace knew the complicated system of guides and presents by which any visitor to the interior of the country had to be passed on from one local chieftain to another if he was to escape attack. Now it had filtered through to tribesmen that their country was at war they would risk attacking even armed convoys under the impression that rewards would be forthcoming for every white they slaughtered. He could speak Arabic, Urdú, "pidgin" French and "pidgin" English, and had a smattering of various other non-European languages, but Danakil, or even Amharic, was utterly beyond him.

"I'm sorry," he muttered. "I can't, and, anyhow, these people don't know one European nation from another—only that it's no longer necessary even to make excuses when they murder white men."

Christopher's thoughts were racing wildly. He was much younger than Lovelace, and this was the first time in his life that he had ever found himself outside the protection of organised law and order. At the first sight of the natives he wondered why they did not use their long, old-fashioned guns or cast their tufted spears. Then he realised that the encircling ring of warriors had crawled nearer and meant to capture them alive. His next thought was the appalling one that Lovelace had had only a few seconds before. He must shoot Valerie first and himself immediately afterwards.

Lovelace had already drawn his pistol. He knew far better than Christopher the terrible mutilations and tortures that all three of them would suffer if they allowed themselves to be captured. He gazed round him, hoping desperately to find one friendly face in the ring of evil masks; a chief to whom they might offer ransom, or a semi-cultured type; but they were all stupid, brutal, bestial; their black hair wild and shaggy, their eyes fierce with the lust for blood.

He raised his automatic. Sweat was pouring off his face in rivulets. With an almost superhuman effort of will he jerked the gun up behind Valerie's shoulder until it was pointing at the base of her skull behind the left ear. She would know nothing about it; feel nothing but a smashing blow and then be beyond all physical joy or pain for ever.

At that instant she turned. She could not see the

pistol, but his raised arm and half-crazed expression told her of his intention. Instinctively, blind terror gripped her. Her mouth fell open, her grey eyes started from her head, and she ducked with such suddenness that she stumbled and fell forward on her knees.

Hardly a moment had elapsed since their first sight of the Danakils. As though her fall had been a signal, the native warriors gave a yell of triumph and, leaping from their cover, came dashing pell-mell across the twenty yards of open ground.

In a second Valerie grasped the full horror of her situation. To fall alive into the hands of these murderous savages meant twenty deaths instead of one. Far better that Lovelace should blow her brains out. She wrenched herself round on her knees and threw her head back.

"All right!" she gasped. "Go on—shoot me!"

Lovelace had let his pistol-hand drop to his side. Now he raised it again until the weapon pointed at her breast. For split seconds, each of which seemed like an eternity, he strove to force himself to press the trigger.

He could have managed it before, when she was not looking; but now that she was staring up at him, her eyes riveted on his, waiting for the bullet to sear through her body, he could not.

Christopher had turned and was shouting something. His black eyes shone feverishly in a face drained of blood. His *Millers'* lethal gas pistol, too, was now aimed at Valerie, but her fall had lost them precious seconds, and before either of the men had time to nerve himself for his terrible act the Danakils were upon them.

At the last moment, Christopher, swerving from his purpose, swung round and discharged his weapon at one of the warriors. Lovelace kept his pistol levelled at Valerie and pulled the trigger, but a huge native leap, upon her as the automatic flashed and took the bullet in his thigh.

After that all chance to kill each other or themselves was gone. They were borne down by a solid mass of black, stinking humanity. It was all over within one minute of the warriors having left their cover. Battered, bruised, breathless, the two white men and the girl were lugged to their feet, alive but captives, to find themselves staring half-dazed into a host of hostile, brutish faces.

Without further delay they were pushed and pulled over the hot stones, past their wrecked plane and on through the wilderness.

It seemed to stretch interminably behind them and on either side, with neither tree, nor shrub, nor waterhole to break the endless monotony of sun-scorched rock, but before them rose a great range of cliffs ; the first step to the highlands of the interior. Black, precipitous, apparently unscalable, they towered up in the near distance, cutting sharply across the skyline.

The prisoners were being taken towards the west, and the morning sun beat down with relentless force upon their backs. Valerie had lost her hat, and only her chestnut hair, now hanging about her head in damp, tangled rats' tails, protected her from sunstroke. As she was hurried along, tripping and stubbing her toes on the hot, uneven ground in the firm grip of two perspiring natives, she thought of that ; then realised how little sunstroke mattered. In a few hours she would be raving mad from the atrocities these animals in human form would practice upon her.

Lovelace and Christopher were both thinking of the same thing, and each was cursing himself for his cowardly hesitation at the moment when he might have shot her. They trudged on blindly, hastened by jabs from spear-points and blows from the muzzles of ancient blunderbusses.

Before they had covered five hundred yards of their terrible journey all of them had lapsed into semi-consciousness from heat, nightmare imagination, and brutal beating. The naked rocks underfoot had given way to tough, dry, desert grass and through this they were half-dragged, half-carried, until they arrived within a hundred yards of the cliff face. There, they sensed rather than saw that they had arrived outside a village.

A swarm of screaming women and a host of naked children came out to meet them, dancing and grimacing with delirious glee, while the warriors broke into a shrill, unmelodious song of triumph at their capture.

The village was no more than a collection of daub-and-wattle huts clustered together at the foot of the cliff. It was so primitive that it had not even an open space at its centre. By the nearest hut an old, old man, with a fringe of white hair round his polished skull and a wizened, monkey-like face, stood leaning on a staff. As the gibbering mob dragged their prisoners before him he regarded them with small, cruel, rheumy eyes for a moment, then muttered a few words in his own dialect. Without further parley they were jostled another twenty yards and flung head foremost into an empty hut.

Immediately the screen was pulled across the entrance it became pitch dark inside, but Lovelace caught a glimpse of Valerie's face before the light was blotted out and saw that she had fainted.

The place stank worse than any kennel; with the mixed odours of goats, pigs, and filthy humanity. Almost instantly the hundreds of fleas which infested it settled upon them.

For a long time they were too broken and bemused even to stir from the places where they had fallen. Lovelace, knowing what was in store for them, was thinking feverishly of the knives of the Danakil women as they would cut into his shrinking flesh, when Christopher roused at last and muttered: "If they're going to kill us, why the hell don't they get on with it?"

Lovelace knew the answer. They were being kept for a night's entertainment. It was highly probable that never before in its history had this village experienced the undreamed-of pleasure which could be provided by the skilful mutilation of two white men and a white woman. If they were dead before the morning they would be lucky and the Danakils intensely disappointed. His one prayer was that they might all go mad and cease to suffer early in the game, but he forebore to voice his thoughts in case Valerie had regained consciousness.

Actually she had never quite lost it, and now she had recovered sufficiently to speak clearly again. With uncanny precision she guessed his thoughts, and said :

"It seems years since we crashed in the plane, but it can't be midday yet. That means we've got a long while to wait until sundown."

Christopher stretched his bruised arms, clasping and unclasping his stiff fingers. Their captors had not troubled to bind them. The ghastly thought had come to him that, since his gun had gone, he had better strangle Valerie, because he loved her. As he moved she spoke again, deliberately and bitterly.

"I wish some of the people who want to go to war to save the Abyssinians were in our place now. They don't understand—they can't. These brutes are worse than animals—worse than reptiles—even a snake doesn't bite you unless you provoke it in some way. I've never seen such fiendish cruelty as stared at me out of the eyes of these loathsome creatures when they dragged us here, and the women who met us looked even more ferocious than the men. They're not human, but soulless devils incarnate whose one delight is inflicting pain."

Her voice rose to a shrill note of hysteria. "I don't care any more for ideals and all the senseless nonsense that is talked about Leagues and Covenants and Treaties. I hope the Italians win ! I hope they wipe these people out, man, woman and child. Destroy them and blast them limb from limb until there's not a single one of them left to pollute the decent earth they tread on."

As she ceased speaking the first bomb fell.

CHAPTER XVIII

DOLOMENCHI OF THE DEATH SQUADRON

THE explosion occurred with such frightful suddenness that for a second they did not grasp what was happening. The ground they lay on shuddered under the impact, a shower of dried mud rattled down from the unseen walls and roof of the hut, the hot dark air quivered, and the crash nearly burst their ear-drums. There came another before the echoing reverberations of the first, thrown back from the cliff face, had subsided.

"Bombs!" yelled Lovelace, staggering to his feet. "Quick—we must get out of this!"

He kicked aside the wicket covering the entrance to the hut, and with the others hard on his heels, dashed into the open. Any guards who might have been keeping watch a moment earlier had disappeared. In the blinding sunlight a ghastly spectacle lay before them.

A third of the village had been blown to fragments. Men, women and children shrieked and screamed as they fled in all directions; here and there brown figures lay in terribly distorted attitudes, some deadly still in pools of glistening blood, others contorted into fantastic shapes by an agony of pain.

Valerie glimpsed one headless body and another with both legs blown away as Lovelace, gripping her by the arm, raced her across the tough grass out into the open.

Another bomb burst behind them. It was not big stuff, Lovelace knew, otherwise there would have been only great craters where the village stood, but extremely deadly, nevertheless. The attacker was using light bombs with instantaneous fuses specially designed for spreading their metal laterally and causing casualties to troops rather than wrecking buildings. Tiny pieces of jagged steel, capable of inflicting frightful wounds, sang past them as they ran.

Three hundred yards from the wreck of the village he pulled up for a second. Christopher was close behind. They halted, gasping for breath after their desperate race.

An intensely bright light that was almost unbearable to look upon suddenly appeared on the edge of the remaining huts. Instantly the whole lot burst into flames like a stand of matches upon which the end of a lighted cigarette has been dropped.

A pitiful whimper in the tall grass near by caused Valerie to switch round just as Lovelace was urging her on again. It came from a naked child, about three years old, who had been scampering away in front of them. A large piece of the last explosive bomb had taken off his right foot, severing it at the ankle, so that it now hung from the leg by only a shred of skin.

She ran to him and snatched him up, regardless of the blood which poured over her soiled skirt. The others seized her by the arms and forced her on while the child struggled wildly in her fierce grip ; more terrified to find itself clutched to the breast of a white woman than at the pain of its shattered limb.

The bombing had ceased and they eased their pace after they had covered another hundred yards. Valerie sank down exhausted with her quivering burden. As she fell she burst into a passionate flood of tears.

"The brutes!" she sobbed. "The fiends!—how could they ? Oh, my lamb, my lamb, what have they done to you ?"

Christopher bent over her. The old fanatic gleam had come back into his dark eyes. "This is war," he muttered. "War! The curse of humanity. The horror we're out to stop. Can you ever doubt again that the *Millers of God* are right ? Oh, how I wish I'd killed that devil Zarrif when I had the chance."

"He's coming down." Lovelace was staring upward

into the fierce blue sky where a single Italian war-plane circled gracefully above their heads. "Look! he's coming down."

The village was now only a smouldering pile of ruins; the surviving Danakils had disappeared as though by magic. As they watched the plane circled lower, seeking an even stretch of the coarse grass on which to land. It came to earth a few hundred yards away.

A man got out of it and walked over to a hummock on which he halted to scan the surrounding country.

Christopher waved, the man waved back, and they started to run towards him, Valerie still clutching the child whose moans had grown more feeble now.

As they approached they saw that the man was lithe and dark and handsome. He wore a pair of beautifully cut breeches, field-boots that shone with the reflection of the sun, an open-necked sleeveless shirt, and an air-helmet. He was smoking a cigarette with quiet enjoyment.

A rifle cracked and the bullet sent up a little spurt of dust just to his left; another zipped a rock in the rear. Some of the Danakils who had managed to retain their weapons had now regained their courage. He lifted the hand that held his cigarette; a machine-gun on the plane began to sweep a rocky patch where the survivors of the massacre had taken refuge, and the feeble attempt at retaliation was silenced.

The dark man smiled as the dishevelled fugitives came panting up to him; bringing his heels together, he gave the Fascist salute as he introduced himself. "Lieutenant Count Giulio Dolomenchi."

Still sobbing, Valerie held out the child towards him. "Look!" she gasped. "Look what you've done! How could you?"

He made a little gesture of distress and spoke in Italian. "Signorina, we are at war. Think, too, of what these barbarous people would have done to *you* had I not seen the wreckage of your plane. I risked the lives of my men and myself to land here on the chance that I might be in time to save white airmen from mutilation."

She knew enough Italian to catch the drift of what he said, and felt that his argument was unanswerable. Her pity for the child fought with her gratitude at the thought of the inexpressible horrors from which Lieutenant Count Dolomenchi had rescued them.

Lovelace was already stammering their thanks and the Lieutenant glanced at him quickly. "You are English—are you not?—but you can tell me about yourselves later. Into the plane, please, now. They will be shooting at us again and we shall get sunstroke if we remain here much longer. Signorina, that child is dead, I fear, so you had better leave it."

It was true. The little Danakil had ceased to moan and struggle. Its life-blood had drained from it and the small body now lay limp in Valerie's arms. She laid it down in the grass and, after a last sorrowful glance, turned towards the war-plane.

The crew of Italian airmen helped them up into the narrow cabin. Lieutenant Count Dolomenchi mounted to the pilot's seat; the machine taxied forward, bumped a little, and they were in the air again. The desert was still and lifeless below them as they climbed. Where the village had been there was now only a pile of blackened ash with a few wisps of smoke curling up from it.

Christopher was staring down at the ruin they were leaving behind them. "How quickly it burnt once it caught fire," he muttered to Lovelace.

One of the airmen overheard him and said in English: "I used explosives first—just to scare them out—but once we saw you running from the village I dropped one of our new incendiary bombs to finish it."

"I thought as much," Lovelace nodded. "From the frightful glare it must have been a pretty big chap."

"No, no, quite small." The Italian smiled. "They weigh only one kilo, about two English pounds, but they are thermite and develop a heat of 3,000 degrees Fahrenheit. Anyone within ten yards of one when it bursts would be scorched to death instantly. They would bore a hole through the steel decks of your most heavily-armoured battleships, and come straight out through their bottoms too, as easily as a rifle bullet would go through an orange."

Lovelace would have liked to have heard more of this new weapon, but the Italian excused himself with the plea that he and his comrades must continue the reconnaissance upon which they were engaged.

The war-plane was now well above the level of the towering cliff, and turned north-by-west in the direction of Dessye. As further ranges of cliffs appeared, they climbed higher and higher while the observers took innumerable photographs of the wild gorges, and hardly discernible goat tracks, beneath them.

The three passengers had fallen silent. They were now feeling the reaction from the excitement of their escape and the minor misfortunes resulting from their grim ordeal. All of them were badly bruised from the blows they had received, and had numerous small cuts from knives and spears upon their backs and thighs.

Many of the fleas which had attacked them in the hut were still upon them, and although they had not been exposed to the sun for any length of time, its rays were so strong that they had been badly scorched about their necks and shoulders.

As the reconnaissance progressed they lapsed into a semi-stupor. Their bodies ached, itched and burned intolerably, yet they were too dead-beat to do anything but crouch on the narrow seats they had been given and pray that the flight would soon be over.

Once the English-speaking Italian roused them and, pointing downwards with a grin, said, "Look, we are over Dessye."

Lovelace peered down. From the air the place appeared much as Diredawa had that morning except, that it was somewhat larger and set in a valley among mountains instead of in a plain. There were the same round native *tuculs*; the same cluster of whitish tin-roofed buildings and churches in its centre; the same lack of plan in its straggling outlay. In the rarefied mountain air, however, this landmap stood out with startling clearness, and he could see swarms of ant-like creatures moving about their business below. To one side of the town several hundred white tents and marquees had been erected; regular lines of little oblong things near them could only be rows of stationary tanks and lorries. The rumour that the Italians had taken Dessye was true, then.

As they flew on they passed over an artillery park and veering northward saw a long, long, snake-like stream of slowly moving transport emerging from the entrance of a mountain pass. Evidently the invaders were forming a new base at the Emperor's old headquarters before pushing on again. They still had a hundred-and-fifty miles to go, though, Lovelace reckoned, before they could enter Addis. Their recent progress had been remarkable, but they were very far from having won as yet.

He closed his eyes and dropped back in his seat: too tired and ill to watch the scene beneath them any longer. Valerie and Christopher were huddled up in an uneasy doze opposite to him. None of them noticed when the plane changed its direction again, after having made three-quarters of a great circle from Assab, over Dire-dawa and Dessye, to head back towards the Red Sea. They did not open their eyes again until it landed at a large, military aerodrome.

Lovelac climbed stiffly out and, seeing the long rows of hangars with the white houses of quite a considerable town beyond in the distance, asked where they were.

"Assab, our port in Southern Eritrea," said Count Dolomenchi. "It is a devilish place, but while the war lasts one must put up with such discomforts."

"Assab," repeated Lovelace dully. "Then we're only just over the border from French Somaliland. Jibuti, from where we started this morning, can't be much more than a hundred miles along the coast from here. We could get there overnight if there's a steamer sailing, and make a fresh start for Addis Ababa to-morrow."

Dolomenchi shook his handsome head. "Observe the condition of the Signorina and the young man who supports her. Yourself, too, you look almost all-in."

It was true. Lovelace glanced behind him and saw that Christopher was now holding Valerie up, although he could hardly stand himself.

"Come." The Count took Valerie's other arm. "In one of the Air Force cars I shall take you all to the hospital. Bed is the place for you at the moment."

The hospital to which he took them was a brand-new building on the edge of the town. It was airy, clean and equipped in the most up-to-date manner. Its personnel was entirely military, but Lieutenant Count Dolomenchi seemed to know them all.

The doctors greeted him with Fascist salutes and a hearty welcome; the Italian nurses smiled and lingered as long as they were able in his vicinity. His request for beds which, as they were for foreign civilians might well have been rejected had it come from a lesser personality, was instantly granted. Was he not Dolomenchi of the Death Squadron, one of the heroes of the Italian Expeditionary Force, the gay and gallant airman who had been twice decorated for his feats of valour at the taking of Adigrat and the storming of Mount Aradam?

Valerie was taken to the nurses' ward and the others to a ward for officers. Willing hands assisted them to remove their tattered clothes. Their bruised and blistered bodies were washed, bandaged, and poulticed with witch-hazel.

Christopher, utterly played out, submitted to the ministrations of the orderlies in silence. His whole body was racked with pain, the skin of his neck, shoulders, arms and back was stretched so taut it looked as though it might burst, and it burned intolerably.

When he had been put in the next empty bed to Lovelace he rallied a little, and said: "First thing to-morrow we'll have to see about buying another plane."

The Italian doctor overheard him and smiled. "I think it will be some time before you need bother about that."

"But we can't stop here," Christopher protested. "It's of vital importance that we should reach Addis Ababa at the earliest possible moment."

The doctor shrugged. "That is unfortunate, as it is quite impossible for you to resume your journey in your present state. Give me your arm, please."

"We must," insisted Christopher feverishly. "We must! So much depends on our arriving there in time. How long did you mean to keep us here?"

"You have had a ghastly grilling, and some of your wounds may be septic, but, if no complications set in, I'll have you up and about again in a fortnight or three weeks." The doctor plunged the hypodermic needle into Christopher's arm and sent him, still muttering, off to sleep.

CHAPTER XIX

THE SECRET OF THE SECOND NILE

FOR seven days they were kept in bed. Both Valerie and Christopher had second-degree burns, and, for the first forty-eight hours, suffered the same agony as if they were being grilled before a slow fire, but, as thousands of similar cases had passed through the hands of the hospital staff since the opening of the campaign, they received expert treatment and were able to get some sleep without the assistance of morphia on the third day.

Lovelace was burnt, too, although less badly, owing to his previous acclimatisation in the tropics, and he would have recovered earlier than the others had it not been for a small wound in the calf of his leg which gave considerable trouble because it had been inflicted by a poisoned Danakil spear.

In the next bed to him Christopher fretted badly. They must get on, he insisted whenever the nurses' backs were turned. Paxito Zarrif was already in Addis Ababa, and the first of May was the date fixed for the signing of the concession. They had been shot down in the Danakil country on April the 18th. It was now the 22nd . . . the 23rd . . . the 24th. Unless they left at once there would be no time to plan any attempt against Zarrif which would have a reasonable chance of success. Money was no object. They must charter or buy another plane; buy one for preference, in order that their movements might be free from the surveillance of a hired pilot.

Fortunately, they had their passports on them when they crashed in the desert, so, although they had lost their luggage, they had no difficulty in proving their identity, and Christopher was able to cable New York for a credit to be opened in his name at the *Banco Italiano* in Assab.

On the eighth day after their arrival they were both allowed to get up and went into the town together, where they purchased immediate necessities, but, with all his money, it proved impossible for Christopher to hire or buy another plane. There were hundreds of machines, yet every one of them was either the property of the Italian Air Force or required for some special purpose by the Government. They telegraphed to Jibuti and found that no planes were available there either; but in neutral French Somaliland Christopher was able to make dollars talk. He got in touch with the United States Consul and asked him to purchase an airworthy plane, regardless of its price. The Consul got busy and reported a four-seater, equipped with a variable-pitch propeller for sale at a sum that would have bought a Schneider Cup winner. Christopher bought it and arranged for it to be piloted over next day so that they might fly it to Addis Ababa, starting in the cool early hours of the following morning, but he had reckoned without their hosts.

Each day the debonair Lieutenant Count Dolomenchi had called at the hospital to inquire after them, leaving gifts of tropical flowers and fruit. He had also called upon Valerie and obtained permission to sit at her bedside each evening after his day's flying was done. When he had realised that she was Valerie Lorne, the famous American airwoman, his courtesies had turned to unbounded admiration. To have rescued her became a double honour, and he insisted that she should dine in his mess on her tenth night in Assab, as the doctor agreed that she should be well enough by then.

She protested that it was impossible, that she had no clothes, and that her hair was in a hopeless mess, but he had brushed her objections aside with a gay laugh.

"The matter of your hair is easily settled. It takes all

sorts to make an army, you know—bricklayers, farmers, porters, clerks, and even criminals—there is a professional burglar in my own unit, an amusing fellow. I shall easily find you a hairdresser—as for clothes—you shall see!" and he departed impulsively to beat up the town.

When Christopher and Lovelace appeared to make known their plans, they found invitations for this gala awaiting them too, and the latter insisted that it was quite out of the question to cut the party.

Christopher was furious at this fresh delay, but he agreed that the extra twenty-four hours of enforced convalescence would make them all the fitter for their journey, and on the ninth day, when their new plane arrived, Dolomenchi was able to have it thoroughly overhauled for them in his squadron's workshop.

Early next evening a surprisingly attractive selection of dresses arrived for Valerie, brought by a local dressmaker who made the necessary alterations to one of them on the spot.

An hour later a hairdresser, in the uniform of a corporal, presented himself and informed her that, as he had spent two years with Duraye in London, she might have every confidence in him.

Their generous host also provided the two men with fresh drill suits and sent a car to bring them all out to the air force mess at eight o'clock.

In her brief career as an airwoman Valerie had been the heroine of many ovations but never one like this. The Italian officers were all practical airmen who had a professional understanding of her records. Moreover it was months since many of them had even seen an attractive white girl of their own class. The band struck up as she entered but it was drowned in cheers and the cheers continued until she thought that they would never stop.

She was the only woman present. A distinguished General who had been asked to meet her sat on her left and the Commandant of the aerodrome on her right. All down the long tables there were rows of tanned boyish faces smiling an enthusiastic appreciation of her presence.

After dinner the health of the King of Italy was drunk, those of Il Duce, Signor Mussolini, the President of the United States, and King Edward VIII of England: then that of Valerie, as an inspiration to the airmen of all nations and their most honoured guest.

The glasses rang; the young men pounded on the tables and shouted plaudits as they drank the toast.

She stood up to reply and ended by saying that her only wish was to see them, with honour, safely home again in their beautiful Italy which all who had ever seen it must surely love.

When she sat down the General had to lend her his big handkerchief; for the thought was unbearable to her that many of these splendid boys might leave their bones in the burning deserts of North-East Africa.

As they left the dinner-table for the big ante-room, Valerie was surrounded by a swarm of young men; all anxious for a few words with her. Those who could not get near because of the crush fastened on Christopher, who, as her fiancé, took on some of her reflected glory, while Lovelace was carried away into a corner by the General.

For a little they talked of conditions in the interior of Abyssinia as Lovelace had given it out that he and his friends were on their way to join a Red Cross unit; a fiction which pleased the Italians as the more neutral whites there were behind the enemy lines the more chance their own wounded and prisoners had of receiving decent treatment.

"Have you been stationed here long, sir?" Lovelace inquired in Italian.

"No," the other replied quickly. "I am recently transferred from the southern front where I was serving under General Graziani."

"You found it interesting, of course? Any soldier would."

The Italian stroked his grey moustache and his brown eyes twinkled. "Naturally. I was stationed in Italian Somaliland for a number of years before the war, too, so I know the country and the people."

"Did you find that the Somalis compare well with other native troops?"

"Yes, splendidly. The "Lions of Juba," as they call themselves or *Doubats* as we term them, are magnificent fellows. Incurably lazy as a people but they're great fighters. A *Doubat* will walk fifty miles in a day and swim a couple of rivers infested with crocodiles if you offer him a chance of cutting an enemy's throat. They're handsome chaps and their women are really beautiful. Black, of course, but without any trace of the thick lips and the flattened nose of the negro. They'd shoot anyone who attempted to interfere with their women without a second thought and their wives follow them up to within a mile or two of the battle line. The Abyssinians are their hereditary enemies, so we've had more Somali volunteers offering to fight with us than we've known what to do with."

Lovelace sipped the drink that stood beside him. "As almost the entire population of the Ogaden province are Somalis I suppose they'd prefer to see it under Italian rule than continue to be fleeced by the Negus's tax-gatherers."

"Naturally. Their own people further south, over the frontier, know we treat them fairly. They're Mohammedans, too, and they detest the Abyssinians' pseudo-Christianity. For years past the people of the Ogaden have only been kept in subjection by a reign of terror which is maintained by the Negus's Amhara soldiery."

"How's the war going down there?"

"As well as can be expected," replied the General non-committally. "Our progress on all fronts appears spasmodic because each time we gain a victory roads must be built through these trackless wastes to carry our supplies, before we can launch a new attack and clear a further section of the country. In the south we are opposed to Ras Nasibu, the Governor of Harar, who is by far the finest soldier among the Abyssinian Commanders. Ras Seyoum, in the Tigre, took a little handling because he is the real, lion-hearted type of Chief we have always heard about; a brave savage, shrewd, courageous and possessing real intitiative, but the others are a joke, little better than stupid children. They get drunk each night and fill their bellies with raw meat while they boast of what their fathers did in the way of killing forty years ago."

Lovelace nodded. "It seems that your Intelligence Service keeps you pretty well informed."

"Why certainly," the General laughed. "As ninety-nine out of every hundred Abyssinians would shoot their own brothers in the back for a handful of thalers they'll part with any information our agents require for the price of a drink. Besides, all the subject races, who form the bulk of the population, detest the Amhara and regard us as liberators. We know everything that goes on and every trench in their "Hindenburg line" is already marked out on our maps."

"D'you mean the line Ras Nasibu is holding?"

"Yes. It is about a hundred-and-thirty miles south of Harar and he is banking on it holding us up. It won't, because it's only an absurd travesty of its namesake; sand trenches connecting a chain of ancient mud forts, instead of reinforced concrete strongpoints linked by fifty-yard belts of barbed wire. General Graziani's troops are already concentrated in front of Sasa Baneh; he is certain to break through there within the next week or so. But that, please, is not for the Press."

"Of course not," Lovelace agreed quickly, "and however brave Ras Nasibu's men may be they couldn't possibly stand up against your massed machine-guns or a concentrated bombardment by artillerv using high explosives. Besides, you have unchallenged supremacy in the air and must be able to break up their masses anywhere, quite easily, before they get to the point of charging."

"That is true," the General concurred, "but the mastery of the air does not give us the same advantage that it would in Europe. Great tracts of Abyssinia are covered by dense jungle. The enemy uses them in which to concentrate his forces and our airmen are often completely baffled. During the day time, too, these blacks have the sense to go to earth; the whole front appears desolate and there's not a figure to be seen for a hundred miles along it. Then at night, when the planes are unable to help us, they come out by the thousand; stripped of their white *shamas*, stark naked and greased all over their bodies. They sneak up to our pickets and massacre them; often before an alarm can even be sounded."

"That sort of thing must prey on the nerves of your men pretty badly."

"It does; almost as much as the attacks of the hyenas."

"The hyenas," Lovelace repeated with surprise. "But surely they don't molest human beings."

The General laughed. "Evidently you have not met the Abyssinian variety. Like the human inhabitants of this miserable country, they far surpass in ferocity the normal members of their species."

"They prowl at nights, of course. I've seen them even in the streets of Addis Ababa, but I didn't think . . ."

"Oh, there, offal would keep down their ravenous hunger, perhaps, but outside the towns packs of them have to be driven off by rifle-fire at times. All our wounded that we fail to get in before nightfall are devoured by hyenas, and often they get the better of little bands of stragglers too. They're much more dangerous than the lions with which the country swarms, or even the tribes of baboons which set upon anyone who crosses their path."

Lovelace made a grimace. "Knowing so much fine Italian manhood would have to be sacrificed in such horrible ways it's difficult to understand how Signor Mussolini ever brought himself to the point of engaging in this war."

"For you, perhaps—but not for us." The General leant forward earnestly. "You are an Englishman of some standing; it is pleasant therefore to have the opportunity of putting the real facts before you. Listen, I will tell you why Italy had no alternative but to advance into Abyssinia. It is this: we did our share in the Great War but got practically nothing out of it. If Mussolini had been present when the Treaty of Versailles was drawn up things might have been different—but he was not. We received no colonies where our population might expand or from which we could secure vital raw materials. Afterwards, for a year or two, everything was anarchy; then Mussolini accomplished the March on Rome and proceeded to clean up our country. He was faced with Bolshevism, graft, indifference, and every kind of roguery. I tell you this—I who am an Italian." The General thumped his chest and Lovelace nodded.

"Good! For ten years Mussolini performed the most incredible labours; then he sat back to take stock of the situation. Order has been brought out of chaos; the great bulk of the people are the better for his reforms and, after years of doubt, now have unquestioning faith in his leadership. He has infused a new spirit into our nation and placed it once more among the leading powers *but*, in spite of all his efforts, he is faced with the cold, hard fact that our country simply cannot support our population. France has 60,000,000 people and Italy 40,000,000, yet France has more than ten times the area of cultivable land that we possess. Unless all that Mussolini had done was to go for nothing, he *had* to find some outlet for our surplus millions. Before the war our people could emigrate to the United States, to all parts of your British Empire, and to most other countries, freely. Since the war all that has been altered. Unemployment problems have forced nearly every nation to restrict or prohibit the immigration of aliens in order to protect such jobs as are going for their own nationals. Where could Mussolini turn without coming into conflict with the other great powers? We had two pieces of seaboard in Africa, both abutting on Abyssinia, with frontiers which have never been clearly defined. If he could advance those frontiers his problem was solved.

"Italy had already claimed and disputed that territory in the war of 1896. The Abyssinians only conquered it themselves in living memory and their title to it is extremely dubious.

"We made a treaty of friendship with them and for years it was our hope that we might assist them in the development of their country. Haile Selassie's authority has never existed, in fact, outside the comparatively small area of Abyssinia proper and in a few of the principal towns. We would have made him and his dynasty paramount throughout the whole Ethiopian Empire. All we asked in return was that he should allow us free immigration and the control of the police in order that we might protect our settlers. Surely, that we sponsored Abyssinia's entrance to the League in the face of Britain's opposition is proof of our honourable intentions. Yet this ill-advised little man has never treated our overtures with anything but prevarication and ill-concealed contempt. Worse, he has not even honoured his own agreement with us. Swiss, Belgians, Swedes are selected for the advisory posts which were promised to Italians. No special facilities which were promised for the development of trade have been given. Our people are singled out for insult and outrage whenever they venture into Abyssinian territory. The position has long been intolerable.

"In addition, the lack of law and order in the country is an open scandal and the native population would fare better under our protection than they do at present. We seek no war with any other European country. We are only proposing to do that which Britain and France have done on innumerable occasions in the past."

Lovelace smiled. "I'll grant you, sir, that you've put up a good case; just the sort, in fact, that Britain has used time and again to justify her own annexations, but honestly, is the country worth it? These miles of waterless desert, dense jungle and barren rock can offer nothing to colonists."

The General shook his head slowly as he lighted another cigarette. "At the moment no; but certain portions of them, in the hands of Italy, could be made to offer much. I give away no state secrets, but look at that map."

Glancing over his shoulder Lovelace saw a big map of Ethiopia pinned up on the wall. "Yes?" he said.

"You see Italian Somaliland to the south of Ogaden?" the General pointed with a thick finger. "That is a good country. It is hot but healthy and it has no disease-carrying insects; on the other hand, it has little water. Only certain sections of the river Juba flow all the year round and the Webi-Shebeli, which is much longer, becomes a mere trickle during the great heats. Look at the Webi-Shebeli again. It is *nearly two thousand miles in length*. If modern engineers could get to work upon it that river could be turned into another Nile and made to fertilise great tracts of territory; *but* two-thirds of it lie in Abyssinia."

"You need the upper reaches before you can build your dams and power stations?"

"Exactly. The whole of the Ogaden must come under the Italian flag. It is not only a question of the people we can settle on the land once it becomes fertile, but towns, roads, villages will need to be built and all the innumerable services necessary to a great modern community installed. At one stroke Italy will have solved her unemployment problem for two generations."

Lovelace nodded. "I see. The campaign in the north from Eritrea is only a feint then?"

The General smiled. "National *morale* demanded that we should avenge the catastrophe we suffered at Adowa as early in the war as possible. That naturally necessitated considerable concentrations of troops on the frontier of Eritrea."

Lovelace noted the smile and returned it. "The opinion of the experts among the neutrals was that you had decided to engage and defeat the trained army of the Emperor there in order to break his personal power, but that strategically those battles in the north were only staged to exhaust the enemy while your southern army advanced through the comparatively easy country of the Fafan Valley, gradually subdued Ogaden, captured Harar, and penetrated to the Jibuti-Addis Ababa railway."

The General's smile broadened into a grin. "The so-called experts said many things. For example, that our first action would be a terrific bombing raid on the railway where it crosses the Awash river in order to smash the bridges and cut Addis off from the outside world. Could any suggestion be more foolish? It would cost us millions of lire to build those bridges again and we shall need the railway for our own use immediately we have conquered the country."

It was obvious to Lovelace that the Italian did not mean to answer the really interesting question as to whether the Higher Command intended to attempt pushing their northern flying columns through from Dessye to the capital or if they would gradually subdue the country from the south as had always been predicted. He returned to wider spheres.

"I think it's a pity, sir, your real intentions about the Webi-Shebeli are not more widely known. Few people could fail to sympathise with your wish to turn a great slice of Africa from useless desert into fruitful farmlands but, from what you tell me, the troops are having a very bad time of it in spite of their victories. D'you think they'll stay the course?"

"There is no doubt of that," the General replied firmly. "The rains, which are due to start any day now, will mean further delay, of course, and conditions are appalling. Our soldiers fight, not only against a merciless enemy, who does not observe the decencies of war, but against heat-stroke, fever, sunburn, dysentery, shortage of water and even the wild animals which seem to be the allies of the Abyssinians; but our organisation is sound and they have confidence in their leaders together with the inspiration of a great national ideal. There has never been any question of our failing to achieve complete and final victory."

Christopher and several officers joined them at that moment so the talk became general. Orderlies carried round trays of Asti-Spumanti and the aromatic, sparkling wine made them disinclined for further serious conversation. A young officer began to strum upon an upright piano; soon a group was gathered round him singing the old songs of Italy and the newest importations from the States.

More Asti-Spumanti—more singing; for a little the war and its horrors were forgotten. The thought of that anxious hour at sundown, when those who were off duty gathered on the aerodrome each evening to count the chickens as they came home to roost and tried to thrust out of their minds the terrible fate which had probably overtaken the missing, was submerged in gaiety.

At one o'clock Valerie declared that if she was to make an early start in a few hours' time, so as to avoid the heat, she must really get to bed.

As she left with Christopher and Lovelace she carried away with her the hearts of a dozen handsome young exiles who might never see Italy again, and the sounds of a last, tremendous ovation followed them nearly back to the hospital.

Only Lieutenant Count Dolomenchi, for once bereft of his usual gaiety, saw them off as the dawn was breaking. He told them that the great attack of the southern armies had just been launched against Sasa Baneh which lay a little above the fork of the all-important Webi-Shebeli. Four and a half hours later they arrived at last in Addis Ababa.

CHAPTER XX

THE LAST BLACK EMPIRE

IF the irregular row of hangars which constituted the aerodrome at Addis Ababa seemed a toy by comparison with the great Italian base at Assab it certainly did not suffer from lack of personnel.

As the four-seater plane came to earth at least three hundred people ran across the open space towards it. Some were in the dirty white *shamas* of the country and others in khaki uniforms of European design, but nearly all were barefooted.

At first Lovelace would not let Valerie leave the plane because, although many of the uniformed men were driving back the crowd with hippopotamus-hide whips, the mob showed a sullen and, at times, vociferous hostility.

A white man arrived on the scene, however, and introduced himself as Henrick Heidenstam; a Swedish pilot in the Emperor's service. He told them that the war with Italy had caused the Abyssinians to develop an intense distrust of all Europeans—particularly those who came in planes, on account of the way in which the population had suffered from air-raids—but that they had no cause to be frightened. It was his duty to meet all arrivals at the airport and he was personally responsible to the Emperor for their safety. He then introduced a bearded, copper-coloured man as Ato Habte Worku; a chief of Customs.

Ato Habte Worku demanded fifty thalers landing-tax and, while Christopher paid him, sent his apparently numberless assistants to rummage the contents of the plane. Valerie handed over a cardboard box containing the clothes she had worn the previous night and Lovelace another which held their united washing and shaving tackle purchased in Assab. They were charged five thalers on the dress but the rest of their things were let in free. When the Customs men returned to report that there was no baggage in the plane, however, there ensued a most excited discussion in Amharic.

Lovelace told Heidenstam that they had been forced to come down in the desert and that robbers had made off with their luggage.

The Swede expressed surprise that they had succeeded in getting away with their lives but Ato Habte Worku was neither sympathetic nor interested. He said that since they had no luggage which he could tax they must pay another fifty thalers landing fee.

Christopher was about to protest at this flagrant injustice but Lovelace nudged him and told him to pay up; knowing that in Abyssinia there was no appeal against such arbitrary decisions on the part of government officials.

The passport officer, a one-eyed black, presented as Ato Wolde Rougis, now asked for their papers. He also had numerous assistants, and these, having glanced at the three passports, said that they were not in order.

What was to be done? Having visited Abyssinia before Lovelace knew the answer and promptly slipped five thalers into Ato Wolde Rougis's hand.

The black official took the bribe but shrugged and shook his head, evidently hoping to obtain a larger sum.

Lovelace knew there was nothing wrong with the passports and considered the tip enough; so he resorted to a trick and produced a document from his note-case which he carried for the purpose. It was a piece of thin vellum with Arabic characters inscribed upon it and a red ribbon attached from which dangled a large seal. The seal was actually a tin plaque lauding the virtues of a brand of Turkish cigarettes but the characters on it looked not unlike those on the vellum, which he had written himself.

"This," he said solemnly, "is the sealed warrant of Ibn' Saud, King of Arabia. The possession of it places myself and my friends above all suspicion. We are people of considerable importance."

With a far more respectful expression on his face Ato Wolde Rougis took the piece of vellum and pretended to read the characters, although it was obvious that he did not understand them. It was the red ribbon and the fine, tin seal which impressed his native mind and made him feel that it might be dangerous to blackmail such people in case, later, they did him some injury.

After a moment he said: "Why did you not show me this at once? It is all in order. I will not delay you further." But he did not offer to give back the money he had taken.

A third man now appeared. They did not catch his name but noticed that he did not rejoice in the title of *Ato*, or Mr. He had the plane run into a hangar and had to be given ten thalers for his trouble. Then, it seemed, they were free to leave the aerodrome.

Henrick Heidenstam took them over to a rickety car with a black chauffeur and, while the airport police kept back the sullen-looking mob, they drove off.

Three minutes later the car stopped outside a petrol station. Heidenstam smiled ruefully.

"I'm awfully sorry," he said. "This fellow's evidently run out of juice and you'll have to buy some if you want to go any further. This is a government car, you see, and one of their methods of getting petrol is to play this game on strangers. I'd buy some myself but I haven't been paid for months so I'm pretty hard up at the moment."

"Please don't worry—it's not your show." Christopher assured the Swede; but the man at the petrol station refused to supply him with less than a *tonika* of four-and-a-half gallons which cost another thirteen thalers, roughly one pound, and he was angered by this further imposition.

"What a racket," he exclaimed as they drove on. "Is all Addis Ababa as full of grafters as that airport?"

Heidenstam shrugged philosophically. "I'm afraid you'll find it so. Abyssinia's a lousy country. With the exception of the Emperor, who is a really wonderful little man, and about a dozen of his Europeanised helpers, there's hardly a native in the place one can respect. They have all the cunning and the greed of orientals but none of the Arabs' love of colour and gaiety and good living. It may be their particular brand of Christianity that gets them down. I don't know; anyhow all they seem to get from it is their morbid killjoy ways. It doesn't prevent them getting drunk or being unbelievably cruel and vicious. They're lazy too—lazy as hogs. You can never get anything done unless you go to the Emperor. Even the highest government officials constantly put you off with *Ishe-naga* which means, 'all right, but to-morrow,' or actually, 'come next week and I'll put you off again.'"

They were driving through well-wooded country with fields, rough gardens, and white, one-storied buildings dotted here and there between the patches of blue-gum trees.

"When shall we reach the city?" Valerie asked.

"We're in it now," Heidenstam replied. "Addis Ababa is a young town. It was started only fifty years ago because the wife of the old Emperor Menelik came and built a palace here. The Emperor followed her and it has grown until its 130,000 inhabitants have spread out over as big an area as Paris."

The white-walled, zinc-roofed houses became a little more frequent as they entered the European quarter. They pulled up outside a big building on a hill and Heidestam said: "This is the Hotel Imperial. There are others, but it's supposed to be the best, and you'll not be uncomfortable here. Also, you will be quite safe, so I shall leave you now. One of the Emperor's people will visit you this afternoon and tell you what you may or may not do during your stay. Haile Selassie is most anxious that all Europeans should be protected from any unpleasantness and, even though he's at the front now, his partisans continue to superintend visitors' arrangements personally in his absence."

They thanked the Swedish airman, who drove away with a cheerful wave of his hand. Lovelace then interviewed the Greek hotel proprietor. The results were far more satisfactory than they had hoped. Three good bedrooms, each with a private bath, were placed at their disposal, and it was promised that a sitting-room on the first floor should be reserved for their exclusive use.

Having viewed the rooms and parked their few belongings, they came downstairs again. Now that the excitement of their flight was over they felt chilly and depressed. Although it was still only mid-morning, a drink seemed the obvious remedy.

A square-faced, grey-moustached man and a red-headed youth were the only occupants of the bar. After ordering drinks Lovelace got into conversation with them. The elder was a Dutchman representing a firm of coffee merchants; the younger a Belgian adventurer who had come out hoping to secure a command in the Abyssinian Army when the regular officers loaned by his Government were officially recalled on the outbreak of war. As he possessed exceptional linguistic attainments, he had managed to get a job as interpreter at the Consular Court where justice was dispensed among alien nationals.

They soon informed the newcomers why it had been so easy to secure accommodation. From September to Christmas the hotel had been crammed from basement to attic with foreign correspondents, armament men, and every sort of shady white who hoped for good fishing in the troubled waters. But the armament people could not find anyone with the cash to buy their goods; the Press-men discovered that even the Abyssinian War Office knew nothing of what was going on at the front, and the job-seekers had found the inborn suspicion of the Abyssinians concerning the honesty of all whites too deeply rooted to be overcome. After three or four months of wasted time and money the editors had recalled their journalists, the munition pedlars had packed their samples, and the funds of most of the others had run out. The place was now two-thirds empty.

When Valerie remarked how surprising it was to find that every room in the hotel had a bath, they both laughed.

"It happens to be built next to a hot spring," the Belgian said. "It's the only place in Addis of its kind. Even the people in the legations come here for a bath once or twice a week. But the food is filthy and the prices extortionate. You would do better at the *Deutches Haus*."

Christopher asked if they had run across an elderly Armenian named Paxito Zarrif, during the last fortnight, but they shook their heads. Neither of them had even heard of him.

Lovelace inquired their opinion of the outcome of the war. They both began to talk at once, but the Belgian was more fluent and won the day. "In less than a week the rains will come. The Italians will be bogged; their communications will be cut, their leading troops will be massacred piecemeal and there will be a stalemate for six months. After that they will advance again, but the Emperor will have had time to reorganise his forces and secure fresh supplies of munitions. The Abyssinians all believe that the League will intervene before then, though, and that Britain will come in on their side. Anyhow, my job's safe for another year, at least."

"How about air-raids? Aren't the Italians making things pretty unpleasant here?"

The young man shook his fiery red head. "There was a great scare at first, but the Italian planes never seem to do much except reconnoitre. They bombed Harar and Dessye some time back, but only as a sort of demonstration, I imagine. They killed a few civilians, but they didn't do much damage. All sorts of nonsense has been written in the Press about their deliberate destruction of hospitals, and so on. That has occurred in isolated cases, but it's not deliberate. The red cross used to be the sign of a brothel in Abyssinia. It still is outside the principal towns. Directly the blacks learned that Europeans regarded it as immune from attack, they painted it on everything. You'll see thousands of red crosses plastered all over Addis."

Valerie shivered in her light, tropical clothes. Lovelace noticed it and said: "We need some more suitable kit. There's plenty of time before lunch. We'd better go out and buy it."

"Mohamedally," said the Dutchman. "That is the place for you to go. Anyone will tell you where to find it. Their store is the only one worth while in Addis, and they have branches all over the country."

Leaving their new friends lolling in the bar, as though time had no significance, they set off on foot to do their shopping.

It was a bright, sunny day, but the temperature seemed almost arctic after the stifling heat of Assab and Jibuti. As they trudged up the steep gradients they found themselves not only cold but oppressed and breathless.

"We should have taken a taxi," Lovelace said. "I'd forgotten that Europeans never walk more than a few hundred yards here. This place is 8,000 feet above sea-level, and that means a big strain on the heart."

They found Addis Ababa, or rather the small scattered European quarter, to be a place of staggering contrasts. Three-story, stone blocks rose, here and there, among a jumble of tin-roofed, brick bungalows and mud-walled huts thatched with straw. In the irregular open space that formed its centre delicatessen shops were selling luxury tinned foods, such as caviare and asparagus, imported from Europe, while before their doorsteps native women squatted, displaying for sale mouldy-looking fruit and vegetables, miserable little heaps of parched corn, and handfuls of red peppers.

There were two cinemas, two indifferent-looking cafés, the *Perroquet* and the *La Secret*. Khaki-clad, white-topee'd policemen at the junctions of the roads were laying about them with heavy, hippopotamus-hide whips—the only method, apparently, of driving the pedestrian population out of the way of the traffic, which was mostly composed of smart taxis driven with reckless speed by fuzzy-headed Abyssinians.

Mohamedally's store provided them with most of their requirements, all at fantastically expensive prices, but Christopher paid without a murmur. He was too cold and too worried about the necessity of finding Zarrif, now that they were at last in Addis, to argue.

He questioned the turbaned Indian who attended to them, and the policemen in the streets, without result. Lovelace took him by the elbow.

"Look here," he said, "you lost the ether pistol with which you meant to kill him when we were taken by the Danakils. We'll have to use ordinary automatics, and we must get another brace of those before we can do anything; even if we can find out where he's got to."

Christopher agreed, and they walked over to an oil-shop which displayed for sale a most extraordinary collection of weapons: scimitars that had possibly been used to lop off the limbs of Crusaders; poisoned spears such as the Mahdi carried when they surrounded General Gordon in Khartoum; ancient arquebuses which had been new when Cardinal Richelieu was beseiging La Rochelle; long-barrelled, beautifully-inlaid pieces from Arabia; wide-mouthed blunderbusses for firing handfuls of old nails; tenth-hand rifles made for a dozen wars of the last century, and, quite incongruously among these museum exhibits, a few modern automatics.

For a quarter of an hour they stood examining the goods among drums of paint and turpentine. Lovelace came away with a heavy, blue-barrelled Mauser, Christopher with an ultra-modern, snub-nosed, American automatic, Valerie with a small but handy Browning, and each had acquired as much ammunition for their weapons as they could carry without inconvenience.

Heavy fatigue still upon them, they carried their numerous parcels to a taxi and drove back to the hotel, where they changed into their new, ill-fitting, but warmer clothes.

At lunch they were given mutton, and Valerie commented upon it, as she had hardly tasted meat since they left Alexandria.

"I am glad that Madam is pleased," said the Eurasian head waiter brightly. "We have mutton every day."

"And nothing else," added Lovelace bitterly. "I remember that when I stayed in Addis for the Emperor's coronation."

They had coffee upstairs in their private sitting-room. Christopher returned at once to the necessity for finding Zarrif.

"Well, we're here at last," he said. "But d'you realise it's the 28th? We've only got two clear days left to work in. We've got to act quickly now or it'll be too late. Somehow we've got to run Zarrif to earth and fix him once for all. If we don't, the concession will go through, and you both know what that means."

"How about trying the United States Legation?" Lovelace suggested thoughtfully. "They must have a big staff here, and somebody there may be able to put us on to him."

"Splendid!" Christopher's dark eyes lit up with their old fanatic gleam. He turned to the door. "I'll go down and call them up now."

It was a long time before Christopher returned. He

was breathless and paler than ever from having run upstairs, but his handsome young face was alight with excitement.

"We're in luck," he panted. "Rudy Connolly is one of the secretaries at the Legation. He's a friend of mine. He's asked us out there to dine this evening. In the meantime he'll pump all his colleagues for us. One of them is certain to know where Zarrif's staying. Men like that can't hide themselves in a small place like this."

Sitting down, he put his hand up to his heavily pounding heart, and went on jerkily: "God! the telephone service here—you'd never believe it. They call the operator by name and have to ask after the health of his wife and family before he'll even consent to give you the first wrong number."

Lovelace grinned. "I know. It's a ragtime country, isn't it? If I were you, though, I'd take it easy. The height here plays the very devil with Europeans. Don't exert yourself more than you absolutely have to, and do everything you've got to do as slowly as you can. If you're feeling dicky, why not have a lie-down on your bed?"

"Good idea," Christopher panted, but at that moment a house-boy arrived to announce that Blatta Ingida Yohannes, a representative of the Emperor, was below and wished to see them.

"Ask him to come up," Lovelace said at once. Then he explained to the others that *Blatta* meant "wise" and was a civil title ranking one higher than *Ato*. It could be taken as Esquire; the next rank above it being *Kantiba*, or Knight.

The Abyssinian proved to be a pleasant young man dressed in European clothes. His hair was oiled back, his face clean-shaved, and he spoke French with an easy fluency.

His first request was rather surprising: he asked for news of the war; but he explained that communications with the fronts were so difficult that even the Emperor usually learnt of fresh movements, when he was in Addis Ababa, through reports brought in from the outside world by neutrals before he heard of them from his own commanders.

"We heard the Italians had opened a big attack at Sasa Baneh this morning," Lovelace informed him.

Blatta Ingida Yohannes smiled. "There they will break themselves against our "Hindenburg line". Many lion pits have been dug to trap their tanks. When these have fallen through the thin, earth-covered layers of sticks into the holes Ras Nasibu's men will overwhelm their infantry and wipe it out. What do they say in Jibuti of the fighting on our northern front?"

"We've heard nothing of that since they captured Dessye close on a fortnight ago."

The young coloured man shrugged his shoulders. "So that silly rumour still persists. We had it here ten days back, but it is false, of course—just one of the many propaganda lies that the Italians send out over their powerful wireless to try and hearten their troops in other sectors. You see, it is quite impossible, because the Emperor is still at Dessye."

Lovelace forebore to contradict him, although he had seen the Italians occupying the town itself from Count Dolomenchi's plane. He feared that the officials in Addis might become suspicious and troublesome if they knew their visitors had just spent some time as guests of the enemy. Spy mania was running high. Their movements might be restricted and the aeroplane seized. It was safer to allow it to be believed that they had come straight from Jibuti. "You feel that the war's going well for you, then?" he asked.

"It is difficult to say," the Abyssinian replied. "We know so little, only that it is certain we shall win in the end. The Italian casualties are far higher than they say, since we contest every inch of the ground, and every one of our soldiers is a crack marksman. Each night we raid their lines, too. They hate that. It is shaking their *morale* even worse than their air-raids are shaking the *morale* of our people. Every mile they penetrate, too, lengthens their lines of communication and makes them more vulnerable. Sooner or later they must collapse. It will happen quite suddenly one night. Then we will chase them out of our country. You will see."

"They won't collapse as long as they keep on sending out adequate reinforcements," Christopher said, "because you cannot possibly hope to beat them in a pitched battle owing to their complete supremacy in the air."

"No." The young Abyssinian gave him a sly glance. "You are right, perhaps, as long as the fighting is on the low levels with only an isolated mountain to be captured here and there; but wait until they reach the high ground. European airmen cannot fly day after day at fifteen thousand feet. Their hearts will give out in the rarefied atmosphere and they will be crashing all over the place. That is why they so seldom attempt an air-raid here. White people cannot even walk here in Addis without their hearts giving them trouble."

They knew that he was right. Every step they had taken since they arrived in the Abyssinian capital had seemed to cost them a special effort.

"You feel very confident of victory, then?" Valerie said.

"How can you doubt it when everybody knows that the British are coming to our assistance?"

"If they did it would mean another World War," Christopher said quickly.

"About that I do not know, but our situation is obvious. A few years ago the Emperor might have been willing to compromise with his powerful neighbour rather than risk a war which must mean much misery for his people whichever side was victorious. Since that time Abyssinia has been admitted to the League. What is the League for if not to protect small nations from aggression? Naturally, after that the Emperor would not consider any form of compromise. He knew that he could rely upon the League to maintain him in his just rights. The machinery at Geneva works slowly. We understand that; and we are perfectly willing to defend ourselves while Britain makes her preparations. But as the champion of the League she is bound to intervene on our behalf before very much longer. Many squadrons of her aeroplanes are already in Egypt waiting for the word to attack."

Valerie sighed. The whole world knew now that the League was a broken reed to lean upon, yet this man's faith in it was apparently unshakable and quite pathetic.

More coffee and liqueurs were sent for. Lovelace took advantage of the interruption to get Blatta Ingida Yohannes off the thorny subject of the League, and asked him about the Emperor.

The young man was one of the *Jeunesse d'Ethiopie*; the society of progressive Abyssinians. He spoke with real enthusiam of the Emperor's reforms, and sadly of how the westernisation of his country was being held up now for lack of funds because the Emperor was being compelled to spend every penny of his money on munitions for this wicked war that had been forced upon them.

Believing them to be ordinary tourists, he expressed great anxiety that they should see everything before they went away and leave with a good opinion of Abyssinia. He said that the Emperor received all visiting Europeans personally when he was in the capital, but in the Emperor's absence it was his duty to entertain them. To start with, he proposed a drive round the town that afternoon and that he should call for them again after dinner to take them to the cinema.

Christopher's face showed his anxiety lest their self-appointed guide would seriously embarrass their movements; but Valerie leaped into the breach by saying that they were all tired after their journey and feeling the effect of the high altitude; for the remainder of the afternoon they would prefer to rest. The evening was already disposed of by their arrangement to dine at the American Legation.

Blatta Ingida Yohannes accepted the situation, but insisted that he should call for them first thing on the following morning. He would take them to see the French and English schools where the children of the Abyssinian aristocracy were being educated on modern lines. In the meantime he would see about securing suitable personal servants for them, to look after them during their stay, and attach a special police guard to them in case they wished to walk in the town; but he begged that they would confine themselves to the European quarter.

The moment he had gone Christopher gave a despairing groan. "What with servants, and police guards, and that fellow hanging round us all the time, we'll never succeed in getting at Zarrif even if we can find him."

"We'll manage somehow," Lovelace said grimly. "These people have plenty of low cunning, but we whites have far better brains. It's not difficult to trick them, and I've been thinking, if we can't trace Zarrif through the American Legation we'll probably be able to get a line on him through his friend Ras Desoum. You go off and have your rest now; you're looking rotten."

"Yes, I feel it too. See you later, then."

As Christopher left the room Valerie looked across at Lovelace. "So we're off on this murder game again, it seems."

Lovelace gave her a quick glance and began to fiddle with a new pipe he had bought. "When Zarrif shot down your plane in the Danakil country he did it with the deliberate intention of murdering us all, so, quite apart from the fact that the *Millers of God* have ordered his execution, to my mind he deserves all we mean to give him."

"Yes—yes," she nodded wearily. "I know."

He stroked his small, upturned moustache and went on slowly: "You're not quite so keen now on this Crusade—as you used to term Christopher's mission—are you? It's a grim business and I've wished all along you were safely out of it. Listen, Valerie. Why not fly back to Jibuti this evening. We'll beg, borrow, or steal some reliable chap from one of the Legations to go with you."

She shook her head. "No. I can't leave Christopher—or you. When I think of my darling Count Dolomenchi and that nice young Abyssinian who was here just now, too, I am more certain than ever that anyone like Zarrif, who deliberately pulls the wires to make them wish to cut each other's throats, deserves death a hundred times. I'm just tired—that's all. When I've rested for a bit I'll feel better."

He realised that her affectionate mention of the Count implied no more than friendship, but all the same, as she made it, Lovelace was conscious of a little twinge of jealousy. She stood up and, as he watched her leave the room, he checked his thoughts sharply. He knew he had no right to think of her that way at all. She was Christopher's. Yet he wished, as he had never wished for anything in his life before, that she were free so that he could tell her how much he loved her.

That evening a car with two special guards picked them up and ran them out to the United States Legation. It was some way from the centre of the town and, like those of the other nations, stood in a fine, walled, private park on land which the Emperor had generously presented for the purpose.

Rudy Connolly received them with shouts of joy and introduced them to his colleagues. For Christopher and Valerie it was grand to find themselves among their own people again, and Lovelace was made equally welcome. It would have been a thoroughly delightful evening if each of them had not had to act a part and endeavour to conceal their secret anxieties.

They posed as tourists who, being in Egypt, had just flown up for a few days out of curiosity, to see Addis now that it played such a prominent part in the world's news.

When Christopher cornered Connolly after dinner, the diplomat said that, of course, he knew Paxito Zarrif by reputation, but he had heard nothing of his being in Addis. So far, inquiries among his friends had proved fruitless, but native spies had been put on the job and perhaps some information might come in the following day.

Connolly showed some professional reticence in speaking about the war. He admitted to knowing that the Italians were actually in Dessye, although the Abyssinians refused to acknowledge it; and said that as far as their own information went, the Emperor was with his troops somewhere between Addis and his old headquarters. Fresh levies were still moving through from the far west to his support, and it was thought that he would hold up the Italians at a point where the road dipped suddenly from the terrific heights of the Abyssinian central ranges to the fringe of the plains bordering the Danakil country.

"Are there any landing-places for aeroplanes on the Dessye road?" Christopher asked.

Connolly stared at him in surprise. "Good Lord, no! but why?"

"I'd like to go there. See a little of the fighting."

"I wouldn't try it if I were you. They won't let you, anyway, without a pass, and I don't think they'd grant you one for a second. The front's somewhere out there now, and they wouldn't even let a single newspaper man go within a hundred miles of the actual operations."

"Never mind. Say I *could* get a pass," Christopher went on doggedly. "How long would it take me to get there by road?"

"You could reach Dessye itself, if the road were open all the way, in about three days. That is, if the weather remains as it is at the moment, and given a good stout lorry with plenty of hired men to pull it out of the gulleys whenever it gets stuck. If the weather breaks, as it may now at any time, you might be ten days on the road, and once the rains have really set in it becomes quite impassable. Honestly, you'd be mad to attempt it. Even if you could get a pass and managed to get to the front all right, as the rains are due, you'd be caught there and unable to get back."

"Thanks," said Christopher. "I was only asking out of curiosity," and he turned the conversation into other channels.

When they were back in the hotel Christopher faced the others just as they were sitting down to a night-cap in their private room.

"Look here. I've thought it all out. Nobody but the Emperor can sign that concession, and he's still at the front; somewhere down the Dessye road. Zarrif must be with him at his new headquarters or on his way there. These Abyssinian officials are bribable, you say. Well, I don't care what it costs, but we've got to get a pass and reach the Emperor so that we're on hand to deal with Zarrif when he tries to do his stuff."

"But we can't use the plane for that," exclaimed Lovelace, "and to talk of covering a hundred miles of this ghastly country in two days any other way is sheer madness."

"I don't care," Christopher said tersely. "I'll buy a dozen lorries and leave each one as it gets stuck for another of the convoy, offering a big reward to the driver who gets through first. It's got to be done."

CHAPTER XXI

THE FLOWERING OF THE PASSION VINE

LOVELACE had warned the others that Blatta Ingida Yohannes would probably call for them at some godless hour next morning to take them sight-seeing. They were not surprised, therefore, to be knocked up at half-past five, but, when they met an hour later at breakfast, Valerie complained bitterly.

"Yes, filthy practice, isn't it?" Lovelace agreed. "But early rising is the custom here. The Emperor always holds his first Cabinet Meeting of the day at five o'clock, except when he has to propitiate his fanatical priesthood by being in church."

"We've got such a lot to do, and such a devil of a long way to go, we need every moment," Christopher said shortly. "These extra hours may prove invaluable."

"You mean to tackle Yohannes about a pass as soon as he turns up?" Lovelace asked.

"Yes, and if he can't give us one I'll bribe my way up from him to the fellow who can. Will you see about getting the lorries and staff for the journey? Don't spare money. I've got plenty. I brought it in case of just such an emergency as this."

"Here comes the young man," cut in Valerie.

Lovelace glanced over his shoulder. "By Jove! you're right, and he's only half-an-hour late. That's the height of punctuality for an Abyssinian."

The young, Europeanised native came hurrying towards them across the dining-room, a happy smile on his coffee-coloured countenance. He seemed bubbling over with some secret excitement which he found it hard to contain.

After greetings had been exchanged, Christopher came

out with his request at once. "Look here, I understand we have to get a pass to motor out towards Dessye; but I want one. Can you fix it for us?"

Yohannes gave him a quick furtive look. "Why should you wish to go there?"

"To see something of the front."

The Abyssinian shook his head. "That is impossible. It is forbidden."

Christopher hedged cleverly. "Well, it's not exactly the front we're interested in, but the Emperor. We're all tremendous admirers of the Emperor, and I'd pay a very high price indeed for the privilege of being allowed to offer him my sympathy in his troubles."

"Behold, then! your wish shall be granted." Blatta Ingida Yohannes spread out his thin hands and began to laugh uproariously. "I have just come from the Emperor. He returned last night from the front."

The reason for the young man's suppressed excitement was immediately apparent. Lovelace thanked his gods that they were to be spared the journey. For Christopher it was something of an anti-climax, but he was quick to realise the reason of the Emperor's return; he had come back to keep his appointment with Zarrif on the first of May. That meant that Zarrif was in Addis after all, or would certainly be there by the following day. Valerie, with the same thought in her mind, asked: "Why has the Emperor returned so unexpectedly?"

"Because the rains, which are expected so soon now, will put a stop to the fighting. He has summoned a council of his Rases for the day after to-morrow, doubtless to make arrangements for securing further supplies of munitions and training new bodies of troops through the rainy season. Directly he has a moment he will receive you. He has said so. In the meantime it is his wish that I should show you everything. Come! let us go."

They set off at once in Blatta Ingida Yohannes' car, which pulled up at the first filling-station. The

Abyssinian explained regretfully that he had forgotten to bring out any money, so Christopher, suppressing a smile at what Henrick Heiderstam had told them the day before of this Abyssinian custom, paid a pound for the usual four-and-a-half-gallon *tonika* of petrol. They then proceeded on their way through the hilly, well-wooded town, which had far more the appearance of an ill-planned suburb than of a capital city.

The War Office, when they passed it, proved to be, not as they might have expected a hive of activity, but a small, tumble-down, almost deserted building, and on Valerie remarking that it hardly looked as if a war was in progress at the moment, Blatta Ingida Yohannes shrugged indifferently.

"All power is centralised in the person of the Emperor, and he is so remarkable a man that he can dictate three letters to different secretaries at the same time. Each ministry has its office, but only for a few clerks; the Ministers are in constant attendance at the Palace, and it is there that every decision on even the most minor matters is taken. See, there it is upon the hill. That is Gibbi, where the Emperor lives and works when he is in Addis Ababa."

In the distance the Palace appeared little more than a rambling mass of buildings clustered upon a high mound which dominated the whole town. As they approached it, Blatta Ingida Yohannes pointed out the dome of the old Emperor Menelik's tomb, the long roof of the Audience Hall, and, between them, the present Emperor's Observation Tower; below these spread a higgledy-piggledy collection of roofs and courtyards sufficient to accommodate the population of a good-sized town. Thousands of white-robed or khaki-clad figures were in constant movement behind the palings which separated the first great court from the street. Here was the explanation of the deserted War Office; all the brain-power and nervous force of Abyssinia was concentrated in Gibbi.

A little further on they met a strange procession. It was headed by a big, black-bearded man, riding on a mule, and beneath an open umbrella which an attendant held over his head. His helmet, shoulders, knees and elbows were decorated with great tufts of lions' fur so that in the distance he had the appearance of some kind of animal. A nearer view, however, showed that the fur was sewn on to a frock-coat of rich brocade, laced with tarnished gold embroidery. Several sinister-looking necklaces dangled on his chest, and altogether he was an amazing spectacle of barbaric valour. Behind him there rode several hundred warriors, somewhat less spectacularly clad, then, in a ragged column, marched at least a thousand men and children, some of whom carried modern rifles, but most armed only with spears and cutlasses, slung, as is the Abyssinian fashion, at their right hips.

"That was the Dedjazmatch Maskassa," Blatta Ingida Yohannes remarked, as he steered his car round the tail-end of the column.

"Is he off to harass the Italians during the rains?" Lovelace asked, thinking of the contrast between this ill-equipped rabble, which must be a fair sample of the bulk of the Abyssinian forces, and a detachment of the smart European-trained Imperial Guard they had just passed outside the palace.

"Oh, no. The Emperor would like him to go, but cannot compel him, as he is one of our great feudal chieftains, and, for some reason of his own, he does not wish to take part in the war for the moment."

"What on earth was he doing with all those armed followers, then?" Christopher inquired.

Blatta Ingida Yohannes shrugged. "He had been to visit a friend, I expect, or is going to do a little shopping in the town. Whether you have five men or five thousand, it is still the custom here for your entire retinue to accompany you wherever you go. Only the younger members of good families who have been educated, like myself, have given up the practice as yet.

"I am hoping that you will lunch at my house to-day," he went on after a moment. "We go now to inspect the Menelik and Ras Makonnen Schools, but we will drive out there afterwards."

As he was virtually their host on behalf of the Emperor, no other course was open to them but to accept his invitation, and for the next four hours they had to hold their frayed nerves in check as well as possible while they visited the two schools which are the pride of the small progressive element in Abyssinia.

In the first all lessons were given in English, and in the second in French. The young pupils spoke these languages quite frequently, and asked a thousand questions of the visitors. The class-rooms, dormitories and kitchens were clean and orderly, the curriculums carefully thought out and on a par with the highest standards of modern European education. Christopher felt that these bright, happy, knowledgeable boys and girls were the living proof of what the Emperor could do if only he were given time, money, and peace; but Lovelace saw these schools for the children of the Abyssinian aristocracy in more correct proportion, as only two oases of civilisation in a vast wilderness of barbarism.

Each time they had to leave the car to walk round or mount flights of stairs they felt the strain on their hearts which ensued from the least effort at this great altitude. Ordinarily Valerie would have taken immense interest in all that she was seeing, but her acute anxiety about the immediate future was too great. Half the time she felt that she was talking sheer nonsense, through inability to concentrate her thoughts on anything but the terrible events that the next few hours might have in store for her, and the other half she was fighting to control her laboured breathing. Christopher, too, talked only in nervy, spasmodic bursts, being almost entirely occupied with his secret thoughts. Lovelace alone managed to maintain at least an outward appearance of calm, polite interest in the things they were being shown.

Afterwards, on their way to another quarter of the town, they passed several of the Legations: clusters of buildings like good-sized villages set in spacious, walled parks that the Emperor had presented to the foreign governments.

Blatta Ingida Yohannes pointed out a number of them and, driving on, arrived twenty minutes later at his house. It was a square bungalow with the usual array of huts and lean-tos about it; all enclosed by a high wall and separated from its neighbours by patches of partially cultivated ground shaded in places by blue-gums.

The house possessed only one reception room, but this its owner showed them with some pride. It was furnished with fumed oak of the variety obtainable from the cheaper shops in the Tottenham Court Road, but probably imported at very considerable expense. There were two long shelves of well-thumbed books, a relic of their host's student days, and a porcelain stove fitted in one corner as a gallant attempt to carry a French atmosphere into this benighted corner of Africa.

The effort was interesting but pathetic, for these European furnishings looked completely out of place, lacking, as they did, a natural background.

Two white-robed servants produced a meal, the principal course of which was *vod* with *intshera*, and Blatta Ingida Yohannes gave his visitors their first lesson in eating this staple Abyssinian dish. The *vod* was a highly seasoned stew and the *intshera* a kind of biscuity unleavened bread. The process consisted of breaking off a piece of *intshera*, then pouring some of the *vod* upon it and getting the resultant mess into one's mouth while spilling as little as possible.

Valerie was surprised that an apparently cultured man should think it amusing to teach his visitors to feed in such a disgusting manner, but Lovelace knew that if it had been their misfortune to have had to accept the hospitality of one of the old-school Abyssinian nobility they would have had to eat raw meat and show their appreciation afterwards by loud, and to Europeans offensive, noises.

The meal suffered an unexpected interruption. Bugles blew and klaxons suddenly sounded. It was an air-raid warning.

Everybody abandoned their food and ran out into the street. Six great, silver planes were sailing high above the town. They circled slowly, keeping perfect formation, divided, each turning in its own track, and then flew round again.

A few anti-aircraft guns opened up and did a little ineffective shooting. The scene was enlivened by a small company of ragged warriors evidently on their way to the front. They had dyed their *shamas* a pinkish brown in the muddy streams of the mountains through which they had passed, so as not to provide such an easy target for the Italian snipers, and each carried a small sack containing enough grain and dried meat to last him a month. The sight of the planes seemed to drive them into a frenzy. They waved their long sabres round and round their heads, screamed all the things they would do to the Italians when they got them, foamed at the mouth, and those who had guns let off their ancient pieces.

An officer on a bicycle dashed up to the leader of the rabble and began to expostulate angrily with him. As Yohannes informed his charges, the Emperor had given strict orders that ammunition was not to be wasted in such a senseless manner.

No bombs fell. The Italians flew off again towards Dessye, evidently content with photographing any new concentration of troops which might be forming in the area of the city.

"When shall we be able to see the Emperor?" Christopher asked when the meal was resumed. He liked the young Abyssinian; preferred him in many ways to the quick-witted, debonair Italian officers he had met at Assab, because he preferred simple to complex personalities and happened to be completely free of all colour prejudice, but they had not yet discovered where Zarrif was, and time was slipping by. Any excuse to break up this sight-seeing party must be utilised.

"*Ishe naga—ishe naga.*" Yohannes shrugged, snapping his strong white teeth into a raw paprika, which flamed red among the dessert. "To-morrow—the day after. What does it matter now that he has returned? He will be very occupied for a little, but he forgets nothing and will send for you in due time. Let us sit for a while in the garden, then I will take you to see the broadcasting station and our beautiful prison."

The garden proved to be a stockaded quadrangle boasting a dozen fruit trees, but completely devoid of flowers or grass. It was, in fact, a chicken run with the unusual addition of a family of goats, one of which was tethered to the trunk of each tree.

With the skinny fowls pecking the bare earth about their feet they lounged there, in faded deck chairs, for an hour. Yohannes kept up a happy monologue about the Emperor's plans for civilising his people; the others, while appearing to give polite attention, were fretting to get away but quite unable to think of any plausible reason that they could give for their presence being instantly required elsewhere in Addis.

In due course, still inwardly fuming, they were driven to see the broadcasting station. It was a fine building but quite deserted. Those treacherous Italians had built it, Yohannes explained, with a view to jamming the Abyssinian Government's own station when the trouble came. Naturally they had to be dispossessed, but they had taken certain vital parts of the mechanism with them, so no one could use it, and the Abyssinians had to remain content with their own less powerful station.

The prison, like many other hastily begun buildings in Addis, was still unfinished. It would be very fine and beautifully sanitary when it was done, no doubt, the visitors agreed. In the meantime, Yohannes declared angrily, all the workmen who were engaged upon it had had to go off to this wicked war.

Valerie and Christopher were duly sympathetic, but Lovelace knew that the whole thing was a deliberate deception got up to pander to the sympathies of the League of Nations. Five years before he had managed to get into one of the real prisons, a courtyard surrounded with rows of cages where the wretched malefactors, often only imprisoned for debt, lived in an unbelievable state of filth and horror. Chained in pairs, or sometimes singly, with just enough loose chain to enable them to crawl out into the main courtyard, they were entirely dependent for food on what their relatives chose to bring, and were dying by the score of typhus. That the same thing was still going on he had little doubt, as Yohannes refused his request to take them to see some of the prisoners who would occupy these delightful modern premises when completed.

At last they got back to the hotel, but still they could not shake off Blatta Ingida Yohannes. He proposed to dine with them and take them to see something of the night life of Addis later.

While Lovelace and Valerie entertained the pleasant, but unwelcome, guest to drinks, Christopher telephoned to the American Legation.

On his return he told Lovelace, in an aside, that Connolly had no definite news but that some white guests were believed to be staying in Ras Desoum's palace. He was having the place watched and would report further late that evening or early the following morning. It seemed that there was nothing more they could do for the moment.

Christopher engaged Blatta Ingida Yohannes for a few moments during which Lovelace was able to pass on the news to Valerie.

"All right," she said. "If we've got a respite in this

hellish business, let's enjoy ourselves. Our host's a terribly nice little man in his way. After we've had dinner we'll go round the town with him and try to forget what we're here for."

Lovelace shook his head. "I don't think you'll like it. The films at the cinemas are six-reel melodramas, and the two bars are the sort of places I think you'd find it rather embarrassing to be in. The native quarter's ruled out, anyway, as quite impossible for you to visit at any time."

"Did you see most of these places when you were here before?" she asked.

"Yes. I went round with a few friends and I've rarely spent a more boring evening. The few French jazz dance-bars are more dreary than anything you could find in provincial England, and the native high spots are terrible. There's nothing to drink except *tetch*, that sickly kind of honey wine we had for lunch, or *talla*, which tastes like bad beer; nothing to listen to except tuneless native music; and nothing to look at, as, from some strange prudery, the Abyssinian women remain sedate and clothed up to their necks even in these haunts of vice and squalor."

"In that case I'd much rather not go," Valerie agreed. "We'll wriggle out of it somehow."

Valerie now occupied the attention of Yohannes for a little, while Lovelace held a brief consultation with Christopher.

"If it's as you say, she'd best not go," Christopher said at once. "But I'm worried; worried out of my wits. We've lost a day—*a whole day*—doing nothing. If I stay here all evening I'll go crazy. Besides if none of us goes the boy-friend will think it funny. Someone's got to stand by the wire in case a message comes through from the Legation. Will you do that, and keep Valerie company, while I go round the town with him? There's just a chance I might hear something of Zarrif in one of these places."

As they went in to dinner Yohannes suddenly remembered the servants he had engaged for them but these were found to be still squatting patiently upon the steps of the hotel, where they had been waiting for the last twelve hours. The troop consisted of two Gallas, a hunchbacked Shoan, and a gentle-eyed Mohammedan Harari who was to act as their interpreter. Lovelace gave them some money, as an earnest of good faith, and dismissed them all until the following morning.

For dinner they ate mutton again but the excellent coffee made up somewhat for the poorness of the meal. Afterwards Christopher went off as arranged with Yohannes while Lovelace and Valerie returned to their private sitting-room.

It was cold now. The temperature had fallen at least forty degrees, as it does each night in the Abyssinian highlands. They were glad of the bottle of fake Chartreuse which stood on the table before them; even if it was poor stuff it at least sent a fresh glow of warmth through their bodies.

For half an hour they talked of trivialities and he had been speaking of the first journey East of Suez that he had ever made when she said:

"Tell me more about yourself, Anthony. You've visited so many strange places yet it doesn't seem to have altered you a little bit."

"From what?" he asked curiously.

"Oh, I don't know, somehow you seem as though you must always have been lean and brown and tall and very attractive, but rather silent, and a little cynical; as though nothing had ever touched you very deeply."

"No," he smiled. "You were thinking I hadn't changed much from that time I can't remember when we met years ago."

"Nonsense," she said airily. "I've already told you that was in some previous existence, although you won't believe me. I want you to tell me what you've been doing in this one."

He stared at her hard for a moment, shrugged, and began to tell her of his past. Usually he was rather reticent about his adventures but with her he talked easily and well; just as though they had been intimate friends for many years.

Outside, the Abyssinian night grew blacker. Below, the watchmen, who were there to drive off the hyenas, sang their tuneless chorus. Time drifted on, the clock struck nine, ten, eleven without their noticing it. All thought of the strange and dangerous adventure into which they had been drawn had left them. They were completely happy in each other's company.

It was Lovelace who, at last, suggested it was time for her to get to bed because Blatta Ingida Yohannes would probably be calling for them at the same ungodly hour again next morning.

"I'm not in the least tired," she said as she stood up reluctantly. "This evening's been a little oasis of delight, Anthony, in a desert of dread and distress. I suppose we must think of to-morrow though, so I'll go to bed now, although my brain is much too active for sleep yet. I'll read for a bit I think."

As she spoke she picked up a magazine which someone had left on a side table. It was a nine-months-old copy of *Country Life*.

He stood beside her as she flicked carelessly through the pages. For a second she paused at an article on Mazes in famous English gardens; then she made a move to pass on but he exclaimed: "One moment!" and seized her hand.

His eye had caught a photograph of the maze at his own home, Fronds Court in Yorkshire. In his mind's eye he saw it again as he had seen it so often—with all its yew hedges trim and orderly—but he saw something else as well. He knew now where he had met Valerie before.

She glanced up at him and the change in his expression

must have given him away, for she said softly: "You've guessed at last—haven't you?"

"Yes," he said slowly, and in a fraction of time he lived again that long past moment of a summer afternoon. The gardens at Fronds had been thrown open for a charity. That was why, wanting to be alone, he had gone into the maze. Lost in its intricate turnings he had found a little girl of fourteen or fifteen, with great, grey eyes and chestnut hair done up in pigtails. She had come racing towards him near tears with distress at not being able to find her way out. He had told her it was a two-hundred-year-old custom that anyone lost in the maze should pay a forfeit if they wished to be led out of it and, upon her agreeing, laughingly demanded a kiss. At first she had refused but, when he had insisted, instead of the childish peck on the cheek he had expected, to his immense surprise the little girl had solemnly reached up her arms, placed them about his neck and kissed him full and hard upon the mouth. As he had led her outward along the green-walled, twisting paths she had told him shyly that she had never kissed anyone like that before and that those sort of kisses were sacred things. He had felt a little bewildered, and a little ashamed, but he had found her parents for her and they had all driven away in a big Rolls-Royce to York, where they were spending the week-end while doing a motoring tour of England.

The episode of that serious child had troubled him a little for a few days before it had slipped from his memory; to return now as clearly as if it had occurred only the day before.

His brown eyes met Valerie's grey ones. She raised her arms and, after a dozen years, he felt them around his neck again. Before he realised what he was doing he had clasped her to him and her soft lips had melted into his.

Suddenly she threw back her head and sobbed:

"Oh, we're a couple of beastly rotten cads—but we can't help it, darling—can we ?"

"No," he said, "no. I've never loved anyone before, but I love you, Valerie—and it's hell that it should happen like this—yet I can't help it." With all the pent-up passion of years he pressed his lips on hers again just as Christopher entered the room.

CHAPTER XXII

THE KING OF KINGS GOES BY

A HEAVY banging on her door roused Valerie at half-past five the following morning and she heard the Greek hotel porter call out; "Blatta Ingida Yohannes has telephoned, lady—he will be here at six." It was the same formula as that with which she had been roused on the previous day.

After a second she realised that she was in Addis Ababa and the awful scene of the night before came sharply back to her. Christopher's demoniacal rage when he had returned from his round of the town to find her in Anthony Lovelace's arms and their long, bitter wrangle afterwards.

It seemed as if he had kept her up half the night and that for the other half she had tossed a sleepless prey to shame and misery. Her mouth was parched and, as she crawled out of bed, she knew that a splitting headache was starting.

Her mirror was no comfort. It showed her smooth chestnut hair tangled and tumbled from her restless night, dark circles under the big grey eyes which stared back at her, and that the climate was playing the very devil with her complexion. Hastily she began to dab on a coat of soothing oil.

The thought of another sightseeing expedition appalled her. As if it wasn't enough that she would have to handle Christopher and Lovelace with extreme diplomacy, that all three of them were engaged on a secret man-hunt which might become an open attempt at assassination within the next twenty-four hours, without having to exhaust herself making polite conversation with the young Abyssinian while they trudged round schools and hospitals.

She began to brush her hair vigorously while she thought over the wretched business that had occurred the night before. Lovelace ought not to have kissed her. He had known from the moment they had met just a month ago, back in the States that she was engaged to Christopher. But had he kissed her? Yes, afterwards, as though he never meant to stop; but she had kissed him first.

Valerie was completely honest with herself. She adored the lanky, brown-faced Englishman; always had, ever since that day long ago when he had made her give him a kiss as a forfeit before showing her the way out of the maze at his lovely old home in Yorkshire. How strange that he should have forgotten it until the night before; yet not strange really as he was already a full-grown man whereas she had been only a little girl with pigtails and a short frock. She had been obsessed with the thought of him for months afterwards, made him her dream-hero, and woven a thousand romances round his tall, loosely-knit figure. It had never occurred to her then that she was being disloyal to Christopher because, in those days, she looked on Christopher as a brother. She wondered now if she had ever really thought of him in any other way. She loved him, had done so as long as she could remember, because of his gentleness and his chivalry and his devastatingly good looks. Later, fascinated by his passionate idealism and touched by his pathetically impractical nature, she had begun to mother him as well, until her admiration and affection for him had led her to believe that she was blessed beyond measure in that he had never cared for anyone but her, and that their marriage could not possibly fail to be a happy one.

Now, that vision of peace and security had been shattered. It had been shaken the very second she came face to face with Lovelace again, for she knew him instantly, and during this month that they had been together his presence had fired in her that positive passion so utterly different from her deep, calm affection for Christopher. Last night her secret feelings had proved too strong for her, the barriers had gone down, and in that wonderful moment of revelation she knew what she had been suspecting for days past: he loved her with the same fierce, possessive passion as that which she felt for him.

Yet she felt sick, miserable and utterly ashamed. She did not wonder at Christopher's white-hot anger when he found them, or that he had abused both her and Lovelace in terms that made them wince. To find the friend whom he admired and trusted and his fiancée, whom he had loved all his life, literally in each other's arms must have been an appalling shock; and he knew nothing of that fateful episode which had established a bond between them a dozen years before.

Lovelace had behaved wonderfully, she thought; but only as she would have expected him to. He took all the blame upon himself, made no excuses, and asked her if she would prefer him to remain or go. Frightened that Christopher might actually attack him she had said she would rather he went to bed and that they would talk things over in the morning. After that she had had to face Christopher's wrath alone.

For an hour he had raved up and down, white-faced and glowering, lashing her with his tongue in so fierce a way that she would have far preferred a physical beating. She did not resent it, feeling that he had the right to do so, and it at least gave her time to make a decision upon the awful problem which faced her; to tell him the truth, that she really loved Lovelace, which would shatter him utterly, or bear with him until she won him round to the belief that she had only been guilty of one of those absurd, unreasoned impulses which carry away both men and women at times and are thought of afterwards only with shame and regret.

While his anger lasted the impulse was strong in her to make a break, tell him the truth however much it hurt, and ask him to release her from her engagement; but suddenly his fury abated and he had sunk down beside her clutching at her knees and moaning, "How could you, Valerie!—Oh, how could you?"

Now, as she bathed her tired eyes, she could feel again on her finger-tips his dark tumbled hair as she had stroked it very gently and begged his forgiveness.

He had cried then until she thought that he was never going to stop. If she could have cried with him he might have ceased in order to comfort her but she could not. She sat there dry-eyed and desperate; praying as she had never prayed for anything in her life before that the ordeal would soon be over that she might get to bed and be alone with her misery.

She no longer had the heart to tell him the truth. She could only repeat again and again that it wasn't Lovelace's fault or premeditated in any way. That there was no affair between them; that it had just been a sudden impulse on her part such as came to every woman at times, to test her powers of attraction; and that he must believe her promise that nothing of the sort should ever occur again.

For a time Christopher had accepted that but then he had begun to torture himself about the past. When she had been making her record-breaking flights she had travelled over half the world. She must have met innumerable men. Hadn't some of them made love to her? She was good-looking, famous, unchaperoned. They must have! How many of them had kissed her—or tried to—and when and where?

In vain she protested that although lots of men had taken her out to dine or dance and had often tried to flirt with her there had been nothing—nothing—nothing to which he could object between her and any of them, yet, in view of what he had seen that night, he simply would not believe her.

Eventually, in order to try and satisfy him, she had been forced to relate a few brief episodes in which she had allowed men to make mild love to her; but very soon she repented of it.

He had demanded details—details—details. What did they look like? What had they said? How far had they gone? That nightmare cross-examination had been painful and humiliating to a degree.

When he had utterly exhausted himself and her he had suddenly seemed to get a grip on himself again, apologised for his behaviour and declared that he knew such impulses came to other people, yet had believed both of them to be different. Now he saw that he alone must be abnormal. He accepted her statement that Lovelace was not to blame and said that they must forget the whole matter; wipe it from their minds as though it had never happened.

It was then he had told her that on returning to the hotel he had found a note waiting for him. Rudy Connolly had found out about Zarrif. He was lying low at the house of his friend Ras Desoum. First thing in the morning they must make their arrangements to get at him.

At last she had been able to drag herself off to her room. There she had found a note from Lovelace pinned to her pillow. It said:

"My dear, I could not have concealed my love for you much longer, and, given the chance, I'd move heaven and earth to make you really *care for me—but you're not free—and so my hands are tied.*

All I seem to have done is to place you in a wretchedly awkward position by taking advantage of that sudden resurrection of an old memory, which we shared, to-night. Christopher must have suffered a rotten shock but, knowing you so well, he'll soon come to accept the fact that I mean nothing to you really.

It is I really who have to pay the price of having

broken into heaven by now being barred out. I'll leave to-morrow, or remain to see the Zarrif business through, just as you wish.

Anthony Lovelace.

Although she longed to keep it she had forced herself to tear his letter up. She scribbled a reply which she pushed under Lovelace's door, returned to her own room, shed her clothes and, bursting into a torrent of tears, crept into bed.

Now, as she dressed, she wondered miserably how this fateful day would end. It was the 30th of April. To-morrow, the concession which would provide funds to strengthen Abyssinia for next year's campaign and give opportunity for involving the whole of Europe in a ghastly struggle, would be signed—unless Christopher killed Zarrif first. If Christopher and Lovelace were caught either before or after the attempt they would be dead by evening and she, probably, under arrest for complicity in a plot to assassinate the Armenian financier. In this terrible secret war the *Millers of God* were waging in their effort to bring permanent peace to the world there would be no mercy on either side.

Valerie knew the best she could hope for was that Lovelace would prevent Christopher throwing his life away through some rash and ill-considered plan. After that it would be on the knees of the gods whether they could reach her at the aerodrome in order that she could fly them out of the country. Even if they succeeded in escaping she would now have to say good-bye once and for all to Lovelace to-morrow; having found him again and just learned that he loved her, after all these years. As she went downstairs she wondered if ever a girl had been placed, through no fault of her own, in a more wretched situation.

Christopher met her in the hall. To her immense relief he showed no sign that anything unusual had occurred between them, greeted her cheerfully and, taking her arm, shepherded her into the .dining-room.

Lovelace was already seated at breakfast, his tanned face an impassive mask as he waited to see if they would join him or go to another table. On their approach he stood up and said, "Good morning."

"Not so good to be dug out of bed at this hour, is it?" Christopher smiled as he sat down and, although she knew well that once he had given his word he never broke it, Valerie felt desperately grateful to him for acting with such perfect normality.

Now the ice was broken Lovelace took up the cue: "Any news from the American Legation yet?"

"Yes," Christopher replied in a low voice. "There was a note waiting for me when I got in last night. Rudy Connolly had found out about Zarrif for me. He's there all right and staying with his friend, Ras Desoum."

"Are the others with him?"

"They are. Eleven of them I'm told. That obviously includes secretary Cassalis and the six gunmen. The others'll be his pilots and servants. It looks as though we shall be up against the whole bunch and Ras Desoum's men into the bargain."

Lovelace grimaced. "Not so easy, and we've only only got twenty-four hours, at the outside, to work in. It seems almost impossible to plan an attempt in that time which'll give us any chance of getting out alive."

"We've got to risk our own necks, at least I have." Christopher's face was white and set again.

"Oh, I'm coming too," Lovelace volunteered with a cheerfulness he was far from feeling.

"It's decent of you to offer—but this is my job—not yours. I'd much rather you stayed behind to take care of Valerie in case anything goes wrong—with me."

Lovelace shook his head. "No," he said. "I still

don't grant you that the *Millers* have the right to slay, however just their cause, but I haven't forgotten my vow of vengeance on Zarrif for the way he shot Valerie's plane down in the Danakil country. You can't involve your Legation in this so we'll leave her in the care of that nice Swedish airpilot who's in the Emperor's service. Henrick Heidenstam—wasn't that his name? If things go wrong he can place her under your friend Connolly's protection later. We're in this together and our first move is to find out where Ras Desoum is living."

"Connolly told me the Ras has a castle in the north end of the town," said Christopher quickly. "I was hoping we might give Blatta Ingida Yohannes the slip this morning and go out there to have a look at it."

"Better not," Lovelace demurred. "It's the very devil we should have to tag around with this chap when time's so precious, but European visitors are so few here, and it's the Emperor's order we should be shown the sights. They're terribly suspicious of all whites, too, so if we go off on our own they'd immediatly jump to the conclusion that we were spies. Within half an hour the police in Addis would be after us and that's the last thing we want."

"Can't we possibly think of an excuse to get rid of him," Valerie urged, "pretend we've all got food-poisoning or something?"

"We might try that later but if we do it means we'll have to stay in the hotel. At the moment we want to get out and see this Ras's place. I see no reason, though, why we shouldn't get Yohannes to take us there."

The red-headed Belgian whom they had met on first arriving at the hotel came over to them. "Have you heard any rumours?" he asked in a low voice.

"No," replied Christopher. "Why?"

"It is said the reason for the Emperor's return to Addis is that his troops broke; and that the Italians have already covered half the distance from Dessye. It may be completely untrue but I wondered if you'd heard anything. It's queer that he should have returned practically alone and I'm told he had to send for a car to meet him a few miles outside the town."

Lovelace shrugged. "He'd hardly be likely to bring a lot of his troops back with him when every man is wanted in the firing-line; and with such bad roads the older methods of travel are nearly as fast and much more comfortable. Still, if a story like that's running round I wonder there hasn't been a panic."

"So many wild rumours have proved false in the last six months that the people don't take much notice of them any more. That the Emperor has called an Assembly of his Rases for to-morrow, too, is enough to allay any anxiety for the moment."

"Say his army has been routed and the Italians manage to push right on to Addis. That will mean the end of the war, won't it?" asked Valerie.

The Belgian laughed. "Dear me, no, Mademoiselle, only the end of my job. The real capital of Abyssinia is not Addis but wherever the Emperor is. He'd just retreat into the mountains of the west until he'd had time to rally his forces."

The arrival of the young Abyssinian put an end to the discussion. After greeting them cheerfully he said that the Emperor was making an inspection of the military college that morning and wished them to be present. They must leave at once.

As they drove out to Oletta, where the officer's school was situated, Lovelace questioned their guide about the rumour.

"It is true the Emperor returned from the front with only a few retainers and on mule-back," Yohannes admitted, "but that was because he wished to travel by short cuts through the mountains and thus avoid demonstrations of loyalty on the way which would have delayed him. As for this tale that his regular army has been defeated, it is absurd. It has not yet been engaged in any serious action. The Emperor has come back to Addis only to make an announcement to his Rases of his plans for the coming months."

Christopher thought he could guess what that announcement was to be. That, in return for a sweeping concession over all Abyssinian oil and mineral rights, many millions of pounds' worth of munitions would be forthcoming from Europe which would enable them to fight the Italians on more equal terms by the opening of next year's campaign.

"What would happen if the Italians did reach Addis?" Valerie asked.

Blatta Ingida Yohannes smiled. "They would find themselves in a pretty mess. What would the good of the city be to them once we had removed our stores? And how, please, would they feed themselves through all the long months of the rains? The road becomes impassable in fifty places between here and Dessye. They could not bring up either reinforcements or supplies except by air. We should harass them from the surrounding mountains until they surrendered."

"It would be a big loss to your prestige if they captured Addis, though." Lovelace insisted. "Don't you think the Emperor might think it better then, to come to terms?"

"No, no. He would agree to no peace except through the League and in whatever part of Abyssinia he made his headquarters, that would be the new capital."

"What would happen if he was killed fighting, or in an air-raid?"

"Ah, that would be different. Abyssinia without Haile Selassie would be like a body from which the head has been cut off."

Shortly afterwards they arrived at the Military Academy and pulled up at the side of a barrack square where numerous companies of natives were drilling.

To their amazement they found that these cadets, who were to officer the armies in a few months' time, averaged no more than fifteen years of age; but Blatta Ingida Yohannes explained that his countrymen reached maturity early and experience had proved them to make first-class soldiers when still in their teens.

The young soldiers performed various evolutions with speed and precision at the orders of their Belgian instructor officers. They were all in smart new uniforms and carried modern rifles, in fact they differed in appearance from the O.T.C. of an English public school only in their black or coffee-coloured faces, and the point that their uniforms ended at their ankles. The soles of Abyssinian feet have been inured to rocky ground for generations, and, as yet, only the Emperor's immediate entourage have submitted to the acute discomfort imposed by the wearing of boots.

As she watched them drilling Valerie's thoughts were taken, for a moment, from her own gnawing anxieties. Unless the war was stopped these children would be flung into the battle in a few short weeks. How could they hope to stand against the Italians and all those vast stores of modern death-dealing equipment which she had seen at Assab and Massawa. It would be sheer massacre and her heart bled for them.

News travels fast in Addis Ababa and it was now evidently common knowledge that the Emperor was expected at the Military Academy, since a big crowd was collecting. As they eddied round the car, which Blatta Ingida Yohannes had driven on to the parade ground, they cast lowering looks at the Europeans, and some of them began to make hostile murmurs.

A booted officer of the Abyssinian Imperial Guard, with tufts of lion fur in his hat and on his epaulettes, noticed them from some way away, came over, ordered back the crowd, and asked the visitors to descend and take up their position in a cleared space near the College building.

They waited there for what seemed an endless time, making polite conversation with Blatta Ingida Yohannes, yet each harried by their secret thoughts of the reason for their presence there, their private miseries, and the terrible work which was to come. The cadets continued their drill without the least sign of fatigue from heart-strain in the now strong sun.

At last there was a murmur in the distance. It swelled and grew into a roar of salutation. The crowd gesticulated wildly and began to shout, "*Habet! Habet! Dshanhoi!*" A Rolls-Royce, surrounded by police and running footmen, who drove back the too enthusiastic mob with their long whips, entered the parade ground. As it drew up a small, erect figure descended from it. The Emperor had arrived.

He wore the undistinguished garb common to the aristocrats of his country; a white *shama* with the ugly black cape of nobility over it, which looked like a bicycling waterproof and was, perhaps, originally designed as a protection from the unceasing rains which stream down on Abyssinia for so considerable a portion of the year. Yet there was no mistaking him for anyone but Haile Selassie, the Lion of Judah.

The band struck up. The cadets presented arms. Lovelace and Christopher removed their topees and Valerie curtsied as he passed within a dozen yards of them on his way to the inspection. He looked full at them for a moment and acknowledged their gestures by a grave inclination of the head.

Valerie thought that she had never seen a sadder face or one more beautiful in sorrow. His big dark eyes held pride and fearlessness; yet something else which she could not quite analyse. Christopher read the deeper meaning of that glance; it was reproach.

Christopher understood the thought behind it as clearly as if the Emperor had spoken and said, "I know that you Europeans despise my people because they eat their meat raw, but a backward race cannot be educated by merely passing a few Acts of Parliament. It will take three generations to civilise Abyssinia but if the Italians had only left me alone for even one I could have set my people on the road from which there would have been no turning back. As it is they have compelled me to abandon my most cherished projects because every penny that I possess must now be squandered on this war they have forced upon me. And you other white men are no better than the Italians. Your rotten little politicians lied to me about the power of their futile League, urged me to resist the Italian demands, and now they are afraid. Yes, afraid to the depths of their rotten little souls to help me defend my people from massacre by poison gas and high explosives."

A wave of shame swept over Christopher. For the moment he forgot that only a few days before he had narrowly escaped mutilation and murder at the hands of the Emperor's subjects—forgot the Italians' plans to turn the Ogaden deserts into fertile farmlands and sweep away a thousand barbarous abuses—forgot the greedy Customs officials at the airport and the hyenas that still made the streets of Addis Ababa dangerous by night. He only burned with indignation at those thoughts which he felt the Emperor had transferred to him in that one long glance and understood how profoundly the lonely, cultured ruler must despise the white races for their treachery and weak vacillation. They had stolen the very jewels for his crown when it was made in Europe and had substituted bits of glass thinking he would not know. Apart from the Red Cross and relief people there was hardly a white in Addis Ababa who had come out during the war to give disinterested help. They all scented jobs or easy money and would rob him of the last thalers in his coffers for dud munitions if he did not defend himself with his wits as well as his courage.

Christopher's slender hands clenched and unclenched themselves spasmodically. He could not help the

Emperor, he could not stop the war, but he could prevent it spreading. The *Millers of God* were right beyond quibble or question. Their cause was a sacred one and he, as their instrument, would not fail them. Before another dawn came to gild the zinc roofs of Addis Ababa he would have killed Paxito Zarrif or have given his own life in an attempt to do so.

CHAPTER XXIII

PREPARATIONS TO KILL AND RUN

THE inspection was over, the Emperor gone, and the crowds in their dirty white *shamas* were melting away again. Valerie caught a last glimpse of the green, gold and red flag of Abyssinia fluttering so bravely over the Military College, then it was hidden by a group of blue-gum trees as they sped back to the centre of Addis Ababa in Yohannes' car.

Owing to the early hour at which they had started the morning was still only half spent, yet Lovelace was conscious of a growing anxiety as the time slipped away. They had formulated no plan as yet for their attack on Zarrif and had not even had an opportunity to reconnoitre the place where the Armenian was staying. Much thought and careful preparation would be necessary if he and Christopher were to stand any chance of pulling off this horrrible job and getting away safely afterwards. Lovelace was no fanatic and, although he felt that he must go through with the ghastly business now, he was determined to take every possible precaution which would give them the least hope of escaping with their lives. In a casual voice he asked Blatta Ingida Yohannes, "Do you happen to know Ras Desoum?"

"Oh, yes," the Abyssinian nodded. "He is one of the younger Rases; an able man who sometimes assists the Emperor in financial matters. He was educated in France but perhaps over-educated in some ways for he is not very popular among us."

"He has a castle on the north side of the town, hasn't he?"

"Yes. It is near my own home."

"I wonder if you'd mind driving us out there. I should rather like to see it."

"There is very little to see," Yohannes replied, glancing at him with some surprise, "but I will do so if you wish."

Twenty minutes later they pulled up in front of a wide-spread rabbit-warren of low-roofed buildings, encircled by a wall, which abutted on the road. "This is Ras Desoum's castle," said Yohannes.

"*Castle!*" echoed Christopher in amazement.

The Abyssinian grinned all over his dark, cheerful face. "Yes. Any building which has three courtyards in this country is a castle. As you know the Ras, perhaps you would like me to see if he is at home?"

"No, please don't trouble," Lovelace interposed quickly. "We don't know him; only a friend of his whom he knew while he was in Paris. We'll write him a line perhaps and ask if we may call in a few days time."

As he spoke Lovelace was thinking of the grim visit they intended to pay there before the night was out and his lazy, brown eyes were seeking to memorise everything possible about the ragged tangle of courts and structures. The place was rather like a miniature of Gibbi, the Emperor's Palace. Through the open gates he could see natives swarming in the first court and passing in and out of long rows of squalid hutments which lined the walls. Further away a few higher roofs indicated more modern one-story buildings and at one spot there was a small watch-tower.

Yohannes drove on again. "As you do not wish to make a visit here," he said, "I will take you now to one of the most beautiful of our old churches."

His companions would have given much to escape this fresh excursion but there was no possible means by which they could do so.

The church proved to be a gloomy, domed building something after the style of a mosque but lacking minarets. Its interior was dark and smelly. A number of incredibly dirty-looking priests squatted about telling their beads. The whole place reeked with decay and semi-pagan superstition.

There were a few mosaics showing scenes from the life of Christ in which the figures had the big heads, great, staring, almond-shaped eyes, and thin, emaciated bodies seen in very early missals and Byzantine paintings.

Yohannes treated them to a dissertation upon the importance of Abyssinia remaining free to develop her heritage of a distinctive culture, during which Lovelace found it difficult not to laugh.

It might be true that with its warring barons, powerful churchmen, and slave population the real Abyssinia was eight hundred years behind the times but it possessed no chivalrous knighthood, seats of monastic learning, or gay-hearted troubadours as had medieval Europe; and to speak of this debased Coptic art, which had not advanced for centuries, as though it held the growing glory of early Gothic was patently absurd.

Climbing back into the car once more they drove to Madam Idot's café bar, where they drank cocktails of a sort.

Valerie was growing used to the sight of lepers now that she had been in Addis Ababa for two days, they swarmed everywhere; but she was nearly sick when, as they left the bar, one woman tried to paw her with pale stumpy fingers from which the nails had fallen away. Yohannes drove the woman off with a sharp blow from his stick. It seemed that whips and sticks were the only method of enforcing order known to the ruling caste in Abyssinia. Even Christopher had realised now that, much as he liked Yohannes personally, his day and that of the class he represented was done. In common humanity it was high time that white men took over the administration of the hopelessly backward black Empire.

For lunch Yohannes took them to the *Deutsches*

Haus, a *pension* run by an honest German couple, renowned for having the best food in Addis.

Over the meal he began to make plans for the afternoon. A visit to the hospital where the Empress herself supervised the tending of the wounded. It was very modern; a real sign of the progress they were making. Then they should see the new palace which the Emperor had built some years before to accommodate the Crown Prince of Sweden during his visit to Addis. But Valerie complained of a splitting headache and declared she was quite incapable of doing any more sightseeing that day. Her pitifully drawn face touched Lovelace to the heart, yet he was profoundly glad of this genuine excuse to get rid of their charming, but most unwelcome, cicerone.

Blatta Ingida Yohannes expressed the most solicitous regret at Valerie's indisposition, drove them back to their hotel at once and, having received their thanks, declared his intention of calling for them at the same hour the following morning.

Christopher watched him go with some regret. In their short acquaintance he had developed a real liking for the sensitive, well-mannered young man, and he knew that it was the last they would see of him. By the following morning they would either be dead or on their way out of Abyssinia. Slowly, his heart working overtime, he followed Valerie and Lovelace up to their private sitting-room.

"It's an inside job," Lovelace said immediately they had got rid of the interpreter and servants Yohannes had hired for them, whom they found lounging about the place.

"A what?" asked Christopher wearily, sinking into a chair.

"I mean there's no hope of our breaking in from the outside as we did at Zarrif's house in Athens. There'll be niggers sleeping all over the place and we'd be certain to rouse some of them if we came in over the wall

On the other hand, if we can once get inside we may succeed in remaining unnoticed among that big crowd made up of Ras Desoum's household and hangers-on."

"How could you?" exclaimed Valerie.

"Oh, not dressed as we are." Lovelace gave her a reasssuring smile. "We'll have to disguise ourselves as natives. I wish to God I spoke the language but I thought out a way to get over that coming back in the car. I mean to rig myself out as an Arab merchant. I can speak Arabic and I've posed as one before. We'll buy a stock of goods from the bazaars and Christopher can come along as my porter. They're used to Arabs peddling goods, all over Africa, so they'll have no reason to suspect we're not what we appear and Ras Desoum's head servants probably know enough Arabic to barter with me for odds and ends. We must move quickly though. If we're not inside that outer court by sundown we'll be done, because they're certain to close the gates then for the night to keep out beggars, robbers and hyenas."

"Aren't we going to have an awful job getting this kit together in the time?" Christopher inquired.

"I don't know. I'm banking on the chance that Henrick Heiderstam will help us. I'm going down to the airport to try and get hold of him now—so long!"

As Lovelace left them Valerie and Christopher stared miserably at each other. After a moment he came over and perched himself on the arm of her chair.

"This is rotten for you, Valerie—isn't it," he said gently, "all your life mucked up because I'm a crazy fellow who must be risking his neck and the safety of his friends because he wants to make a better world; but I'll do my best to see that he gets out."

"*He*," she repeated dully.

"Yes, it's my show—not his, and I can't help liking him, although there're moments when I'd gladly see him dead after what he did last night."

"Oh, Christopher!" she moaned. "I thought you

promised you'd forget about that, and it wasn't his fault—really."

"I know, I know," he stood up impatiently, "but it needs two people who're drawn to each other to make love, just as it needs two people who're angry with each other to make a quarrel. Never mind about that though. He's taking his chance with me when he might well remain here with you and leave me to do this ghastly job on my own. There'll be time enough to talk of other things if either of us comes out alive."

"Oh, Christopher, don't! don't!" she pleaded and began to dab her eyes.

Instantly he was all solicitude and knelt down to comfort her. For a long time they remained like that and Lovelace found them still huddled together when he returned.

"It's all right," he announced abruptly. "I had the devil's own job to persuade Heidenstam into helping us as, naturally, I couldn't give away what we are up to. He consented in the end though; after I'd sworn by everything I hold sacred we intended nothing which could possibly harm the Emperor. Once he'd agreed he proved a real trump. He's at the bazaar now getting us the merchandise we shall require and the kit necessary for us to rig ourselves out as Arabs. I got the stain for our faces at the chemist's on the way back and I've hired a small car, in which we can drive ourselves out there, to be here at five o'clock. We'll park it near Ras Desoum's place so it's handy for a quick get-away if our luck holds out. Heidenstam's coming here immediately he's got the goods and whatever happens he's promised to take care of Valerie. He'll take her to the airport directly we've gone and help her to see her plane's fit to leave at a moment's notice without any bother from the aerodrome people. If we fail to turn up he'll place her in the care of Connolly at the American Legation by breakfast time to-morrow. The thing that worries me though is these cursed mountains.

If we do get away dare we risk a flight through such difficult country by night?"

"It's that or a hundred to one on our being arrested for murder," Christopher said slowly. "You see, we've got to leave here dressed as Arabs in daylight; there's no time now to arrange for our changing anywhere. Even if we're not recognised someone's certain to notice us on our way out. Ras Desoum will raise the whole place directly I've had my talk with Zarrif and, as everyone knows everybody else's business in this wretched town, the hotel people will remember Valerie paying the bill here and that they never saw either of us leave. Then someone'll remember the two Arabs and guess they were you and me. Our only chance is in the lead we may be able to get by making a dash for the airport in this car you've hired, but if we wait there till dawn orders are certain to arrive to stop all planes leaving."

"The only alternative is to go to earth, but that's going to be mighty difficult among a native population. We'd never be able to get hold of the plane again then and we'd be almost certain to be recognised if we tried to get away later by the railway."

Valerie sighed. "Don't worry. I only wish a night flight through the mountains was the worst we had to face. The plane's a good one and there's only about eighty miles of dangerous country to cover. After that we shall be able to follow the valley of the Awash river. If you can only reach the airport I'll back myself to do the rest."

"Bless you," said Christopher, while Lovelace looked his admiration and his thanks.

She shrugged. "That's nothing. I've tackled far more difficult flights in these last few years. It's Anthony we should thank for having made all these arrangements so skilfully."

"Yes, he's a wonder," Christopher agreed.

"No." Lovelace shook his head. "Just fairly

competent, that's all, and as nervous as a two-year-old. I wish to God we were all safe out of here. Let's have tea, shall we?" He rang the bell and slumped into a chair.

Valerie thought her heart would break as she looked at him. He seemed years older than he had the night before; the lines about his mouth and eyes were deeper now. She felt she could not possibly let him go—yet she knew that she must.

Over tea they spoke little, although Lovelace strove to keep the conversation going. He did not feel like a pipe. Somehow even smoking seemed an effort at this high altitude but he put one on, after his second cup, in order to try and appear normal, while he talked of the difference between the show-places they had seen and the stagnant poverty which met the eye in every street.

Soon after, Henrick Heidenstam arrived with a big suit-case and the three men went into Lovelace's room to change.

When they returned Valerie would not have recognised either of her lovers if she had met them in the street. Lovelace had transformed himself into a fine-looking Arab and Christopher into an unusually handsome black with a hump on his back; which was actually formed by a ruck-sack beneath his *burnous* containing certain kit they might require.

Henrick Heiderstam looked at her. "You know, of course, the work your friends are engaged upon?"

She nodded silently.

"Will you add your assurance to theirs that they intend nothing which could harm the Emperor? The fact that he cannot afford to pay my salary any more does not affect my loyalty to him and I must be certain on this point."

"I give you my word of honour," she said slowly.

"Thank you." The young Swedish airman smiled at her before turning to the others. "My servant has put the goods from the bazaar into the back of your hired car. I went down to see to that while you were dressing, so all is ready for your departure now."

Christopher took both Valerie's hands in his and gave her a long, steady look while he pressed them so hard that she thought he would crush her fingers. He raised them to his lips, released them suddenly and strode out of the room.

Lovelace hesitated for a second, gave her a last smile, and made to follow; but Valerie raised one hand to stay him and he caught her jerky whisper: "I meant every word I said in—in my letter."

"Letter?" he repeated in a puzzled tone. Then Christopher's voice came impatiently from the corridor, "Come on! We don't want the whole hotel staff to see us in these clothes."

"Coming!" Lovelace sang out. Heidenstam was still with them in the room and there was no time to ask her now to explain what she meant. With a murmured, "Good-bye—my dear," he left her.

Valerie pushed past Heidenstam and ran to the doorway. She was just in time to catch a last glimpse of the two white-robed figures as they turned out of the corridor to go down the service staircase. She closed her eyes and leant against the wall wondering if she would ever see either of them alive again.

CHAPTER XXIV

THE MILLS OF GOD GRIND SLOWLY : : :

LOVELACE and Christopher saw that they would have no difficulty in getting into the first courtyard of Ras Desoum's so-called "castle." They had escaped all but casual glances from the numerous servants as they left by the back entrance of the hotel, found Heidenstam's man waiting round the corner with their hired car, drove out in it and parked it ready for immediate flight under cover of some low trees. Now, with a miscellaneous assortment of goods dangling from their arms and shoulders, they walked towards the entrance of the Ras's residence.

A stream of natives was constantly passing in and out, the big doors in the low wall stood wide open, and no guards or porters were present to challenge newcomers. The two pseudo-Arabs trudged through the gates, bowed under their burdens, and glanced cautiously round.

The scene was not unlike that in a mean quarter of Baghdad or Damascus, Lovelace thought, except that it lacked colour. These people seemed cursed with a dreary spirit in addition to their poverty and hardly a splash of red, blue or green broke the monotony of black, white and grey. The court proved far larger than it had appeared from outside as the many buildings in it tended to obscure the full view. In one corner there was a big corral for cattle; further along one into which several hundred mangy-looking sheep were tightly packed. Humans swarmed everywhere, men, women and children; all but the latter robed in clothes to their necks. They wandered slowly and apparently aimlessly about; stood in groups heatedly disputing or sat on their haunches gazing listlessly before them. There were mules, donkeys, goats, chickens and half-starved dogs all over the place, the beasts of burden tied up casually to anything that came handy, the rest scavenging among the offal that stank to heaven.

Christopher noticed two negroes chained to each other. They squatted side by side and were chatting quite happily together. Lovelace caught the direction of his glance and muttered, "a debtor and his creditor; they'll be chained like that until the debtor pays. These people are Gallahs, Guragis and Beni Shankalis—mostly freed slaves, I expect. Come on, let's try our luck at getting into the second court."

They made their way slowly through the maze of squalid hutments until they reached another gate. It was open but a fierce-looking Gallah warrior leaned indolently against the heavy, wooden door post. As they approached he barred their passage by lowering his long spear.

Lovelace spoke to him in Arabic but the man obviously did not understand so they began to display their goods and act a pantomine of selling with a handful of small money. Still the fellow shook his head with a sullen frown. Lovelace slipped a few *gersh* into his hand, about a shilling, upon which he bared his white, even teeth in a fearsome smile and allowed them to pass.

The second court seemed to be allotted to Ras Desoum's household troops and their families. They were better clad, more prosperous-looking, and many of the men carried rifles slung over their shoulders.

Here, Lovelace made a pretence of trying to sell some of his goods, brass bangles and anklets from Birmingham, tawdry trinkets from Hamburg, and oriental knives made in Sheffield. Over a quarter of an hour was wasted haggling with one man who coveted a murderous-looking dagger, but he could not pay the price Lovelace demanded and to give it away too cheaply would have immediately drawn unwelcome attention to the two traders.

About fifty horses were stabled in the second court, but any number of domestic animals ran riot, and filth was everywhere. Behind a row of shacks a rough circle of men had been formed and, in the centre, two enormous blacks were wrestling stark naked on the ground among the refuse and manure. In a corner near by an old man sat facing a ring of about forty children. He wore a ragged sort of turban and his face was engrained with dirt. Each time he pronounced certain words with a sonorous roll the children chanted them in a high treble after him. "He's a priest," breathed Lovelace. "Teaching them bits out of the *Kebra Nagast*, their version of the Old Testament. Learning that stuff off by heart is about all the schooling most people get in Abyssinia. Very different from what we saw yesterday—isn't it? Come on, let's try and wangle our way into the Holy of Holies."

The gate of the inner courtyard was more carefully guarded. Two soldiers stood by it leaning on their rifles and a third, an officer apparently, since he wore a dirty white duck suit, a blue bus-conductor's hat and a Sam Browne belt to which was attached a revolver holster, lounged near them.

Lovelace bowed himself almost to the ground and Christopher followed his example. As the officer walked over to them Lovelace addressed him in Arabic, "Illustrious and Valorous Master, we have goods to sell. Permit us, I beg, to enter; that we may show them to the Noble Lords whose sweetness makes this court a place of perfumes."

The answer came in halting Arabic. "Show me what you have."

With a deep obeisance Lovelace spread his wares out upon the ground and, for the next five minutes, Christopher marvelled as he stood behind him. Every trace of the quiet, reserved Englishman had disappeared;

instead, a born Oriental rattled on unceasingly in flowery Arabic and gesticulated graphically with both hands.

The Abyssinian displayed no emotion until Lovelace produced a miniature automatic, held it pointing at his own heart, and pressed the trigger; an Egyptian cigarette shot out of the barrel. He caught it deftly, placed it between his lips and, pressing a button, lit it from an automatic lighter concealed in the butt of the toy pistol.

The black man's eyes glinted with desire. "How much?" he asked.

"Twenty thalers," said Lovelace.

The officer shook his head, but his fascinated gaze was still on the miraculous toy.

Lovelace held it out to him by the barrel. "It is yours, Master, if I may show my wares to the Illustrious *Ferentshis* who are within."

"How do you know that there are foreigners here?" the black asked suspiciously.

"Rumour has a long tongue, oh begetter of many hundred handsome children," Lovelace countered. "All the world knows the exalted Ras extends his regal hospitality to these bringers of Evil," he spat suddenly, and added, "but their thalers are as numerous as the fleas upon a donkey—and I am poor."

After a quick glance round the inner court the man in the soiled dungarees snatched at the pistol and motioned them inside. As ever, in the East, cupidity had unlocked the door. They snatched up their goods before he could change his mind and genuflected past him.

The third enclosure was almost as large as the others, but its buildings were more massive and it was a little cleaner. In the centre rose a single-storied, stone block, evidently Ras Desoum's own dwelling. At one end of it the observation tower dominated the whole human ant-heap from its top platform at the modest height of thirty feet. A separate building was, perhaps, a banqueting hall, and another the stables that held the

Ras's chargers. Against the walls were the same wattle-and-daub shanties as in the outer courts, except in one place, where a long, low, modern bungalow was raised on a concrete platform a few feet above the ground. On its stoep four Europeans were sitting, and, even in the distance, Lovelace recognized them as some of Zarrif's gunmen.

"Now we're inside I want to talk to you," Christopher whispered.

"Shut up," snapped Lovelace. "That chap at the gate's still watching us. It's devilish risky, but we're sunk now unless we do our stuff." With a slow but firm step he led the way over to the bungalow.

As they advanced they saw that a machine-gun on a tripod had been placed at one corner of the veranda. The weapon commanded all the open ground of the inner court, yet none of the gunmen was within twenty yards of it.

"This is where Zarrif hangs out all right," Lovelace whispered; "but you see he takes his precautions, even here."

"If we could grab that gun and reverse it we'd have the whole party cold," Christopher muttered in sudden excitement.

"Good God, no!" Lovelace muttered back. "There're five hundred men with rifles in this place. They'd pot us when we tried to climb out over the wall as easy as sitting rabbits. We've got to wait till after dark. Steady now! Try and think yourself into the skin of a native. We've passed muster as Arabs with the Abyssinians, but some of these chaps have seen me before, face to face, and if they once smell a rat they'll bump us off without even waiting to ask Zarrif."

With a forced, ingratiating grin he produced his goods and called out to the bodyguard in exceedingly bad French:

"Hi! Masters! Souvenir of Abyssinia yes! Very fine, very cheap. Necklace for pretty girl. All are pearl come from Persian Gulf. Ivory elephant bring plenty luck. Come, Masters, look!"

One man murmured to another: "Here's a chance to buy a few things. I'm going to spend a bit as we're leaving to-morrow." The man spoke in Spanish, but Lovelace knew enough of that language to catch the drift of what he said, and redoubled his enticements.

The second man shook his head. "Save your money, friend. Who can say when we'll be able to earn any more now?"

In spite of the pessimist, Lovelace succeeded in unloading thirty-five thalers' worth of goods on to two of the thugs after the usual haggling that was expected of him in his part.

He was just collecting his things again when his heart almost missed a beat. Cassalis came out of one of the doors of the building and fixed him with a suspicious stare.

Christopher, recognising the secretary from Lovelace's description, felt his hair prickle on his scalp. If the Frenchman noticed that the features of the Arab trader were exactly the same as those of a gentleman who had eaten quite a number of meals with him under the name of Jeremiah Green, the next few seconds would see certain bloodshed. He fumbled under his *burnous* for his pistol, while Lovelace, with the audacity born of desperation, proceeded to badger Cassalis to examine his stock.

Cassalis seemed worried and distrait. After a quick glance at the goods he ordered them off, and began to talk excitedly to the others about arrangements for their departure from Abyssinia the following day.

The pseudo-Arabs beat a hasty retreat. Lovelace let out a quick sigh of relief and nudged Christopher's arm. "Now we've got to hide before somebody spots us and turns us out. Look! Over there, between those two huts, by that big pile of straw."

"I've got to talk to you," muttered Christopher urgently.

"You can talk all you want to in a minute." Lovelace's lazy glance was fixed on the apathetic soldiers who guarded the entrance to the court.

A high note on a horn sounded from out near the roadway and some native drums began to beat. "What's that ?" Christopher asked jerkily.

"Curfew. They'll be closing the gates for the night in a few moments now. Hadn't you noticed the sun is just about to set ?"

It was true. The strong shadows had been lengthening even when they were talking with the officer at the inner gate. Twenty minutes had elapsed since then, and now all the gimcrack buildings were bathed in the pinkish glow of twilight.

As they reached the big pile of loose straw and wriggled down into it, Christopher's voice was more urgent than ever : "Listen !" he pleaded. "You've got me in here which I could never have done for myself. I know the lie of the land and where Zarrif is. I'm—well, terribly grateful. Now, you must get out before it's too late."

"Get out—why ?" asked Lovelace in surprise.

"That's why !" Christopher produced a paper from inside his robe and passed it over. "That's a letter from Valerie to you. She pushed it under your bedroom door late last night. I happened to see her and I was half-crazy with jealousy. I fished it out with a thin piece of stick—then read it. Cad's trick, I suppose, but at least it's given me the truth about the situation."

By the last light of the dying sun, while the native drums were still rolling, Lovelace read the pencilled scrawl.

My dearest one,

I have your note. If anything could help me to face the future it is that you understand. Christopher is so weak, so helpless, so very much alone. He put me through hell this evening, but I'm so fond of him that I stood for it and I shall never give him further cause to doubt my faithfulness to him.

He has promised to forget how he found us and is still determined to go through with his mission. I've no right to ask you anything, but—if you can bear to remain with us—please carry on to-morrow as if nothing had happened.

Afterwards, we must never meet again. I couldn't bear it. But, in case anything goes wrong, I want you to know that I have loved you from the very first moment we met years back in England and that I shall never love anyone else with real love as long as I live.

Valerie.

Lovelace sat silent with the letter in his hand; his thoughts racing and chaotic. So she did love him—after all. Those precious kisses the night before had not been born of impulse or a sentimental weakness welling up from schoolgirl memories, as he had imagined on receiving no sign of any kind in reply to his own note. She loved him. Had loved him for years in secret; and here he was trapped in an undertaking he had always hated and in which all the chances were that he would lose his life. If only he had known a few hours earlier; but if he had, could he . . .

Christopher seized his arm and shook it, breaking in upon his thoughts. "Quick, man—you must get out. In a minute it'll be too late."

"It *is*—too late."

"Nonsense! They haven't closed the gate yet."

"I mean it's too late for me to back out of this thing."

"It's not. For God's sake! Don't you see that once I'd read her letter I never intended to ask more of you than your help to get in here. You must go back so you can look after Valerie."

Lovelace shook his head. "I can't. I could never look her in the face again if I left you on your own here now."

The rolling of the drums ceased. The horn sounded

again. In the deepening shadows a score of men slowly thrust-to the heavy wooden gates of the inner court.

For a long time Lovelace and Christopher crouched under their thin covering of straw in silence; each sunk in his own thoughts. The brief twilight gave place to darkness, but fires were lit on the bare ground and flaming torches placed in sconces round the walls. From the outer courts there came the murmur of discordant singing, the clopping of hoofs as the horses stamped restlessly, the wailing of a child, and all the other occasional noises which make up the night sounds of an Eastern village.

"How long must we wait?" asked Christopher at last.

"Until they sleep. Our only hope lies in complete surprise. To do the job and be away over the wall before they realise what's happened."

"We may have to shoot some of the bodyguard."

"I can't help it." Lovelace's tone was bitter now. "They're hired mercenaries paid to deal death or risk it in the service of their master. It's the same gang that tried to murder me in Alexandria and who shot down Valerie's plane without the least compunction. There must be no stupid weakness. Once we go in we've got to shoot to kill."

An hour, two hours, drifted by. Their vigil seemed endless. Christopher was beginning to think the dawn might come before they would be able to carry out their business, but when he got out his watch he was amazed to find it only a little after ten. Lovelace was not surprised; he had a fairly accurate idea of the time from the movement of the bright stars overhead.

The outer courts were quieter now. The great bulk of Ras Desoum's followers was already fast asleep, but near his house, the bungalow, and the inner gateway, occasional figures still moved and were thrown up for a second in sharp silhouette against the brightness of the fires.

"We'll give them another hour," Lovelace murmured

as Christopher told him the time, "then see if we dare risk it."

The hour dragged by. At the end of it all movement in the inner court had ceased, most of the torches had burnt out to blackened sticks, and the fires were dying down.

Christopher stirred restlessly in the heap of straw. Suddenly he muttered: "For God's sake let's get on with it."

"All right." Lovelace stood up and got out his heavy automatic. "Come on, then. Stick to the shadows as much as you can and, if you hear anyone coming, go dead as a log."

With cautious steps they moved from their hiding-place, edged round the hut, back to the wall again on its far side, and so on; following the outline of the court round two of its sides until they were within twenty yards of the bungalow.

One window, which had been concealed from them before by an intervening angle of the house, was still lighted. The glow from the window faintly illuminated the stoop. The machine-gun was still upon it, trained on the open space and gate, yet, to their surprise, not a single gunman was on duty.

"The room with the light will be Zarrif's," Lovelace whispered. "No one but that scheming devil would work so late. Queer none of the bodyguard is about. Perhaps he considers Ras Desoum's men and the two outer courtyards sufficient protection. That's not like him, though, because the wall the bungalow backs against has nothing on its other side; only an open field."

Christopher pressed his arm. "If you can grab that machine-gun to cover our retreat, I'll break in and do the job."

"Let's think of our retreat first. See that low shanty leaning up against this end of the bungalow. Think you could swing yourself up on to its roof?"

"Yes," Christopher breathed. His pale face was set and he was trembling with excitement now.

"Right, then," Lovelace went on quietly. "From that roof you can easily hoist yourself on to the wall. Don't wait for me. I'll take care of myself and I'll probably be out before you are. The second you've killed your man you're to dash out and over. It's no more than a twelve-foot drop on the other side. Pick yourself up and beat it for the car as though all the devils in hell were after you . . . Sssss—what's that?"

At the same second Christopher heard the soft footfalls. Instinctively they both drew back into the deeper shadows. A watchman came into view swinging a lantern.

Lovelace pressed himself against the side of the hut. It gave behind him. He staggered and nearly fell, put one foot inside the door that had swung open, to save himself, but it met empty space instead of ground. Next second he had pitched backward in the darkness and was falling! falling! falling!

In those brief, frightful seconds he expected to be smashed to pieces when he reached the bottom of that infernal pit, but he brought up on a soft and yielding substance that gave beneath him.

By the mercy of Heaven the safety-catch of his automatic was still down so it had not exploded. For a moment he lay on his back, wondering what in heaven and hell could have happened; then Christopher's voice came in an urgent whisper from above: "Lovelace, where are you? What the . . ."

"Quiet!" Lovelace cut him short. "If you've got your torch handy, close that door and shine it downwards."

A moment later a beam of light cut into the pitch-black darkness, and he saw that he was sitting on a great mound of loose grain. He had fallen backwards into an Abyssinian storage-pit, and the sheer, dark tunnel of it showed over his head to Christopher's light a dozen feet above.

He could not get up again by the way he had come down. That was certain. Fearful now that he was trapped unless Christopher could find something with which to haul him up, he replaced his pistol underneath his robe and, getting out his own torch, flashed it round to see if the place had any other exit.

To his relief he found that he was at one end of a large cellar. Arms, ammunition, bales of cotton, root crops and all sorts of other things were stored in it besides the pyramid of grain on which he sat. A set of stone stairs at the far end and two ladders leading to trapdoors in other places showed that the cellar had several entrances. He slid down the heap of grain, hurried to the steps at the far end and up them. Pressing gently on the wooden door at their top, he found that it was unlocked and gave on to a dark corridor. Hastening down the steps, he ran back to the grain-shaft and peered up to where Christopher was still holding the light.

"There's another way out," he said in a swift whisper. "We must stick together. As I can't get up to you, you'd better come down to me. See the safety catch on your pistol is set before you jump."

He stood aside and as Christopher landed with a soft thud, ankle-deep in the grain, shot out a hand to steady him.

Flashing their torches before them, they made for the cellar stairs. Lovelace was leading, but it was Christopher who spotted the grim thing that lay just to the right of the lower steps.

"Half a minute," he exclaimed. "What's this?"

Lovelace paused and lowered the beam of his torch. In his hurry he had not noticed it before, but a body lay there huddled in a limp, unnatural attitude, which suggested that it had been thrown there dead.

"Someone they've bumped off," he muttered, staring at the vivid splashes of blood which stained the white *shama* at the level of the dead man's chest. Then, with a sharply indrawn breath, he stooped lower. The still face was dark brown and half hidden by a native head-dress; but a deep scar ran from the left corner of the mouth to the chin.

"Good God!" he breathed. "It's the Austrian we met in Jibuti. The chap I saw for the first time outside Zarrif's house in Athens."

"Why, yes," Christopher muttered. "The fellow who calls himself Baron Foldvar. I recognise him now in spite of his disguise. What the deuce can he have been doing here dressed up like that?"

"God knows! He's one of Zarrif's people. Perhaps they caught him double-crossing them. Whoever he was he must have been a decent fellow once, though, so let's straighten him out. He looks too terrible like that."

The Baron could not have been dead for many hours, as *rigor mortis* had not set in. His chest was riddled with bullets, so he must have died instantaneously. They arranged his body decently, drew a piece of sacking over his face, and left him. Their nerves keyed up to the highest pitch, they tiptoed up the steps.

The corridor on to which the cellar gave was dark and silent. The torches showed it to be like that in a modern house, and they guessed they were now in Ras Desoum's own residence. The ground-floor passage ended in a door fifteen feet away.

"Put out your light," whispered Lovelace, and, as he switched off his own, they crept down the passage, their guns grasped ready in their hands.

The door was not locked, and opened to his touch. He saw at once that it gave on to a large room; the starlight was sufficient to outline a row of windows which showed faintly in contrast to the solid blackness of the opposite wall.

Suddenly a deep growl sounded. Lovelace switched round. Two bright, yellow eyes were gleaming at him in the darkness. It was not a dog and, next second, came the appalling realisation of what those fierce yellow eyes portended.

It was a lion! In this country almost given over to wild beasts, the Abyssinian nobles kept lions as a protection in their houses. The Emperor himself had had a couple which used to lie across the doorway of his workroom until the British Minister complained and they were removed in consequence.

There was no time to think. Christopher flashed the torch he still held in his left hand as the great beast gave a full-throated roar. As it sprang they pressed the triggers of their pistols and poured half the contents of their weapons into its face and body.

The brute crashed to the floor within a couple of feet of them, writhed, turned on its back, stabbed the air wildly with its unsheathed claws, and thrashed its tail in its death agony; but those crashing shots in the silence of the night had roused every man, woman and child in Ras Desoum's house and courtyards.

Shouts of alarm and the patter of naked, running feet sounded almost before the acrid smoke had ceased to drift from the pistol barrels.

"Quick!" yelled Christopher. "Zarrif! I've got to get him!" He dashed for the door which gave on to the court.

With desperate fingers he wrenched back the bolts while Lovelace lit him with his torch. They both tumbled outside.

"The gun," shouted Lovelace. "Make for the machine-gun."

Side by side they sprinted across the open towards the bungalow. In one bound they were upon the stoep. Lovelace flung himself flat and grabbed the tripod as though it was a Rugby football. Christopher burst in through the door of the bungalow nearest the lighted window. The crack of a pistol sounded from the room—then another. One of the bullets shattered the window.

There was a scream as it hit someone in the court. Flashes began to stab the darkness by the gate, and the bullets of the native guard smacked into the brickwork above Lovelace's head. Next moment he had his thumbs on the buttons of the machine-gun, and its staccato clatter made the night hideous.

The horn that had been blown for the closing of the gates at sunset sounded again. Shouting and clamour came from the outer courts. Ras Desoum's retainers thought that Zarrif's white gunmen were attacking their overlord. The gates were flung open and they came streaming in.

Lovelace knew his position was untenable. Behind him more shooting and sounds of commotion came from the bungalow; any second Zarrif's men might dash out and take him in the rear. He ceased fire, grabbed the heavy gun, and staggered with it to a new position twenty yards away where he could cover either the gate or the bungalow. As he set it down a stab of pain shot through him like the searing of a white-hot iron; a bullet had hit him in the shoulder.

Suddenly Christopher appeared in one of the doorways of the bungalow. A gunman came out of another at the same instant. He was pulling on his coat, but, taking Christopher for an attacking native, he fired at him from the hip. Christopher jumped just before the flash, half-turned, shot the fellow down, and raced over to Lovelace.

"Zarrif wasn't in either of those rooms," he panted, his heart beating as though it would burst from the triple strain of excitement, exertion, and the altitude.

"Perhaps he's in the house," Lovelace gasped. He fired another burst in the direction of the gate, knowing that if they could not keep the natives back they would be overwhelmed and torn to pieces.

Shrieks of agony told him his shots had found their marks, but hundreds of warriors from the outer courts were now forcing the front ranks of the mob forward.

Bullets sang over the spot where Christopher and Lovelace lay crouched, but the main fire of the Abyssinians was directed at the bungalow.

Zarrit's men, believing that the Abyssinians intended a midnight massacre, were barricading themselves in. One of them was yelling commands in Spanish. The lights which had been lit at the first alarm were put out again and a second machine-gun was brought into action from one of the windows.

Christopher grabbed Lovelace by the arm. "The house !—the house ! I've got to get Zarrif."

"All right ! One moment !" Lovelace fired a final burst from his machine-gun which exhausted the belt of ammunition. He was cursing the evil luck which had caused them to misjudge Zarrif's whereabouts as he slipped a fresh clip of bullets into his automatic. If they had been right Christopher would have done his work by now and they might have stood some chance of escaping over the wall unobserved in the confusion.

"Come on ! come on !" Christopher urged, springing to his feet.

"Crawl, man, for God's sake !" Lovelace shouted, but his warning came too late. Christopher grabbed at his arm and then sank down on his knees.

"I'm hit !" he muttered. "Hell, how it hurts—bone's smashed, I think, but—but it's only my left arm—I'm not done yet." He began to wriggle forward on his stomach.

Lovelace's shoulder was paining him badly and he knew that he was losing blood. As he edged his way towards the house a new clamour caught his attention. Something was happening out in the roadway. Shouting, shots, and a fresh pandemonium came from the outer court, adding to the general din. Fighting had broken out there as well, some private feud, perhaps, but he had no time to pause and wonder ; they had nearly reached the doorway of the house. It was still open and they both stood up to rush it.

Christopher threw a quick glance over his shoulder.

The court was lit by the continuous flash of rifles. Bodies lay twisted and hunched in all directions. The machine-gun in the bungalow had ceased fire. The Abyssinians were charging across the open, trampling down their wounded comrades as they ran. The gunmen were still using their pistols, determined to sell their lives dearly. The place was a shambles.

As he turned he saw Lovelace stagger, hit again, this time in the thigh; to save him further exposure to the flying bullets he thrust him through the door of the house and flung himself in behind him.

In the flickering light caused by the flashes Lovelace saw that the hall was empty except for the dead lion. A sudden sound in his rear caused him to lurch round. A figure crouched in the angle behind the open door. It was Cassalis.

Half-dazed by pain and weak from loss of blood, Lovelace strove to jerk up his automatic, but the Frenchman was already holding a pistol levelled at his face. A thick, black cylinder on the end of the barrel was less than six inches from his mouth. He recognised the weapon instantly as an ether pistol which could discharge poison gas, like those the *Millers of God* issued to their appointed executioners.

Lovelace knew then that the game was up. There was no time to duck or charge even if he had had the strength to do so. Yet in that split second the words "VENGEANCE IS MINE—SAITH THE LORD" flamed through his tired brain as he realised that he was to die by the very means they had intended for Zarrif.

Suddenly a fist crashed on his wounded shoulder. The pain was agonising, his knees gave way, and he slid to the floor.

The last thing he glimpsed was Christopher's clear-cut, cameo-like features surrounded by a misty halo of the deadly gas. By striking Lovelace down from behind he had been forced to receive the discharge of the pistol full in his own face.

When Lovelace came round he was first conscious of the clean, astringent smell of disinfectant and the crackle of spasmodic rifle fire coming faintly from a distance. The sound brought back the fact that he was wounded; his thigh and shoulder began to throb. He tried to ease his position by turning over, but found himself apparently strapped down; only his left hand was free and the fingers of it met the cool linen of a sheet.

A freckle-faced, sandy-haired man, clad in a white coat, bent over him. "So you've roused at last," he said with a strong Scotch accent. "It's near on five days ye've been lying like a corpse."

"Where am I?" Lovelace managed to murmur.

"In the hospital ward of the British Legation." The orderly held out a glass. "Drink this now; the doctor said I was to give it you the moment you came to."

Lovelace knew there was some question which he wanted desperately to ask, but his mind seemed to have gone completely blank. All he could do was to stammer, "What—what does that shooting mean?"

"The heathen are killing each other and looting their own toun. It started the day after they brought you in: within an hour of the wee Emperor abandoning the war and them to their own evil devices. He went off in the train to Jibuti with his family and friends; to travel to Europe, they say, and ask help of the League. But you must'na talk. Drink this now."

"Wait!" Lovelace turned his face away. He remembered now the thing he had to know. "Miss Lorne—an American lady—have you heard anything about her—is she—is she safe?"

The orderly grinned. "Ai, and she's been here every hour of each day to look at you. She's safe and so are you. Safe as if you were in the ould Castle on the rock in Edinburgh. Haven't I told you, mon, that you're in the British Legation."

Lovelace drank off the yellow fluid. His body was

now one great pain and he felt very, very tired. The effort to think coherently was too much and, after a moment, he gave up the struggle.

When he opened his eyes again it was the following morning and Valerie was beside him. She stooped and kissed him on the mouth.

"Chistopher?" he asked in a whisper.

"Dead," she said, and he saw that her eyes were almost burnt out with crying, so that she could cry no more.

"How—how did I escape being butchered—after I fainted?" His head was clearer now and the details of that last scene of carnage were coming back to him.

She leaned nearer. "I couldn't stand it, Anthony—I couldn't stand it. I stuck it out for six hours and every moment I thought I was going mad; then I caved in and made Henrick Heidenstam take me to the Emperor.

"I told him everything—the whole truth about the *Millers of God*—and he understood. He was wonderful, oh, wonderful. He sent troops at once to arrest Zarrif's gunmen and both of you. They arrived in time to save you, but poor Christopher was dead. He gave his life for Peace."

"He gave his life to save mine," Lovelace said softly. "Later I'll tell you about it; but we failed, you know—failed to get Zarrif. He'll be well on his way back to Europe with the concession in his pocket by now."

Valerie shook her head. "No, my darling. If only we'd known it we might have all slept tranquilly in our beds that night. Zarrif was already dead by four o'clock in the afternoon."

Lovelace closed his eyes. That explained a lot, he was thinking. The gunmen were all sleeping, then, because they had no one left to guard. It accounted, too, for Cassalis having been in such a state of dither at sunset. In a faint voice he asked, "How—how did Zarrif die?"

"Heart, darling. You know how it troubles even us at this height; the strain must have proved too much for him at his age. I was still at the Palace waiting for news of you when Ras Desoum was brought in by the soldiers and told the Emperor. I suppose that's why he decided to leave Addis the following day."

"Poor little man." Lovelace's voice came stronger now. "If his deal with Zarrif had gone through he'd have been in funds again."

"Yes; although things were in a far worse state than we knew. His troops were mutinying and his army going to pieces under Marshal Badoglio's ceaseless attacks."

"Perhaps, but the Italian main line was still nearly two hundred miles away. If the Emperor had been able to collect the funds from Zarrif to satisfy his greedy, thieving Rases the Abyssinians would have hung together and the rains would have given him six months to reorganise. As it is, Badoglio's exploited his victories in the genuine Napoleonic manner and the Emperor's thrown his hand in. So the war's over, eh?"

"Yes, the war's over," Valerie agreed quickly. "The Italians are marching into the town now, and they'll do more in ten years to make life safe and human and decent for the people of the country than poor, priest ridden Haile Selassie could have done in a century. Giulio Dolomenchi arrived with the advance guard. I saw him this morning. He went straight to the American Legation to inquire after our safety, and then he came on here. He's such a dear. I'm terribly glad he's come through all right."

Lovelace grinned feebly. "So am I. I'm glad the Italians have won, too. They were bound to in the end, and this sudden finish saves thousands of lives being sacrificed on both sides in another campaign next autumn. Above all, I'm glad that concession never went through. For the moment, anyway, we've no longer cause to fear another war in Europe."

"Events have proved how right the *Millers* were," Valerie said slowly. "Zarrif's death *was* necessary. But that he should die of heart failure at the eleventh hour makes you think, doesn't it? Perhaps it was God's business and not ours—really."

For a long time Lovelace was silent. At last he spoke again. "Did it ever occur to you, sweet, to wonder at an organisation like the *Millers* leaving the affair solely in the hands of a boy like Christopher when such tremendous issues depended on its outcome?"

"No," she said, "I never thought of that; but now you raise the point, it does seem rather strange."

"Well, I don't believe they did. Cassalis killed Christopher with one of the *Millers'* special gas pistols. Where could he have got hold of such a weapon? Christopher and I found the body of a white man who had disguised himself as a native in Ras Desoum's cellar. It was hardly cold and riddled with bullets. We recognised it as that of poor Baron Foldvar who you met in Jibuti. Perhaps the pistol Cassalis used was taken from the Baron and I did him a great injustice. It may be that the Baron killed Zarrif with it before the gunmen shot him down. We shall never know for certain, now, and it *was* God's business; but I believe he *did* send one of His *Millers* to do His will."

Khartoum
Italian
ANGLO EGYPTIAN SUDAN
Adowa
Makale
Magdala
Blue Nile
Lake Tana
Dessye
Addis Ababa
Endpapers for
THE SECRET WAR
Designed by Joan & Dennis Wheatley
and Diana Younger
Scale 0 50 100 200